THE PERFECT SISTER

BOOKS BY SHERYL BROWNE

The Babysitter
The Affair
The Second Wife
The Marriage Trap

THE PERFECT SISTER

SHERYL BROWNE

bookouture

Published by Bookouture in 2020

An imprint of Storyfire Ltd.
Carmelite House
50 Victoria Embankment
London EC4Y 0DZ

www.bookouture.com

ISBN: 978-1-78681-898-0
eBook ISBN: 978-1-78681-897-3

For Snoops, who offered me unconditional love and companionship through so many of life's ups and downs. Love you, little Noop.

PROLOGUE

His mind lurching frantically from thought to disjointed thought, he couldn't tell if he was awake or still dreaming. A moment ago, he'd been running, the long landing in front of him stretching on to eternity, the door ahead of him growing more distant, the floor like treacle beneath him, sucking his feet in. The room he was trying to get to was empty when he reached it, stark walls, nothing to tell him why he was there. And then the door slammed behind him and the dark descended, and there was no door, no window, no way out of his nightmare.

Guessing he was awake, as the sounds of the night reached him – the resident in the adjoining room coughing, the lonely hoot of a tawny owl – he raised his head from his pillow, and a new sense of panic started to take root inside him. He wondered at first whether the figure on the other side of his room was a figment of his imagination. When it approached, he didn't recognise the person looming over him. The features were familiar, yet not. Fleetingly he had a memory, but it floated away before he could grasp it, disappearing into the night like a soft white djinn. Tormenting him. Always the memories tormented him, hovering on the periphery of his recollection.

But he wasn't hallucinating, he soon realised. This person was real, tangible. He could hear the controlled breathing, as if they were holding their rage in. By the amber glow of the fire escape light spilling in through the bay window, he could see the seething sheen of malice in eyes that seemed to be looking right into his soul. He smelled the cloying odour of floral cologne, and he knew it; knew who it belonged to. He groped for the name of the face that danced just out of his reach, sifted through the quicksand in his mind. He couldn't catch hold of it before the face was lost to him.

This individual meant him harm. Cold certainty settled like an icicle in his chest. 'What do you want?' he rasped, his throat thick with fear.

The loud silence that followed was filled with tacit threat. And then, 'I know what you did,' the person whispered. The voice, tight with suppressed emotion, tugged at the frayed edges of his consciousness.

Another soundless minute ticked by. And then the figure moved, its penetrating gaze holding his briefly before it turned away from him. His heart thrashing wildly, he strained to hear the sounds above it: soft footsteps; the window opening; rain plopping heavily from the roof. Her name – the woman who was long ago lost to him – he heard that, too, carried mournfully on the wind that whistled through the trees in the grounds. A distant dog howled, soulful, blood-chilling, the primeval cry of an abandoned animal. And then…

'She's here, Bernard,' his visitor said softly. 'She's waiting for you.'

CHAPTER ONE

Winter 1992

There was always one. Eyeing the ceiling, Cathy sighed in despair, then came around from behind the bar to peel the last hanger-on away from the jukebox. Whitney Houston belting out 'I Will Always Love You' wasn't helping Jimmy O'Conner's maudlin mood any.

'Come on, Jimmy.' Hooking an arm through his, she steered him towards the exit. 'Whitney will still be here tomorrow.'

'Yeah, but my bird won't, will she? Dumped me, she did, after only three weeks. Did I tell you?' Jimmy said dejectedly.

'You did, Jimmy. About a hundred times.' Cathy manoeuvred him another stumbling yard forward, collecting up his cigarettes and motorcycle helmet from his table as they went.

'Bought her a hairdryer an' all for her birthday. Cost me a day's soddin' wages, that thing did.'

'Ungrateful mare, she doesn't deserve you.' Cathy oozed sympathy, although after a long night pulling pints in platform shoes that were killing her, and with her daughter waiting for her in the living room, her patience was wearing thin.

'Should've stuck with you, Cath.' Jimmy emitted a nostalgic sigh. 'We'd have been good together, you and me.'

God forbid. Jimmy was clearly remembering their relationship in a way that did less damage to his ego. After an excruciatingly long six months going steady with him, Cathy too had dumped him. She had her sights set higher than a farmhand whose idea of a romantic night out was a lager and lime followed by a ride on his clapped-out Honda 650 and a quick shag in the sand dunes. A bloke who never had oil under his fingernails or stank of pig shit was more Cathy's type.

'Yeah, we would have, Jimmy.' She encouraged him the last few feet towards the door, opening it and ejecting him into the crisp night air. 'That boat's sailed, unfortunately. I'll probably be getting engaged soon.'

Jimmy laughed scornfully as she handed him his helmet and fags. 'Oh yeah, who's that to then? Not that tosser who's been stringing you along for the last God knows how many years?'

'He hasn't been doing anything of the sort,' Cathy informed him sniffily. 'He's been very good to me, paying my rent and everything.'

'Least he could do, innit,' Jimmy commented, flicking his fag packet open and sticking a cigarette into his mouth. 'Given what's on offer.'

'Piss off, Jimmy.' Cathy scowled, offended at the implication. She'd rather have her gas bill paid and the odd posh meal out than a poxy lager and lime any time.

Eyeing her thoughtfully over his cigarette, Jimmy lit up. 'Still can't believe you dumped me and went back to him,' he said, taking a tight draw. 'Broke my heart, you did. I loved you, y'know, Cath. Still do.'

'No you don't.' Cathy sighed tiredly. She really wished he'd stop doing this; hanging around every night like a jealous spurned lover in the hope that she and her bloke would split up again. 'You just want what you can't have.'

'Strikes me you do an' all. Nice little house with a white picket fence? Roses round the door and a faithful hubby to snuggle up in bed with?' Jimmy curled his lip in a sneer. 'Ain't likely to get it from some bloke who turns up when he feels like it, are you?'

'Get lost, Jimmy.' Cathy made to close the door.

Jimmy, though, clearly wasn't going anywhere. 'Give us another chance, Cath, go on,' he said, stumbling forward and making a grab for her.

'Jimmy…' Cathy pressed her hands to his chest, trying to keep him at bay. 'Get off!'

'Oi!' Mike, the landlord, appeared behind her as Jimmy attempted a clumsy kiss. 'Sling your hook, Jimmy, or I'll get the law to see you off.'

'What?' Letting go of her, Jimmy stepped back, looking surprised. 'I was only after a kiss. She was well up for it a few weeks ago, weren't you, Cath?'

'Jimmy, you're drunk,' Cathy pointed out, exasperated. 'You're embarrassing yourself. Just go, will you, before Mike calls the police.'

'Right. Like that, is it?' Jimmy wiped an arm across his mouth and looked her up and down disdainfully. 'You're going to regret it, Cath, trust me. You don't want a bloke pissing you about like that prick you're seeing. I'd have seen you all right. You know I would.'

Cathy eyed the sky. 'What, on your income? And living in that smelly flat above the curry house?' She laughed in bemusement; then, noting the flash of humiliation in his eyes, decided she should perhaps be a bit more careful of his feelings. It was clear he still had a soft spot for her. It wasn't his fault he was a loser. 'I know you mean well, Jimmy, but let's face it, that's just not my style, is it?'

Jimmy swept his gaze over her again, taking in her cow-print platform shoes, short black satin skirt and metallic top – all brand new and purchased from her catalogue. 'Nah, suppose not. Think I prefer the old style, though. Less tarty.' Giving her another disdainful sweep of his eyes, he shrugged, and turned to amble towards his motorbike.

Cheeky bastard. Cathy noted the definite weave to his walk as he went. God, what an idiot. Tall, if a bit spindly, he was reasonably good-looking, in a dark, broody biker sort of way. She might have been flattered he was so jealous if he didn't insist on acting like a complete dickhead. 'Don't forget your helmet, Jimmy,' she called after him. 'Wouldn't want you damaging your one brain cell, would we?'

Now considerably miffed, she banged the door shut after him and went through the bar to the private quarters where her little girl waited for her. Poor thing, she would be exhausted. Cathy hated having to bring her here while she worked but, with no money to pay for a childminder, she didn't have any choice.

'Come on, sweetie,' she said, rousing her daughter, who was curled up on the sofa in the living room, the book she'd been reading abandoned on the floor.

'Are we going home now, Mummy?' she asked, sitting up and kneading her eyes sleepily.

'We are, sweetheart,' Cathy assured her, picking up the book and placing it on the coffee table, then taking her by the hand to lead her back to the bar.

'I'm off, Mike,' she said, collecting their coats and her bag. 'See you tomorrow.'

Mike paused in his glass-washing. 'You all right?' he asked her.

Cathy fed her little girl into her coat and straightened up. She noted the concerned furrow in his brow, and was glad he cared enough to have intervened. Drunk or not, Jimmy had been well out of order tonight.

'Yeah, I'm fine,' she assured him. 'He's just jealous. He doesn't mean any harm.'

Mike didn't look convinced. 'Just watch what you're doing with him,' he warned her. 'Likes his booze too much, does that one. And watch how you drive, as well. There's black ice on that road into Meliton. It's always treacherous at this time of year.'

'I will, don't worry. I'm a big girl now, I can look after myself.' Cathy gave his arm a grateful squeeze as they walked past him to the door.

Clip-clopping across the car park, she paused to ferret in her bag for her car keys. Finally locating them amongst the debris at the bottom, she approached her little van, opening the back doors for her daughter to climb inside and then went around to the driver's side. Then stopped as someone shouted her name. 'Catherine Tyson! Wait! I want to talk to you.'

Cathy turned, her brow knitted curiously. 'About?'

'My husband, you little slut,' the woman growled.

Her…? Hang on a sec, what had she just called her? Stunned, Cathy might have demanded to know where the cheeky cow got off calling her names but for the fact that the woman was now advancing menacingly towards her. Shit! Sensing trouble, she whirled back around, fumbled the key into the lock and wiggled it frantically.

'Keep away from him,' the woman seethed, the flat of her hand slamming the driver's-side door shut just as Cathy had wrenched it open.

What the hell was she doing? 'Let go!' Cathy cried, attempting to grapple the door open again. 'Leave me alone.'

'I'll leave *you* alone when you leave *him* alone,' the woman spat, her face so close to Cathy's that she could almost taste the pungent aroma of floral perfume.

'I dunno what you're on about.' Cathy tugged uselessly at the handle. 'I haven't been anywhere near your husband.'

'Lying little trollop. Do you think I'm *stupid*?' the woman snarled. 'If you don't stay away from him, I swear to God I will claw your pretty eyes from their sockets and feed them to the landlord's fucking dog.'

Oh God. Hearing the malevolence in the woman's voice, Cathy's blood froze in her veins. She was stark raving mad. 'I don't have a clue what you're talking about,' she whimpered, feeling dangerously close to wetting herself. 'Let go of my door, or—'

'Or what? What will you do, hmm? Run? In those ridiculous shoes?' There was a mocking edge now to the woman's voice. 'Scream? Cry?'

Icy fear prickled the length of Cathy's spine as she felt the woman's hand lock around the back of her neck. 'Please…' she croaked. 'My daughter…'

'Do *not* see him again.' Sharp fingernails dug mercilessly into Cathy's flesh, the woman increasing the pressure. 'Don't ring him. Do not go anywhere—' She stopped, sucking in a sharp breath as one weighty-soled shoe stomped heavily down to grind her toes into the gravel. '*Bitch!*'

Cathy wasted no time. As the woman stumbled backwards, she yanked the driver's-side door open and threw herself inside, dropping the lock fast.

'Mummy? What's happening?' her little girl said bewilderedly from where she was curled up with her Sindy doll in the back of the van.

She was scared. Hearing the tremble in her voice, Cathy cursed her incompetence. She'd known that bringing her here was a bad idea. She'd witnessed all sorts of things a child shouldn't, and now this. 'Stay down,' she hissed, lunging across to drop the lock on the opposite side, and then flicking the headlights on.

Halfway around the front of the car, framed in the full beam, the woman fixed her gaze hard on Cathy's, a wild, feverish glare that chilled her right down to the bone. She meant to hurt her. Cathy's heart thrashed against her ribcage as she watched the woman look frenziedly around. Looking for something to smash the windscreen with?

Oh, sweet Jesus. 'Stay down, baby,' she whispered, shoving her key shakily into the ignition and turning the engine over, only for it to splutter and die.

At once, the woman's gaze snapped back to hers, a surprised expression crossing her face, which soon gave way to a petrifying smile of quiet triumph.

Sweat popped out on Cathy's forehead. With a sharp knot in her windpipe, she watched the woman turn back to her own car – a great Mitsubishi Shogun – moving with surprising agility despite a now obvious limp. What was she going to do?

But Cathy knew. Swallowing back the acrid taste of terror, she pictured it: the Shogun ramming into her tin-sided van, crushing it like an eggshell. Nausea sweeping through her, she turned the key again, eased out the choke and tried desperately to start the vehicle once more. The engine coughed, a coarse, throaty sound like an old man who'd smoked too many Woodbines, but still it stubbornly refused to spark. *God! Please!* Tears spilling down her cheeks, Cathy prayed with all her might as she eased the choke further out, then closed her eyes, relief crashing through her like a tidal wave, when the van finally juddered into life.

Cautioning herself not to stall it, she reached for the gearstick, crunching through the gears then plunging her foot down to reverse sharply before yanking the wheel around and screeching out of the car park. The woman wouldn't follow her, surely? Attempt to run her off the road?

Drive, Cathy instructed herself. Panic twisting her stomach, the small wheels of her van jolting through potholes on the neglected country lane, she glanced in her rear-view mirror. Bright light slicing high across her vision confirmed that the Shogun was behind her, intent on possibly doing just that.

Shit! She snapped her gaze back to the windscreen and switched on the wipers, but they only made the smear of muddy ice on the glass worse. Her water container was empty. She'd meant to fill it up. *God, please help me.* She leaned forward, using her cuff to try to make a big enough hole in the condensation on the inside to see through.

The motorbike came out of nowhere.

Losing traction on the blind bend ahead of her, it skidded sideways across the front of the van like a hockey puck across an ice rink, before Cathy even had time to blink.

CHAPTER TWO

Claire

2019

Yanked from a dark, dream-filled sleep, Claire snapped her eyes open and then sat bolt upright, flicking on her lamp as she heard scuffling followed by a dull thud outside her bedroom door. Her panic subsided a little when she remembered the baby gates she'd installed at the top and bottom of the long oak staircase, but still she wasn't confident her father wouldn't get past the gate at the top and tumble down it. Without carpet, in keeping with the rustic decor of the house, those stairs could be lethal. A haunting image of her mother lying like a broken ragdoll at the bottom of them flashed chillingly through her mind, and she shook off the shiver that ran through her, threw back her duvet and scrambled out of bed.

What on earth was he doing? It was obvious it was her father wandering about, but she'd moved everything he could possibly bump into on his incessant trips to the loo. Flying to the door, she dashed out – and then froze, her heart leaping into her mouth as she came face to face with not one, but two men on the landing, one of whom was close to being forced over the stair rail.

'Dad!' she cried, launching herself towards them. 'Dad, let him go!' She tugged on his arm, to no avail, then attempted to prise his hands from her husband's throat before he throttled him. 'Dad, *please…*'

'Call the police, Ruth,' Bernard growled, and Claire's heart started the downward trajectory it always did when he addressed her by her mother's name. 'Thieving piece of scum, breaking into decent people's homes. Ought to be—'

'Dad, for God's sake, *stop*!' Claire shouted, her desperation rising as she heard her husband gagging. 'It's *Luke*.'

Bernard faltered, his gaze perplexed as it flicked towards her. 'Who?'

'My husband,' Claire clarified, a hard lump clogging her throat. 'Please stop.'

His forehead furrowing into a puzzled frown, Bernard looked back to Luke, blinked in bemusement and then, mercifully, relaxed his grip.

Oh God. 'Luke…' Claire moved to help him as, clearly shocked and disorientated, he struggled upright. 'Are you okay?'

'For fuck's sake…' Luke rasped. 'Are you *insane*?' Stepping away from the rail, causing Bernard to blunder backwards into the landing wall behind him, he eyeballed the older man with a combination of disbelief and palpable fury. 'What the *hell* were you doing?'

Bernard's expression was now nonplussed. 'Going to the bathroom,' he supplied innocently.

Claire felt her heart ache for him. A proud man, he'd always carried himself tall, but his posture was now stooped in defeat, his once sharply intelligent brown eyes rheumy and awash with uncertainty.

'Bloody maniac,' Luke muttered, fixing him with a disdainful gaze.

'I beg your pardon?' Bernard's mood switched in an instant, as it tended to. Pulling himself up to his full height, he stepped towards Luke again, his eyes narrowing.

Nerves knotted Claire's stomach. Fearing a stand-off, she readied herself to intervene, and then almost wilted with relief as, after scanning Luke's eyes briefly, her dad's mood appeared to shift again, confusion crossing his face before he turned away to walk back to his bedroom.

Luke laughed scathingly and shook his head. 'Yeah, no problem, Bernard,' he called angrily after him. 'Apology accepted.'

'Luke, don't make things worse,' Claire whispered, her heart sinking.

'Me?' Luke stared at her, in disbelief. 'He bloody well attacked me! He could have *killed* me.'

'But he didn't realise it was you,' Claire pointed out. It was well past midnight, and Luke would have crept in. He and his mates had no doubt been the last to leave the local pub again. Luke had apparently been appointed chief organiser of his best friend's upcoming stag night, and judging by the smell of beer, he'd had a fair few while he was at it. Claire tried not to mind him going out. She couldn't help thinking that he might have volunteered for the job, though, preferring to be at the pub rather than here. She hadn't said anything, possibly because she'd felt too tired to pursue it, but she'd been devastated when she'd joined him there one night and noticed a group of girls, also on a boozy night out, one of whom was blatantly giving Luke the eye. She was sure she could trust him, but a nagging seed of doubt had taken root inside her when she'd caught him glancing in the girl's direction.

'Who the bloody hell else would he think it was?' Luke grumbled, as Claire tried again to ignore the awful knot of uncertainty in her tummy. What would she do if he did more than look? If her best intentions to care for her father drove her husband away?

'He thought there was a stranger in the house,' she said, and then immediately wished she could reel the words back in.

Luke's expression said it all. *I rest my case.* He sighed. 'He doesn't *know* me, Claire. He has no idea who I am.'

'He's confused,' she reminded him. 'You obviously startled him.'

'He's not the only one,' Luke muttered.

Guessing where this was leading, Claire felt her heart sink another inch.

'What are we doing here, Claire?' Luke asked, on cue.

He didn't want to be living in her father's house; that was glaringly obvious. He'd been dead set against them moving in when she'd suggested it, and had only relented when she'd pointed out that if they sold the place, the entire proceeds might end up paying for care home fees. Plus, there was the fact that she'd actually wanted to look after her father. Luke wasn't likely to be any happier about the situation now he'd been half strangled to death. Claire felt awful for him. She could see the livid bruises forming on his neck already. There was no point going into it all again now, though. They would only end up arguing, and that would wake Ella, leaving her tired and fractious in the morning.

'I know why you're doing this, and I understand,' he went on, working to control his agitation, 'but it's becoming impossible. He's not just confused any more. He's aggressive. Dangerous. Surely you can see it's time to organise some proper care for him? Professional care. Ella's only four years old. Quite apart from the psychological effect it might have on her, she's haemophilic, for God's sake. What if he turned on her in the middle of the night? Or left the front door open again? He's not safe for a child to be around.'

Claire reeled under that attack. Did he think she wasn't aware of Ella's illness? That she'd hadn't struggled, as he had, to accept the cruel twist of fate that had given their precious daughter the mutated gene that made her a carrier? With her own mother dead and buried and no other family history of haemophilia they'd been able to trace, did he imagine she didn't somehow blame herself, every minute of every day? Ella's symptoms were mild, thank goodness, but did he really think Claire didn't worry about her and watch over her constantly, terrified she might cut herself? Bruise herself and bleed internally? She lived in terror that she might not get her daughter to a hospital in time for the blood-clotting-factor injections to be administered.

'That's not fair, Luke,' she retaliated, hurt and defensive. 'I never leave her on her own with him. I'm always here when—'

'Because you've given up your job,' Luke reminded her, exasperated. 'You've given up your *life*. You can't do this, Claire. It's not fair on you. Not fair on anyone, least of all Bernard. He needs twenty-four-hour care. With the best will in the world, it's just not possible for you to give him that any more.'

'I *know*.' Claire's voice rose in frustration. She was becoming increasingly aware of that. She wanted to scream with exhaustion sometimes, but what good would that do? The two of them were constantly at loggerheads. She couldn't blame Luke for being annoyed and frustrated. She had so little time for him lately. And with her perpetually tired and her dad just the other side of the bedroom wall, the intimacy between them had dwindled to non-existent. He was worried, clearly, wondering where this would end, but right now, she needed his support.

'I've been…' *looking at various options*, she was about to say, when Ella's door squeaked open and she emerged nervously onto the landing.

Guessing she'd been woken by the noise, Claire stepped towards her, but Luke was quicker. 'Hey, gorgeous girl,' he said, bending to sweep her into his arms. 'What's up?'

Ella looked worriedly at him from under her long eyelashes. 'I heard shouting,' she said, her voice tremulous. 'I was frightened.'

'There's nothing to be frightened of, pumpkin.' Luke gave her a reassuring smile. 'It was just Grandad and me. We bumped into each other in the dark.'

Ella eased back to study his face. 'Were you frightened?' she asked him, her expression uncertain.

'A bit,' Luke admitted. 'He caught me by surprise. We're all good now, though. Come on, let's tuck you back up with Flopsy and Gruffy. They'll protect you.'

'Gruffalo and Flopsy are frightened too. They think there's a monster,' Ella confided, her little brow furrowed in consternation. 'Will you tuck up with us, Daddy? You could fight the monster off then.'

'I'll always fight your monsters, sweetheart,' Luke promised softly. Hoisting her higher in his arms, he carried her back to her bedroom. 'Say night night to Mummy.'

Ella waved from the door. 'Night, Mummy.'

'Night, baby.' Claire managed a smile. She didn't miss the pointed glance Luke shot her as he closed the door behind him, leaving her barefoot on the landing, feeling guilty and lonely.

Taking a second to compose herself, she stared at the ceiling, then padded after her father. When she tapped on the open door and went in, she found him sitting on the side of the bed with a deep furrow in his brow, studying the carpet intently. 'Come on, Dad. Let's try and get some beauty sleep, shall we?' she said encouragingly. None of this was his fault.

Bernard looked up as she approached. Seeing his anxious expression, Claire smiled and reached past him for the duvet. 'It's not morning yet, Dad,' she said, working to inject some cheeriness into her tone. 'Why don't you pop back into bed and—'

'Don't see him again,' Bernard said suddenly, his hand shooting out to catch hold of her wrist.

'Dad…?' Claire's gaze snapped to his. '*Dad*, you're hurting me.' Bewildered, she tried to pull away, but he clung on, his fingers digging into her flesh.

'Don't do this to me,' her father begged. 'He'll never be able to provide for you; never love you the way I do. I will tell her. I promise I will.'

Fear clutched Claire's stomach. Tell who what? It wasn't her he was seeing in front of him. Uneasiness crept through her as she noted the desperation in his eyes, and she wrenched her hand away from his grasp and stumbled back.

'Dad?' she said, feeling tearful. 'Who are you talking to?'

But Bernard was staring at the carpet again. When he glanced back at her, after a second, he looked as confused as she felt. 'Sorry, dear?'

'Nothing.' Claire swallowed back the pain lodged like a stone in her throat. 'Let's get you comfortable, shall we? It's really late. I think we could all use some sleep.'

Finally managing to get him settled, Claire went wearily back to her own room. She would have to organise more specialised care, she knew. He was undoubtedly becoming more aggressive. That had happened almost overnight, after a series of transient ischaemic attacks associated with vascular dementia, according to his consultant. He was also more unpredictable, his memory becoming less and less reliable. Was what he'd just said a true recollection? A conversation he might actually have had? One he'd wanted to have? She might never know, because he might never accurately remember.

Desperate for sleep, which she knew wouldn't come easily, she reached for her phone to reset her alarm, and noticed she'd received a new message. She flicked to it, thinking she could use a friendly ear about now, and her heart froze.

Are you Bernard Harvey's daughter? If you are, I'm your half-sister. The message was from someone called Sophie.

Hands trembling, feeling as if the breath had been sucked from her lungs, she went to the sender's profile. The photograph showed a pretty woman with short cropped hair, similar in age to herself. Seeing she was a friend of a friend, Claire had friended her when she'd realised she lived in Rhyl, a place her father had taken her to as a child while on one of his many road trips. Sophie had commented on a message Claire had posted on Facebook about her dad and what a cruel disease dementia was. *I feel for you, Claire*, she'd said.

She had commented on several other posts after that. Claire had thought she'd been reaching out to her, sympathising, that was all. A tight lump expanded unbearably in her throat as she recalled her father's ramblings, the conviction in his tone, his frightening grip on her wrist, and she typed a short reply: *I don't have a sister*.

Are you sure? the woman pinged back.

CHAPTER THREE

Claire

Shaking inside, feeling emotionally and physically drained, Claire crawled into bed. She couldn't do this now, couldn't process her thoughts. Couldn't think. Craving sleep, if only for a few hours, she closed her eyes and tried to empty her mind.

She couldn't stop listening for sounds in the night, though: bangs and shuffling footsteps, creaks on the stairs. Her mind drifting as it played over the message, she was transported back to the day she'd tried so hard to forget: her seven-year-old-self peering up through the stair rail in the hall, panic gripping her tummy as she listened to her mum and dad arguing on the landing above; her dad shouting furiously, 'Do you think drinking this stuff helps?'; her mother screaming, 'It's your fault, you bastard. You drove me to it.' She heard afresh the strange yelp of fear, the few seconds' silence that followed, the dull *thud… thud… thud* of a soft body tumbling and bouncing off each step of the stairs. She scrunched her eyes tighter; tried hard to think of pleasant things: walks in the park with Ella, their last family holiday together. Still the darker memories pervaded.

Somehow she must have finally dozed off, only to be jolted awake by a crash from downstairs, accompanied by a male voice loudly cursing.

Luke? Yet again, Claire shot out of bed, grabbing her dressing gown and stuffing her arms into it as she raced to the landing.

Oh no. Peering over the stair rail to see Luke hauling himself up from the hall floor, she hurried down the stairs. 'What on earth happened?' she asked, negotiating her way around the collapsed gate at the bottom.

'I would have thought that was fairly obvious,' Luke muttered moodily.

'Are you all right?' She looked him worriedly over, then bent to retrieve the gate from the floor.

'Ecstatic,' Luke growled. 'First I'm attacked by your father, then by the bloody baby gate. And now I'm going to be late for work.'

'Well, that's hardly the end of the world, is it?' Claire tried not to react. She was feeling fragile and really didn't want to start the day with an argument.

'It is when I've been late once this week already. At this rate, I won't have a job either, and then we'll really be in the—'

'Luke! Please will you just *stop*,' Claire said tearfully. 'I'm doing my best. You're not the only one struggling here, you know.'

'I *know*,' Luke shot back. 'That's my point. You can't cope. You need to do something about the situation. *Now.* You can't go on like this. *We* can't.'

Claire felt her heart skip a beat. 'Which means what?' she asked warily.

Luke scanned her face, his expression one of discernible agitation. 'Coming to live here was a mistake, Claire,' he said, point blank. 'It's not good for us, and it's not good for Ella. She's vulnerable, for God's sake. And yes, I know we agreed she should live as normal a life as possible,' he went on, as Claire opened her mouth to try to defend herself, 'but this is *not* normal.'

'So what do you want me to do?' she asked, fighting back her tears. 'I can't just make things different overnight. I'm trying, but—' She stopped, her nerves jangling as yet another crash shook the floorboards above them.

'Shit!' Fear flooding his features, Luke lurched towards the stairs.

Oh God. 'Ella!' Claire whirled around to fly up ahead of him. 'I'm coming, sweetheart.'

Her legs almost buckled with relief as Ella appeared at her bedroom door. 'I'm all right, Mummy,' she said. She knew that she had to tell them if she'd fallen or hurt herself. 'It's Grandad. He's pulled his wardrobe drawer out again.'

Her heart rate returning to somewhere near normal, Claire carried on up the stairs.

'You need to think about what choices you want to make, Claire,' Luke called after her.

Cold trepidation gripping her, Claire turned on the landing. 'I don't *have* any choices right now,' she pointed out. 'I can hardly just walk out. He doesn't have anyone else.'

'Right. Which pretty much means you've made your choice, doesn't it?' Shaking his head despairingly, Luke turned towards the front door.

'Luke! What are you talking about?' Claire called. 'I'm not making choices. I'm simply trying to do what—'

'Forget it,' he said curtly. He picked up his keys from the hall table, then cursed as he dropped them.

He was limping, Claire noted, her heart sinking. 'Luke, don't be so ridiculous,' she pleaded, as he retrieved the keys and yanked the front door open. 'Can't we just talk about this later? Sensibly?'

'I'm out later,' Luke said shortly, and stepped outside, slamming the door shut behind him.

CHAPTER FOUR

Luke

'Not going to be up to quad trekking on Friday, are we, shunshine?' Steve slurred, parking another beer on the table and slinging an arm around Luke's shoulders.

'Nope.' Luke sighed, and shifted his leg under the table to ease the nagging pain in his ankle. At least it wasn't as crippling as it had been earlier, when he'd limped into work and Steve had insisted that he go straight to the hospital. It had been throbbing like a bastard when they'd come into Birmingham town centre to meet the other lads and check out a few of the bars on Broad Street. Several bars later, and plenty of alcohol consumed, they'd moved on to the Basement Club to make sure the 'urban vibe' and dance scene was what they had in mind for the stag night. Luke wasn't doing much dancing, but he was doing plenty of drinking, which was probably going a long way to numbing the pain.

'You want to go easy on the booze,' Steve said, nodding towards him over his beer. 'You'll be legless.'

'Yeah, very good, Steve.' Luke eyed the ceiling and took a swig of his own drink.

'Won't have a leg to stand on.' Steve, who was clearly on a roll with the rubbish jokes, grinned and knocked back the rest of his beer, then blew out a low whistle as a pretty young woman who was passing on her way to the dance floor gave him the eye.

'Later,' he muttered to Luke, then wiped a hand over his mouth and promptly about-faced to follow her.

Much later, Luke guessed, which meant he was going to sit here like a lemon for at least another hour. He sighed and tried not to mind. As well as being his boss, Steve was a good mate. They'd worked in the construction industry together for years, a job Bernard had derided, viewing Luke as an unskilled labourer who built houses for other people but couldn't afford one of his own. Steve had taken the initiative a few years back, buying up properties for refurb and selling them on. Now that he was offering to help Luke get on the ladder, going fifty-fifty on a property, the least Luke could do was make sure his stag night was organised.

Some of the guys were going on to a lap-dancing club after. Luke definitely wasn't up for that. He wanted to get home, try to convince Claire that he was on her side, though he wasn't sure how to do that when every time he broached the subject of looking at a care home for Bernard, she shot him down. It was as if he was the enemy suddenly, which hurt when his concern was for her. And Ella.

He couldn't believe Claire couldn't see that Bernard was an accident waiting to happen where their daughter was concerned. He'd come home late from work one night to discover the front door wide open and Bernard standing in the middle of the kitchen, no doubt having forgotten what he was doing there. Bounding up the stairs in a panic, Luke had found Ella sound asleep in her bed. What had bothered him was that Claire wouldn't have noticed if she had wandered off. She was fast asleep too, on the sofa. There was an empty wine glass on the coffee table, he noted.

He had been worried sick ever since. There was danger everywhere out there for a four-year-old on her own. Not to mention a four-year-old who would need the right medication immediately if she sustained an injury that caused bleeding. He knew Claire was exhausted, he could see that, but still he couldn't believe she'd been so irresponsible. Did she not realise that social services might become involved again if Ella was found on her own in the street? Their lives had been a living nightmare for a while before Ella's haemophilia diagnosis. The doctor at the hospital they'd taken her to, several times, hadn't believed them when they'd told her they had no idea what was causing Ella's sudden bruising. She'd raised concerns about the possibility of non-accidental injury, meaning that one or both of them was suspected of harming her. Child protection had been involved, for Christ's sake. Did Claire really want to go down that route again?

Fresh agitation washed over him, as it did every time he thought about the possible scenarios. He remembered how Bernard had left the door into the garage open a couple of weeks back, and shuddered when he thought about what harm Ella might have come to playing around in there. He knocked back his beer and reached for another of the several he had lined up. He understood why Claire wanted to try to care for Bernard herself – she was his only child, after all – but to have uprooted the family and moved them into his house lock, stock and barrel? He couldn't fathom why she'd insisted on doing that.

She'd pointed out that it was too far for her to drive every day from their rented cottage in Herefordshire to Bernard's house in Solihull. But then she'd made the decision so suddenly, he'd got to thinking that maybe she hadn't wanted to live in the cottage in the first place. Sure, the place had needed a hell of a lot of work, but he could have done that, over time. Maybe it was that she didn't want to live with him. He would never be able to provide for his family the way he wanted to on his current income, and married life thus far hadn't exactly been smooth sailing. They'd had each other, though. That was something they'd held onto through the rough times. But now it didn't seem they even had that any more, only ever having rushed conversations, arguing whenever they did talk. Sex seemed like a distant memory, which he tried hard not to mind. After running around after Bernard and Ella all day, Claire was hardly likely to be in the mood. He missed it; missed the closeness it brought them.

Claire wasn't missing him, though, it seemed. She hadn't even replied to the text he'd sent apologising for not being able to get back early. He hoped Bernard didn't leap on him again when he did get back. He wasn't sure how he hadn't lost his temper completely when he'd tried to strangle him.

Running a hand over his throat, which was still bloody sore, he debated whether to send her another text, and then decided to leave it. She was probably busy. Or else she might be sleeping. He hoped it wasn't with the assistance of alcohol. Reaching for one of the whisky chasers someone had kindly bought him, he realised he was being a complete hypocrite. He was on his way to getting well plastered. Correction, he'd actually arrived. He'd be seeing double at this rate. Christ, he wished he and Claire could get back to where they used to be. In their own place, no matter how modest. Some privacy. Each other. Clearly, though, she didn't share his sentiments.

Attempting to curtail his frustration, he swallowed a mouthful of the whisky, wincing as it burned its way down his oesophagus, and concentrated on the action on the dance floor, on the periphery of which was a young woman who looked vaguely familiar. Luke tried to place her. Swaying her hips provocatively to the music, she was definitely eye-catching. He swept his gaze over her, noting the long raven-coloured hair she was now scooping up onto her head, showing off her long, slender neck and the dress she was just about wearing: a slinky white halter-neck affair that fitted in all the right places. Or possibly not. As she reached to pile her hair higher, revealing most of her full breasts, Luke almost choked on his drink.

At least he had some entertainment while he sat on the sidelines, he supposed. Closing one eye, he tried to focus. She had some interesting moves. Realising she had clocked him watching her, he smiled and raised his drink in appreciation of her dancing.

Smiling back, she hesitated for a second as the beat slowed, and then made her way off the dance floor. Luke tilted his head to one side and tried to fathom where it was he'd seen her before. One of Claire's friends or work associates maybe? He thought not. As drunk as he was, he was sure he would remember if she was. He felt guilty for thinking it, but she was an attractive woman. He took in the swing of her hips as she walked in his direction, the grey snakeskin stiletto boots that showed off her long, tanned legs.

'Hey,' she said, stopping in front of him.

'Hey.' Luke dipped his head in greeting and racked his brains. Still he couldn't place her. 'I know this is going to sound like the corniest line ever,' he said, 'but haven't we met before?'

She laughed. 'It does, but yes, we have met, sort of. You and your mates were at the club I work in the other night. I couldn't help but notice you all there.'

'Ah.' Luke nodded. 'We do tend to get a bit loud, don't we? Sorry about that. We're organising a stag night for one of the guys.'

'I gathered.' She looked him over thoughtfully. 'Are you not dancing?'

He shook his head. 'Incapacitated. Sprained ankle.' He indicated the walker boot he'd been given at the hospital.

She winced in sympathy. 'Ouch. Definitely a bit of a hindrance. Painful too, I bet.'

'And some,' Luke concurred, sighing inwardly. He got that Claire had been distracted, but she hadn't even noticed he'd been injured.

'Not too much of a hindrance where it counts, though, I bet?' she said, her smoky dark eyes full of implicit meaning as they focused on his.

Floored for a second, Luke scanned her face, noting the smile playing around her pink-glossed lips. They were full and sensual, and he found himself imagining what she would taste like. *Shit. Pack it up, Luke.* Chastising himself, he reached to take another gulp of his drink, only to end up almost missing his mouth.

'Whoops, you spilled some,' she said, leaning towards him.

Uncertain where to put his eyes, Luke attempted to keep his attention on her face as she wiped a drip from his chin with her thumb. 'I don't suppose you fancy getting out of here, do you?' she asked him, her gaze holding his. 'My place for coffee, maybe? It's not far from here. I'm renting a little apartment on Waterfront Wharf.'

Jesus. Luke's heart skipped a beat. 'I, er… Thanks,' he said awkwardly. 'It's a nice offer, but…'

'You're not interested,' she finished, looking crestfallen as she straightened up.

'No, it's not that,' Luke said quickly. 'You're an attractive woman. Very. It's just…'

'It's fine. I get it,' she said, now clearly embarrassed. 'You're probably already spoken for.' She stopped as Luke's mobile rang. 'I'll leave you to it.' Giving him a sad smile, she turned away.

Luke sighed inwardly, then pulled himself together when he realised it was Claire calling. Hitting answer, he struggled clumsily to his feet. 'Claire… I can't hear you,' he shouted, a hand clamped over one ear to drown out the noise and the phone pressed to his other as he limped towards the exit.

He was almost there when he was distracted by some bloke shouting, 'You *what*? I was nowhere near you, you bloody nutter.'

'Just stay away from me!' a woman screamed back. 'I'm warning you, don't you come anywhere near me or I swear to God I'll call the police.'

It was her. Luke stopped. The woman he'd just been talking to. And she was considerably upset. What was going on here? He narrowed his eyes.

The guy looked her over as she glared tearfully at him, her fists clenched and her arms glued rigidly to her sides. 'Don't worry, darling, you're perfectly safe,' he assured her with a sneer. 'I wouldn't come near you with a bargepole. Fucking mental case.'

'Oi!' Luke moved towards him. 'That's enough,' he warned. 'Back off.'

The man appeared nonplussed for a second, then he looked Luke up and down in much the same way he had done the woman he'd been bad-mouthing. 'For your information, chum, I have as much right to be here as *she* has.' He jabbed a finger towards her as she headed for the foyer, wiping tears from her face as she went. 'Unless you're telling me otherwise.'

'That's exactly what I'm doing, *chum*,' Luke assured him, his anger mounting. The bloke was obviously an aggressive git. 'I'd piss off if I were you, while you still can.'

The bloke laughed out loud at that. 'Right,' he said. 'And you're going to make me, are you? What you gonna do then? Kick me to death with your spazzie boot?'

Offensive little prick. Luke held onto his temper, just. 'Possibly. While *they* hold you down.' Smiling flatly, he nodded to the man's side, where Steve and three of their mates stood, arms folded, expressions stony.

The man glanced towards them and then back to Luke. 'I was nowhere near her. She's got a fucking screw loose,' he muttered, though he'd clearly got the message, turning and heading moodily towards the exit.

Luke breathed a sigh of relief , not least because one of the bouncers was now striding towards them, no doubt about to intervene. He didn't fancy being manhandled out of the club.

'All right, Luke?' Steve asked, stepping towards him.

'Yeah, good, thanks,' Luke assured him, grateful for his timely intervention. 'I just need to go outside.' Indicating his phone, he smiled and headed onwards. Claire had obviously cut the call. He couldn't blame her for that.

He looked for the woman as he made his way through the foyer. No sign of her. She might be in the toilets, he supposed. Or else she'd left, which was a shame. He would have liked to have made sure she was okay.

Reaching the street, he was about to call Claire back when he realised she'd texted him. As he read the message, he felt a knot of bewilderment tighten inside him.

You're clearly having a riot. As you're so keen on being out with your mates rather than home with me, you can go and stay with them.

What the hell was that all about? Leaning back against the outside wall for support, he hit call. He waited, staring at his phone, frustrated when she didn't pick up. She was making a point, obviously, but really? While he was stuck in the middle of Brum with a sprained ankle?

His frustration growing, he texted her back. *Which means what, exactly?*

Exactly what it says, she answered after a minute. *You clearly love your mates more than me and I've had it, Luke. If this is what marriage is all about, then I don't want it. Please don't come back here. I don't want any more upsets.*

Un-bloody-believable. Luke laughed, incredulous. She was telling him not to go home. Which was a bit of a joke considering he hadn't actually got a sodding home to go back to. Pulling himself away from the wall, he ran a hand agitatedly over his neck and wondered whether to try to phone her again, or whether to simply text back *Fine*, which was about as juvenile as this could get. Arguing by text, for Christ's sake.

Sighing heavily, he turned to go back into the nightclub – and very nearly fell over the woman from inside. 'Crap, sorry.' He righted himself with a hand on the wall. 'I didn't see you.'

'I'll let you off.' She smiled, unperturbed. 'Since you're so wobbly on your feet.'

He was certainly that, feeling the effect of drinking heavily on top of painkillers, and disorientated by Claire's texts. He wished he'd stopped and gone on to soft drinks.

'Are you okay?' he asked. 'Whoever that guy was, he was well out of order.' She still looked upset, her eyes watery and her make-up smudged.

She nodded and took a shuddery breath. 'An ex,' she explained, 'who thinks he has a right to harass me, unfortunately.'

'Prat,' Luke growled. 'Have you informed the police?'

She shrugged forlornly. 'For what it was worth. Thanks for riding to my rescue. Many men wouldn't have.' Then, taking him by surprise, she threaded her arms around his neck and leaned in to press her lips lightly to his. Luke felt her perfume invade every one of his senses, as she lingered a second or two too long.

'My pleasure.' He coughed to clear his throat as she eased away. 'Like I say, the man was well out of order.'

Again she nodded, glancing down and back. 'I'll be fine now,' she said. 'That is, I will be once I'm in a taxi. I don't suppose you'd do me a favour and hang around until I find one, would you?'

Luke squinted at her, now very concerned. She thought the bloke would come out after her? Christ, there really were some pathetic bastards about. 'No problem,' he said. 'You sure you're going to be okay once you get home, though?' He was thinking of his mother and the prat she was with. He was like a bloody boomerang. Every time she threw the skiving, thieving piece of scum out, he would come back and wheedle his way in again.

'That's sweet of you, but I will be, I promise. If he's hanging around outside the apartment again, I'll call the police. Not that they'll do very much unless *he* does anything, but…' Trailing off, she glanced past him, and then stepped towards the kerb to flag down an oncoming taxi.

Feeling uncomfortable about leaving her, Luke watched her climb in. Then, 'Wait,' he said, as she reached to close the door. 'That coffee, does the offer still stand?'

She looked at him curiously.

He shrugged. 'I wouldn't be much of a white knight if I rode off when you might still be in trouble, would I?'

CHAPTER FIVE

Luke

'So, your wife doesn't mind you going out clubbing with your mates then?' Anna asked, glancing back at him as she made him a coffee and poured a red wine for herself.

'I don't think she cares what I do right now,' Luke answered wearily, and then immediately regretted it.

'Oh dear.' Her expression concerned, Anna walked across to him and handed him his coffee. 'Problems, I take it?'

'A few,' Luke admitted awkwardly. 'My daughter is sick; she has haemophilia. Not that that's a problem. Hers is what's called a mild case, so it doesn't affect her day-to-day life.'

'But you're worried about her?' Anna guessed.

Running a hand over his neck, Luke nodded, half wishing he hadn't entered into the conversation. It felt like a betrayal of Claire and Ella. He shouldn't be here. He should have left once he'd made sure Anna was in safely. But then he'd been concerned, particularly when she'd confided on the way here that the Neanderthal from the nightclub had forced his way in once before. He'd been angry, too. And bewildered. Had Claire really been telling him their marriage was over simply because he'd tried to explain that the way they were living was impossible? He couldn't get his head around it. He'd had no idea where he was supposed to stay tonight. He could have crashed at Steve's, but his fiancé had not long moved in with him. Steve rolling home drunk with a mate in tow he suspected might not have gone down well with Lauren. Also it would have meant sticking with the guys until the bitter end, and there really was no way he was up for the lap-dancing club. Anna had offered him her couch. It was a bad idea, but he was beginning to wonder whether he cared any more.

'We've, er, been living with my wife's father,' he offered by way of explanation, as Anna studied him curiously. Debating how much to say, and then guessing it really didn't matter since he probably wouldn't see her again, he placed his cup on the worktop and went on, 'He has Alzheimer's. Early onset. Claire…' He faltered, now definitely feeling like a traitor. 'My wife has been caring for him. Trying to. The thing is, it's almost impossible. She's running herself ragged. He's deteriorating rapidly. Becoming unpredictable.'

He stopped and blew out a breath. He hadn't meant to say all that. He'd opened his mouth and it had all come spewing out. Maybe he hadn't realised how badly he needed someone to talk to.

'Violent?' she suggested.

'Definitely that.' His hand went involuntarily to the side of his sore neck.

'And you're worried your daughter might get injured in some way?' Anna suggested. 'I get that. My grandad had it,' she added, compassion in her eyes as she scanned his. Hers were mesmerising. Burnt umber in colour, Luke would describe them, but darker; so dark they were almost black. He could barely distinguish the pupil from the iris. 'Trying to keep up with him was an absolute nightmare, and that was without a vulnerable child to care for,' she went on.

Luke blew out a breath, feeling a huge sense of relief that someone else could see what was blindingly obvious to him. That it might be Ella who ended up a casualty in all of this. How was it that that someone was a stranger, and not her mother?

'Have you tried talking to your wife about how you feel?'

He smiled at the irony of that question. 'Until I'm blue in the face. We only ever seem to end up arguing. I'm beginning to think she sees me as the enemy, as if I want her to stop caring for him for my own selfish reasons. I mean, I do, obviously. I'd quite like to have a relationship with her, but… I don't know.' He shrugged despairingly. 'She doesn't seem to be hearing me. Maybe she just doesn't want to.'

'I'm sorry, Luke. That's so unfair on you.' Looking him over sympathetically, Anna stepped towards him. 'I wondered about those bruises,' she said, reaching out to trace her fingers delicately across his throat. 'Your father-in-law?'

She stepped closer as he nodded uneasily.

'Poor you,' she said, her eyes holding his.

He should have resisted as she moved closer still, her arms looping around his neck, her mouth seeking his. Her kiss was soft, the tip of her tongue tantalising as it slid into his mouth. Her torso pressed close to his, her breasts firm against his chest. Luke felt his desire spike. His urgency driving him, he closed his mouth hungrily over hers, tasting her, paying no heed to the warning voice in his head. Tongues now shamelessly seeking each other's, he wove a hand through her hair, twining it around his fingers, tipping her head back to expose her slender neck. He was barely aware of her hands gliding under his shirt, until he felt sharp fingernails scraping his flesh.

Jesus. His conscience finally kicking in, he stopped. 'Anna… we… I can't,' he said, his voice hoarse. 'I'm sorry, I shouldn't have… I'm married, Anna. I…'

'I know. I just thought that, as you'd come in…' Her eyes flickered down and back. 'I wasn't expecting anything more from you, Luke,' she said, smiling reassuringly. 'I would never cause another woman that kind of emotional pain, not after all I've been through. I thought that maybe we could offer each other some mutual comfort. Ships that pass in the night, that's all. I'm not ready for more than that. Not yet.'

Twenty minutes later, she followed him to the front door. 'You're an extremely sensitive and caring man, Luke,' she said, trailing a hand softly down his cheek. 'Don't let anyone tell you otherwise.'

Luke felt anything but. Guilty was how he felt, on all fronts. 'I should go,' he said with an apologetic shrug.

Anna nodded sympathetically. 'You have my number if you need to talk. No strings. I'm always willing to listen. Any time,' she added.

Cursing himself for his juvenile behaviour, for not going home to talk to Claire calmly and sensibly, he smiled his thanks at Anna for being so understanding and closed the door quietly behind him. He wasn't sure where he was going to go at this time of night, but taking up her offer to stay was out of the question. He guessed he should go back to Bernard's house; shout his apologies to Claire through the front door if necessary.

Sighing at how badly he'd handled the whole situation, and swearing never to drink so much again – the alcohol had obviously addled his brain – he limped along the canal towpath, heading back to the main road. After trying unsuccessfully to hail a taxi, he googled local companies and called one, only to be told it would take a cab forty to fifty minutes to reach him. Sighing again, he found a bus stop, which at least had a shelter, and settled down to wait.

He was half asleep, slumped uncomfortably on the damp pavement against the shelter, when his phone rang. Not recognising the number, and wondering whether it might be the taxi firm, he pressed the phone to his ear, and then, his heart jolting in his chest, pulled himself to his feet.

'She asked us to call you,' the doctor from the City Hospital said.

The shock rendering him numb, Luke was still trying to digest what the doctor had already told him. 'What happened?' he asked, after a second, his voice emerging as a dry croak.

'We're not entirely sure. As I said, she sustained a head injury,' the doctor said. 'You should know she has some self-inflicted injuries too. She could really use a friendly face about now.'

CHAPTER SIX

Claire

With no hope of sleeping, Claire sat in the kitchen nursing a large glass of wine and wishing to God she could cancel the stupid texts she'd sent Luke. She'd as good as told him their marriage was over. It had been a knee-jerk reaction. She'd been so hurt and confused by the comment he'd made before he'd walked out this morning, which had sounded very much like an ultimatum: him or her father. He must have known he was putting her in an impossible situation. He'd actually limped out, she recalled guiltily. He'd been attacked, humiliated, injured, and she hadn't even asked how he was. She'd been selfish coming here, not factoring in the disruption to Luke's life, to Ella's, but she really hadn't had any other choice. Her father had no one else but her. She'd had no one but him since she was seven years old, until she'd met Luke. And now she was driving Luke away.

The time had come to find someone else to look after her father. Her chest ached at that thought. She'd imagined she would have more time, but this insidious disease was no respecter of that, ravaging his mind with unremitting cruelty. Stripping him of his memory.

Looking again at her phone, she hoped there might be a response from Sophie, the woman who claimed to be her half-sister. Feeling as lonely as it was possible to be, even with her father and

Ella upstairs, something had compelled her to message her back. She'd asked the only question she could: *If you are who you say you are, then presumably you won't mind sending me a copy of your birth certificate?*

No reply. She felt peculiarly disappointed. Even knowing the can of worms this would open, which she could hardly bear to contemplate, a part of her wanted it to be true, wanted not to feel so alone with all of this. She sighed, finished her wine, and then headed upstairs in the hope of an hour's rest before daybreak.

Wary of waking Ella, she crept along the landing, freezing for a second as she heard the distant creak of a floorboard. Pausing to listen, she soon realised it wasn't her father, whose snores indicated he was dead to the world. The wood settling, that was all it was. Her dad had always tried to reassure her of that when she was little and her monster under the bed was the body that thudded down each step of the stairs to land bruised and broken at the foot of them. Feeling a tear roll down her cheek, she wiped it away. She hadn't cried for her mum in a long time. She supposed she was doing so now because of the awful aching loneliness she felt inside.

Why had they stayed here? Her dad had talked about moving to a new house not long after her mum died. They'd been outside, sitting on the patio, looking out over the garden. Her mum had loved her garden, hanging bird feeders and nesting boxes, planting wild flowers and hedgerows to encourage wildlife. She would spend hours out there. It had seemed to Claire in the months prior to the accident that that was the only time she was really happy.

She wished her dad had talked more about Mum, shared his memories of her while he was lucid. Claire knew so little about her. Grief she'd thought she'd buried long ago suddenly overwhelming her, she walked across to her bedside table, flicked on her lamp and picked up the photograph she kept there. She had been just six months old when it was taken. Her mum was cradling her in her arms, smiling down at her. She must have been happy then too.

'What happened, Mum?' she whispered emotionally, asking the same question she'd asked over and over, never getting answers. What was it her mother had accused her father of driving her to do? Claire might have assumed she was blaming him for her drinking but for something else she'd heard her mother say before that last awful day: *What happened was because of you, Bernard Harvey! Live with the consequences. I have to. Claire will. Your sordid little skeletons in cupboards are going to come back to haunt her one day too!*

It had never stopped playing on her mind. Her father had said it was nothing but drunken rambling when she'd finally found the courage to ask him. Was it, though? Claire so needed to know what her mother had meant, especially now.

Shaking off the ghost that trod silently over her grave, she placed the photo back and went across to the dresser, opening the top drawer and pulling out the memory box she kept there: a shoebox containing mementos and photographs, one of which she had taken from her parents' wedding album. In his light grey suit and blue tie, her dad had looked very dapper and handsome. Her mum, wearing a short silk shift dress, was standing on tiptoe, leaning in to kiss him. It was a beautiful photo of a couple seemingly very much in love. What had gone so badly wrong?

Delving deeper, she pulled out the few other photos she had, odd snapshots of away days and holidays, including some of her and her dad on their long-ago trip to Rhyl – the same town in which this Sophie lived. He'd been going on a business trip, one of many dealership visits he had to undertake as part of his job as regional sales manager for a leading car distributor. Claire had been on her long summer holidays and her mum had had one of her headaches, so he'd taken her with him, as he occasionally did. They'd visited the SeaQuarium, the miniature railway, the fun park. She'd been terrified of the sea, all the slippery, jellified things that might wriggle between her toes, but all the same, she'd learned to swim in it that day. Her dad had been so proud of her.

She'd relished his attention, which she didn't often get with him so often away on his road trips.

He'd treated her to a 'grown-up' meal as a reward, calling at a pretty little village pub on the way home. She'd felt very important as he'd introduced her to the lady behind the bar and asked for the best table in the house. He'd been chatting and smiling to the woman, she remembered. Wearing an animal-print blouse, pedal pushers and strappy leopard-skin shoes, the barmaid wasn't easily forgettable. Claire had told her she thought she looked like Madonna. Her dad had winked at the woman and said, 'But prettier.' Claire felt a flutter of anger run through her as she realised now the innuendo passing between them.

Was this the woman he'd been pleading with when he'd grabbed hold of her wrist last night? She'd wondered whether he'd been imagining he was talking to her mother. Whether it was her mum who might have been seeing someone else. And if it had been? Would that make the secrets that seemed to be bubbling under the surface any more bearable?

She closed her eyes. She couldn't think about all of this now. She so wished Luke was here. That she could lie safe in his arms while he held her. His presence was always enough to reassure her; his breath warm on her neck as he eased her close. He wasn't likely to be here now, though, after she'd sent him those childish texts.

A deep sense of emptiness engulfing her, she returned the photographs to the box and reached for the perfume that was in there, a heady floral aroma somewhere between jasmine and mandarin. It always comforted her and reminded her of her mother. Spraying a little on her wrists, she sniffed it, and then closed the box and checked her phone again. She was about to click on Messenger when the screen indicated a message alert, causing her heart to jump.

She stilled her jittery nerves and opened the text. It was from her friend Gemma, who was out tonight checking out venues for her hen night. At the same time, she was doing Claire a huge favour. Opening the message, Claire quickly scanned it – and then froze.

So sorry, Claire. You did say you wanted to know, Gemma had sent, along with an attachment. *Will ring you in a sec, sweetheart.*

Claire's breath hitched in her chest as she stared stunned at the attachment. Luke's words rang sickeningly loud in her head: *You need to think about what choices you want to make*. Her husband, the father of her child, who'd evidently been paving the way to announcing that he'd already made his own choice. The absolute *bastard.*

Her heart twisting painfully, she took in the details of another harrowing image that would be indelibly scorched on her mind. His tongue probably halfway down her throat, Luke was kissing a woman. Not the blonde woman who'd been eyeing him up in the pub. This one was dark-haired, slimmer, judging by what Claire could see of her. Was he fucking her? Her heartbeat sped up, thudding erratically against her ribcage. Both of them?

Oh, dear God. Attempting to contain a sudden violent surge of nausea, she pressed a hand over her mouth and scrambled off the bed to dash to the bathroom, where she bent over the toilet and vomited the contents of her stomach.

Please don't get up. Please don't let him have heard me, she prayed silently, glancing in the direction of her father's room as she padded tearfully back to her own bedroom, where she stood quite still, her body shaking, her arms wrapped tightly about herself, with absolutely no idea what to do.

Subduing the sob climbing up her throat, she picked up her phone again. There were several missed calls from Gemma, who would be worried and desperately trying to get hold of her instead of enjoying her evening as she should be. And a reply from Sophie. Blinking hard, Claire tried to focus.

There's no named father on my birth certificate, the message read. *If you think about it, though, Bernard wouldn't have wanted his name on it, would he?*

Claire stifled a near-hysterical laugh. No, he wouldn't – *if* there was any truth in it. That would have meant him having responsibilities other than those to his wife and legitimate child. And cheating wouldn't have been half so exciting if he'd been found out.

She didn't respond to the message. She wasn't capable of responding, not now. It *couldn't* be true. He wouldn't. No, and neither would Luke.

She couldn't speak to Gemma either, not tonight, so instead she sent her a quick message assuring her she was all right. Then she drew in a tremulous breath, stepped towards the wardrobe mirror and took a long, critical look at herself. She was a mess. Her face was blotchy, which always happened when she cried. With her pale complexion and shock of red hair that refused to be tamed no matter what she did, and wearing one of Luke's old T-shirts – her staple comfy night attire – she couldn't look less enticing if she tried.

Her chest tight, the huge lump in her throat threatening to choke her, she stayed where she was for a minute, then a ragged sob escaped her and she dropped to her knees to ferret underneath the bed for the overnight bags stored there.

He had to go. She didn't want him here if he didn't want to be here.

Oh God, she wanted him. So badly.

Sitting back on her haunches, she dragged a pillow from the bed and buried her face in it, muffling her harsh, stomach-wrenching sobs. She felt as if her heart was splintering. And so, *so* alone.

She didn't know how long she sat there, stifling her cries so her baby wouldn't hear them. She was blinking at the ceiling, praying quietly, trying to think what to do, how she would survive – how she would get through this day, let alone the lonely days that would follow – when her phone vibrated, alerting her to a text.

Her heart palpitating wildly, she got to her feet, retrieved the phone from where she'd left it on the bed, and checked her texts.

Not going into work, Luke had sent. *Back in a couple of hours. Think we need to talk.*

Talk about what? The end of their marriage? Swallowing back the knot expanding painfully in her throat, Claire hesitated before answering, not sure what to say, and then decided to hold onto at least one scrap of her dignity and pre-empt him. *Did you stay with her?* she texted back. *Don't lie to me. I have a photograph of you kissing her.*

He didn't reply immediately, and then: *It's not how it seems, Claire. I need to explain.*

CHAPTER SEVEN

Luke

'Claire, please let me explain,' Luke begged into his phone, pressing the heel of his hand hard to his forehead.

'I don't want to *hear* it!' Claire screamed, her voice raw – from crying, no doubt. Luke's heart plummeted to the pit of his stomach. 'Your excuses. Your lies. You really do think you can add insult to injury, don't you?'

'It wasn't how it *looked*,' Luke tried desperately. It was a cliché, he knew it was, but what the hell else was he supposed to say? 'Nothing happened, Claire, I swear. I—'

'Everything happened!' Claire yelled over him. 'You were *kissing* her. Do you honestly expect me to believe it was a chaste kiss on the cheek? That that's all it was?'

'Yes! No. *Jesus.* How much did you see, Claire? Were you there? Because if you were, you would have seen what happened in—'

'What?' Claire gasped, disbelieving. 'Is this some sort of joke? Are you really trying to turn things around here?'

'No.' Luke sighed heavily. 'I'm just—'

'I was *here*, Luke, looking after our child, as you know very well. Gemma saw you. She sent me a photograph. Irrefutable evidence, I'd say, wouldn't you?'

'Gemma. Right.' Luke laughed scornfully. 'Well, that was a really shitty thing to do, wasn't it? Still your best friend, is she?'

'You're treading on very thin ice, Luke,' Claire warned him.

Luke knew she was right. 'Claire, look, I'm sorry. Please let me come over so we can talk properly.'

Claire was quiet for a moment, then, 'There's not much to talk about, though, is there?' she said flatly. 'You've made your feelings perfectly clear. I'm going. Ella needs me.'

'Claire…' Luke trailed off, cursing quietly as he realised she'd ended the call. Now what did he do? Pulling the phone from his ear, he scrolled to his home page, his gut wrenching as he looked at the photo of Claire and Ella smiling back, and then wiped a hand quickly across his eyes, as Anna emerged from her bedroom.

Forcing a smile, he turned to face her. 'Okay?' he asked.

She nodded, but she looked far from it. She'd had a shower, as best she could with bandages on her wrists, washed the blood from her hair, put some make-up on. She was still deathly pale, though. He couldn't believe that a beautiful, vibrant woman had been made to feel so bad about herself by a man that she would attempt to take her own life. Yeah, and he was doing an excellent job of making Claire feel great about herself, wasn't he? He sighed in complete despair at the mess he'd created.

The ex-shit-of-a-boyfriend had apparently watched him leave Anna's flat. When her doorbell had rung two minutes later, she had answered it, thinking he'd come back to take up her offer of staying the night. The bastard had rammed the door into her, forced her backwards. Attacked her before she could pull herself up from the floor. He'd spat in her face, she'd confided tearfully at the hospital, done Christ knows what else. She wouldn't meet Luke's eyes as she'd recounted some of what had happened. The piece of human flotsam had then told her she was a slag, that she deserved all she got. That he would always be watching her every move. She hadn't called the police. It was her word against his. She couldn't face it, the interviews, the statements, not being believed. Going to court, if it ever got there. Couldn't take any more, she'd said.

Seeing her physically jump as the letter box flapped and what sounded like post landed on the hall floor, Luke felt his blood boil.

'I'm fine,' she said as he ran his eyes worriedly over her. 'Getting there, thanks to you,' she added, not very convincingly. She had her arms folded so tightly across her chest it was a wonder she could breathe. 'Are you okay?'

Luke shrugged despondently. 'She doesn't want me back,' he said.

'Oh no. I'm so sorry, Luke.' Anna came towards him, placing a hand on his arm. 'What will you do?'

Again Luke shrugged. If Claire didn't want him there, he could hardly demand to be allowed access. It wasn't his house. 'I'll go and see her,' he said. 'Try and talk to her.'

'And if she doesn't want to listen?'

'I don't know,' he admitted, running a hand tiredly over his neck.

'It's all my fault,' Anna said, tears welling in her eyes. None of this would have happened if it hadn't been for me.'

Jesus. Make her feel even worse about herself, why don't you? 'No, it isn't, Anna.' Taking hold of her hand, he gently squeezed it, and then turned it over. His heart broke for her, seeing the watery red stain bleeding through the damp dressing. 'I was so wrapped up in myself last night, I wasn't considering anyone else. I should have been. None of this is your fault.'

She answered with a small smile. She didn't look very reassured.

'Do you have anyone you could call?' he asked her. 'A friend, maybe, who could stay with you for a while?' He'd already established that she had no family she could call on. She'd lost her father young, apparently, and her mother now lived with her second husband in New Zealand, which was why she'd asked the hospital to call him. As much as he needed not to be here, he didn't want to leave her on her own, not in the emotional state she was in, and with the possibility that the bastard who'd attacked her might come back.

She shook her head. 'I haven't lived here that long, so I haven't made many real friends yet. Not people I would want to know about this, anyway,' she said, glancing down embarrassedly. 'My closest friend lives in London. She's married now, with a little one. I'll be okay, Luke. Don't worry.' She looked back at him, smiling bravely. 'You go. Talk to your wife. I'm sure you'll find things will be all right once you've had a chance to explain properly.'

Luke doubted that. Doubted also that Anna would be okay. She needed help. Someone in her corner at the very least. 'Will you call the police if he shows up again?' he asked her.

'Yes,' she said, but her eyes were troubled, reluctant.

Would she? Considering what she'd told him, Luke had serious doubts. He was worried. Scared for her. 'Promise?'

'Promise,' she assured him. 'You're a lovely person, Luke. Thanks for caring.'

'Yeah, not sure my wife would concur, but… I should go.' Smiling half-heartedly, he scanned her face again, reluctant to leave her.

She nodded sadly. 'Can I ask you something?' she said, walking him to the door.

'Ask away.' Luke stopped as he reached to open it.

'I know you'd probably rather I didn't, and it's okay if you say no, I completely understand, but…' She hesitated, her eyes flicking nervously down and back.

'But?' Luke urged her, trepidation rising inside him.

'Can I call you? Or text you maybe? It's just…' Again she faltered, and then rushed on. 'I get frightened sometimes, when I hear a noise. You know, in the corridor outside, even on the street sometimes. It's usually nothing, but it would really help knowing I had someone to talk to.'

She waited, her huge brown eyes so full of hope that Luke couldn't bring himself to say no. 'I was going to suggest it,' he said, his heart sinking as he realised this wasn't the best way to try to save his marriage.

CHAPTER EIGHT

Claire

Her eyes puffed up and red raw from crying and lack of sleep, Claire was attempting to put on a brave face. Her father would be completely destabilised if she did what she felt like doing, breaking down and crying like a baby. She was managing, just, until Luke turned up. As she settled her dad in his armchair, she glanced out of the lounge window and saw him approaching, and her heart reeled inside her, turning over nauseatingly in her chest.

'I'll get you some tea, Dad,' she said brightly, working to keep the insane edge from her voice. She handed him the TV remote and dashed into the hall, her heart going into downward free fall as she caught sight of herself in the mirror. She looked like she felt: broken, frightened; a complete mess, on the outside as well as the inside. Wiping the heels of her hands across her eyes, she reached to scrape her mass of bedraggled hair back, and tried for some level of calmness as she walked to the front door.

She expected him to use his key. He didn't. He knocked and waited instead, reinforcing the fact that what they'd once had together was no more. She felt desperate, had no idea how she would cope with everything that was coming at her, how she would ever fill the deep, lonely void inside her, but she couldn't just take him back, even assuming that was what he wanted. She felt sick contemplating the possibility that it might not be. That she might have been living a lie. *Might* have? Of course she had. His emotions had shifted before he'd felt compelled to kiss another woman, no doubt have sex with her too. Hadn't it been obvious from his moodiness, his absence, that he was growing tired of Claire, of their life together? How long it had been going on, she didn't know. Rather than see it, she'd closed her eyes, despite a nagging little voice in her head, and waited for him to spell it out, issuing her with his damn ultimatum.

Marshalling her defences in readiness for him to blame her for his infidelity – the situation here, her neglect of him, the way she looked, who she was – she pulled the front door open, and immediately felt her resolve weaken. He was wearing some kind of support boot, and he looked so very tired. His eyes full of remorse, he appeared to be as desperate as she felt. Was she overreacting? All marriages hit a blip, didn't they? Could she take him back if he begged, swore it was a moment of madness, that he loved her? Or would she be sad, weak and pathetic to even consider it?

'Hi.' He glanced nervously down and back, as Claire debated whether to let him in. 'Is it okay if I, er…?' He nodded past her to the hall.

Claire hesitated, and then nodded shortly and stood aside.

'Thanks.' Clearly relieved, Luke offered her a small smile as he limped past her.

'That's okay,' she said, forcing the words past the tightness in her throat. 'We don't want to do this on the doorstep, do we?' She wanted to ask about his injury, but how could she show that she cared for him when he clearly didn't give a damn about her?

He nodded, his expression one of resignation, as if he'd expected her hostility. He should. Did he realise, she wondered, how hard she was working to keep her emotions in check, to stay strong for the people who needed her when she felt like breaking down? Her heart was tearing apart inside her, seeing him here, feeling this sudden vast distance between them. She didn't feel strong. She was terrified about facing the future without him. Without anyone.

'We'll talk in the kitchen,' she said, leading the way, 'assuming you have anything to say worth listening to.'

In the kitchen, she turned to face him, her arms folded, her stomach twisting with painful apprehension.

'Where's Ella?' he asked.

'You remembered she exists then?' Claire couldn't help herself.

Luke swallowed. 'Don't, Claire,' he said quietly.

'Don't *what*?' She stared at him, unable to comprehend the hurt in his tone. 'Remind you it's not just my heart you're breaking?'

Luke fixed his gaze on his shoes and said nothing.

'She's with Gemma. I didn't feel well enough to look after her this morning. Gemma offered to take her for a couple of hours.' Seeing his obvious guilt, Claire relented. If he didn't care about her, he would always care about Ella. She was sure of that. He would need to know she was with someone who knew about her condition.

Nodding, Luke looked up.

Claire didn't miss him clocking the empty wine bottle on the table. Was he judging her? After he'd been out nightclubbing, picking up women? 'Well?' she said, her sympathy waning fast.

He drew in a long breath. 'Nothing happened, Claire,' he repeated. 'I swear it didn't.'

'We've done that bit, Luke,' she pointed out, looking at him coldly. 'And this *nothing happened* even though you stayed with her?' she added, before he had time to insult her with yet more lies.

Luke massaged his forehead, looking as shamefaced as it was possible to be. 'There was an incident in the nightclub,' he said. 'I intervened, and—'

Claire's heart hardened. 'So you went back to her place presumably, had a chat about the weather over a nice cup of tea, and then what? Played fucking *tiddlywinks*?' she spat angrily.

Luke winced as if she'd just slapped him. She wanted to. It was taking every ounce of her willpower not to. He really was going to do this, wasn't he? Stand there and tell her barefaced lies.

'I didn't sleep with her, Claire,' he insisted throatily, locking earnest eyes on hers. 'Please believe—' He stopped as his mobile beeped with an incoming text.

Claire noted the look of panic that flitted briefly across his face. 'Prove it,' she challenged him. 'Let me see your phone.'

'What?' he said, now clearly alarmed.

'Your phone.' Keeping her cool, though her heart was beating so rapidly she felt it might burst through her chest, she nodded towards where it was beeping again from his jeans pocket. 'If you're telling the truth, then you've nothing to hide, have you? I'd like to see it, please.'

CHAPTER NINE

Claire

Claire averted her gaze as Luke walked out through the front door. She didn't want to look at him and see him for what he was, a cold-hearted liar. Just like her father? Closing the door behind him, she inhaled deeply, attempting to stop her emotion spilling over before facing her dad.

She couldn't avoid seeing him, as he stepped out into the hall, a confused look on his face. Always it was there, his utter confusion. He hadn't been confused once. He'd known exactly what he was doing. But *she* didn't know yet. She was judging him and finding him guilty and she didn't have all the facts.

'Everything all right, dear?' he asked, his eyes filled with worry as they met hers.

Claire manufactured a smile. 'Yes,' she managed. 'I'm just popping to the bathroom. Won't be a sec.' She hurried up the stairs, leaving her dad to his own devices for a while. He couldn't come to much harm in a few minutes. She needed some space. She needed to talk to Sophie. She needed more information.

Once in her bedroom, she wiped the back of her hand across her wet cheeks and fetched her phone from her bag. She hadn't replied to the message about the birth certificate. Sophie had sent another since.

Can we meet and talk? she'd asked. *Please? I promise you it's the truth. Why would I have contacted you otherwise?*

Claire hesitated. If only Sophie knew how much she did need someone to talk to right now. Taking a deep breath, she messaged her back. *About what?*

Bernard. Us, Sophie answered straight away, almost as if she'd been waiting for Claire to respond. *I think you may be the only family I have. My mum died years ago, sadly.*

That resonated painfully. Claire wiped again at the tears that were rolling steadily down her face. Could Sophie be telling the truth? It was possible. If there was any substance to what she was saying, though, then presumably she must have something to back it up, information about her father.

Where did they meet? she typed warily. *Your mother and my father?*

Mum lived in Meliton, just outside Rhyl. Bernard combined visits w/business trips, I assume, Sophie replied.

Claire felt as if she'd been punched, immediately transported back to the pretty little village pub he'd taken her to, her father chatting and smiling to the woman with the leopard-print shoes and the red-painted lips. An icy sense of foreboding ran through her.

Will message again later, she sent. She needed to digest what she'd discovered. He'd been involved with the woman. Of course he bloody well had. Swallowing hard, she glanced at the ceiling, trying to summon up the courage to go back down, talk to him as if everything was fine when it quite clearly wasn't. Had he been in love with her? Her heart weighed heavy in her chest. Had she been the cause of the escalating arguments she'd witnessed? One of the 'sordid little skeletons in cupboards' her mother had referred to?

Any time, Sophie sent back. *And Claire, I know you're going through some awful stuff right now. Just so you know, I don't want anything other than to be there for you.*

Claire was about to respond, though she wasn't sure quite how, when something slammed loudly outside. The back gate? But it was locked. She always kept it padlocked, lest her dad wander out that way. The key was on a hook inside the utility room door. She hadn't thought he was aware of it.

She dashed to the window, cursed loudly when she couldn't open it. That was locked too, the key missing. She didn't keep the windows locked, though. And she would *never* remove the keys. She didn't dare, in case her dad set fire to the house.

'Dad!' Pressing her face close to the window, she scanned the garden. There was no sign of him. 'Dad?' she called again, spinning round to thunder down the stairs.

Where in God's name was he?

'Yes, dear?' he answered curiously from his armchair as she flew past the lounge door.

CHAPTER TEN

Claire

Two weeks later

Ella was sitting at the kitchen table when Claire came down from her shower. She was playing with one of Bernard's old board games, which they'd fetched down from the loft while looking for familiar things he might like to have around him at the care home. Noting that she hadn't quite got the hang of the rules, Claire reached to slide her counter back to the tip of a snake's tail, much to her daughter's dismay. 'It's up the ladders and down the snakes, sweetheart,' she reminded her.

'But Mummy, I won.' Ella pointed to the number 99 square she'd landed on, her little forehead knitted into an uncomprehending frown.

'But not fairly. It's no fun playing if there's no challenge,' Claire pointed out, picking up her phone from the work surface and checking it. Still no reply from Luke to the text she'd sent him reminding him he was due to have Ella today. Now what should she do? There was no way she could take her to the care home with her. She didn't want her upset when they had to say goodbye to her father.

'Yes it is,' Ella insisted. 'I like sliding up the snakes.'

Claire couldn't help but smile at her earnest expression. Sliding up snakes would be a bit of a challenge, she supposed. 'Why don't you go and help Grandad sort through his photographs?' she suggested, nodding towards the lounge, where her dad was engrossed in a lifetime's worth of distant recollections, miraculously preserved in the most intimate detail. His more recent memories, though, were falling from his mind like snowflakes in spring, melting away to be lost forever. How long would it be before she too was gone from his past? And what about Sophie? Did she exist in his memory?

'Okay.' Seeming to understand that Claire needed her support, Ella nodded good-naturedly and slid from her chair. Having a wise head on her shoulders, she seemed aware that her grandad was diminishing alongside her growing up. With her own sad memories of childhood, Claire had wished dearly that Ella might be untouched by such heartbreak. More than anything, she'd wanted to make sure her baby was surrounded by the security blanket of the family she herself had never had. With her mother dead, her father had been the only constant in her life. He was still here physically, a living, breathing entity, but this man, whose mind was being stolen, whose moods alternated between forgetfulness and frustration, childishness and anger, wasn't the person she knew. It was as if his personality had been drained from him, leaving just a shrunken shell.

Would he recall details she was desperate to know about if she asked him? Trying to decide whether she should, Claire sighed and wandered across to the fridge to check what she had in for lunch – his last lunch here. She should probably ask him what he fancied, since he'd decided the chicken liver pâté she'd served him yesterday was fish paste and had promptly spat it out.

Hearing him chatting to Ella as she headed for the lounge, she paused at the open door, her breath catching as she took in what would appear to be a normal, happy family scene. Her father was sitting on the sofa, Ella tucked up close to his side, studying the photo album that was open on his lap.

'Who's that strange boy, Grandad?' she asked, pointing at one of the photographs and then glancing expectantly up at him.

'That's no stranger.' Bernard turned to eye her with surprise. 'That's me.'

Twirling a strand of hair around her finger, Ella looked at him thoughtfully and then back to the photo. 'It's not.' She giggled, unconvinced. 'You've got a lived-in face, Grandad.'

She was repeating something he'd told her. 'Old faces are lived-in faces,' he'd once said, when she had asked him about the deep grooves in his forehead. 'Behind these lines is a lifetime of experience,' he'd assured her. Claire gulped back a lump in her throat. What good did that experience do him now?

'It is so,' her father insisted. 'Look, see the name underneath? What does that say?'

A furrow knitting her brow, Ella slowly enunciated the letters of the name written beneath the photo. 'B... e... r...'

'Bernard,' her dad finished. 'That's right. Aged nineteen I was then. And that...' he indicated the photograph, 'was my first motorbike.'

His pride and joy. Claire felt her heart ache for him as she saw the nostalgic glint in his eye. It was still there in the garage: a BSA 250cc. She imagined it would be a collector's item by now. Up until a year or so ago, he would tinker with it most weekends, before the merciless disease stripped away his ability to do anything that brought him any kind of contentment.

'Do you still ride it, Grandad?' Ella asked.

He frowned. 'No, petal, not any more. Not for some years now.'

Claire hesitated; then, since he seemed to be having a period of clarity, she decided to broach the subject she was burning to ask him about. 'Do you have any photographs of Sophie, Dad?' she said, making sure to keep her tone casual.

Her dad's gaze snapped to hers, a combination of alarm and bewilderment in his eyes. 'Who?' he asked.

Claire's stomach knotted nervously. 'Sophie,' she said. 'I just wondered...'

But he had looked away, his face clouding over. He reached for the remote control from the occasional table, flicked the TV on and settled back to watch it almost as if he hadn't heard her.

Claire felt a prickle of apprehension run through her. But she'd noted his glazed expression and realised there was no point in pursuing it. He'd moved on, or back possibly. His mind was elsewhere.

'I'll just pop to the loo,' she said, sighing inwardly. 'And then I'll get us some lunch. Ham salad all right, Dad?'

He glanced at her, puzzled. 'Sorry?'

'Ham salad, for lunch,' she repeated.

'Perfect.' He smiled and turned back to the TV.

Claire tried to quash the doubt niggling away at her. For a second or two, she'd thought he'd recognised the name. In reality, she'd probably just confused him. Throwing something randomly into a conversation was bound to do that. Reprimanding herself for not approaching the subject more carefully, she determined not to mention it again until she'd gathered more information.

Leaving her dad to the house makeover programme he seemed engrossed in, she extended her hand to Ella. 'Need the loo, sweetheart?' she asked her.

He would never intentionally do anything to harm or upset Ella, she was sure of that, despite what Luke had said. The fact was, though, sometimes he didn't know what he was doing. One minute he would be sitting, apparently content, watching TV. The next he would bawl at it. That frightened Ella, who couldn't possibly understand. As did his hiding his slippers in cupboards or behind cushions in case someone stole them. It had been funny at first, until he'd accused Ella of doing the stealing.

Once upstairs, Claire took the opportunity to remind Ella that her grandad would be going to live in his nice new home today.

Ella nodded slowly, and then went quiet. It was obvious she was thinking it through and would no doubt have questions.

They were heading back along the landing when she asked the inevitable one. 'Why does Grandad have to go and live in another home, Mummy?' Her summer-blue eyes were troubled, and Claire felt her heart dip.

'Because he'll be safer there, darling,' she answered softly. 'There are nurses there who will look after him. He'll make loads of new friends, too. That will be nice for him, won't it?'

'But we'll still be his friends, won't we?' was Ella's next anxious question.

'Of course. We'll visit him lots.' Claire squeezed her hand as they reached the hall.

Ella appeared to digest this. 'Mummy,' she said after a second, 'will Daddy be coming back to live here?'

That floored Claire, coming as it did completely out of the blue. Before she was able to formulate an answer, Ella spoke again.

'I think he's lonely,' she said sadly.

'I… don't know, sweetheart,' Claire said. 'We both need some time to have a think. We're still friends, though, so we'll see him whenever you want.'

Again Ella nodded, but this time she dropped her gaze, telling Claire she wasn't wholly convinced.

God, Claire hated this, pretending to their child that her father hadn't broken her heart. When she'd spoken to him on the phone about access arrangements, he'd promised he would be there for her. That he would see Ella on alternate weekends and help out during the week if she needed him to. He'd also said she could call on him if she needed to in an emergency, which this was. Disappointed, she checked her texts again, wondering whether to ring the care home and let them know they were delayed.

She was surprised to find her dad in the kitchen when she went in, busying himself with the preparation of the salad. Noting the sharp knife he was chopping vigorously away at the cucumber with, she approached him with caution. 'Careful, Dad,' she warned him. 'We don't want to be fishing fingers out of the salad.'

He paused and glanced at her questioningly. 'We're not having fish fingers, are we?'

She smiled sadly. 'No, Dad. Ham, remember?' Pointless question. He'd already gone back to his task.

'Clear the board game up, sweetheart,' she said to Ella, fetching the ham from the fridge. 'Lunch is nearly ready.'

'In a sec,' said Ella, rattling the dice cup. 'I just want to climb up the big ladder.'

'Now, please.' Claire gave her a no-nonsense look as she walked back across the kitchen.

And then stopped dead as Bernard said, 'Do as your mother says, Sophie.'

CHAPTER ELEVEN

Luke

'We could go for lunch at the Canalside Café, if you fancy it,' Anna suggested, and Luke's heart dropped.

'Anna, I have something work-related on,' he reminded her. 'A property to look at, remember?'

'Oh.' Her expression was a mixture of hurt and disappointment, and Luke wondered again what the hell he was doing. Seeing the crushing pain in Claire's eyes when he'd declined to hand her his phone, he'd felt like the biggest shit that ever walked the earth. How could he have shown it to her, though, when Anna had texted him: *Good luck. I hope your wife's not too hard on you.* Her timing couldn't have been worse. He'd been desperate to talk to Claire, hoping she might give him the chance to explain. He didn't get that chance before his phone started pinging with messages.

He'd read the bloody things once he'd left. *How did it go?* was the next one she'd sent, followed by *I'm really sorry I kissed you in public. I should have thought that someone you know might see us.*

He'd have stood no chance if Claire had read those. The next text had jolted him. *He was outside the apartment when I went out just now. He said if I tell tales to the police he'll kill me. He means it, Luke. I don't think I can do this. I'm terrified. I don't want to live like this.*

It's not your problem, he'd told himself. Tried hard to convince himself he should have nothing to do with it. But how could he not? From what he knew, there was no one else she could turn to. The fucker who'd hurt her might still be hanging around her apartment, and she was inside on her own. Feeling suicidal? He wasn't sure that was what she'd meant, but when her phone had gone repeatedly to voicemail… What kind of man would he be if he walked away from that? *He* should have damn well called the police. Would have but for the thought that he might be placing her in further danger.

She'd texted and called him constantly since. And no matter how hard he tried to convince himself she would be okay, still he dropped what he was doing and came over when she asked him to. Because he was scared too. Because he felt responsible and wasn't sure he could live with it if he didn't turn up and then found out she'd taken her own life.

He shouldn't be here now; it was sending out the wrong messages. His hope was to persuade her to get some sort of counselling, to enlist the help of the police, but meanwhile, he felt he'd no choice but to be around for her. He had no way to explain any of this to Claire, as if she would want to hear it. He just hoped she was coping. She'd answer with a short 'Fine' when he asked her how she was. He doubted that was true. Prayed she wasn't drinking too much. She never had in the past, but recently he'd noticed too many glasses left about with wine dregs in the bottom, which worried him. He was concerned she wouldn't hear Ella if she got up in the night. And with Bernard wandering aimlessly about…

'Pickle?' Anna said.

'Sorry?' Luke realised he'd been miles away.

'In your cheese sandwich. You can't go off to a building site without any lunch.' She walked from the kitchen to the lounge area, butter knife in hand.

Luke groaned inside. 'Anna, I really do need to go,' he said apologetically.

'Oh,' she said, eyes flicking down, disappointed. 'Not to worry. I can always put it in the fridge. It will keep. Do you fancy going to the pub later?' she asked, returning to the kitchen. 'There's a live band on.'

Luke was about to test the waters, see how she would react if he said he might not be able to get back later, when she went on: 'I've got my doctor's appointment this evening. I thought maybe we could meet up afterwards.'

'Doctor's appointment?' Luke felt hope leap in his chest.

Anna gave him a smile over her shoulder. 'He's going to refer me to a counsellor.'

Thank God. Luke's relief was considerable.

'So? Do you fancy it? We could have a quick bite to eat and then go on there.'

'Er, yes. Why not?' He tried to inject some enthusiasm into his voice.

'Brilliant.' Anna sounded pleased. 'How's your little girl, by the way?' she asked, as Luke collected his car keys from the coffee table and glanced around for his phone.

'Okay, I think,' he answered evasively. 'Confused, obviously.'

'Poor thing. She's bound to be,' Anna said with an understanding sigh. 'You'll have to bring her round soon. We'll take her on a nice day out or something. Cheer her up a bit. I'm actually quite good with children.'

'Yeah.' Luke wasn't so sure about that. 'I'll have a word with Claire, check her schedule and see if we can organise something.'

'Is Claire doing okay?' Anna enquired. 'Coping with her dad, I mean. It must be really hard on her with him declining so rapidly.'

'It is.' Luke really wished she wouldn't keep asking about Claire – she felt guilty, she said, blaming herself for the situation he was in.

'She should probably think about a care home,' she went on. 'I know she's done her best, but with little Ella to look after, she—'

'Crap!' Luke said over her. *The care home! Please God tell me that's not today.*

'Problem?' Anna came back to the lounge.

'Major,' Luke said, now searching under cushions and down the sides of the sofa for his phone. 'I'm supposed to be looking after Ella today. I bloody well forgot.'

How could he have? Because he was hardly getting any sleep at Steve's place, which wasn't conducive to a restful night since they'd just got married and the walls were thin, and he'd forgotten what the date was. Why hadn't Claire called or texted him?

Feeling frantic, he glanced around the room again. 'Haven't seen my phone, have you?'

'On the kitchen table.' Anna nodded towards it.

'Cheers.' Luke walked past her, picked it up and checked urgently for missed calls, finding several, as well as texts. *What the…?* His jaw tensing, he glanced back at Anna. 'You put it on silent?'

Her face flushed with guilt. 'You were dozing. You looked so tired, I thought I would let you sleep,' she said. 'I didn't realise you were expecting a call. You should have said. I would never have muted it if—'

'Forget it. It doesn't matter.' Luke tried to keep his immense agitation from his voice. He had said. He'd told her specifically that he never muted his phone. He had a four-year-old daughter, for Christ's sake. Anna was aware that Claire might need to call him at short notice. He needed to be contactable at all times. 'I have to go.'

'But you're coming back later?' Her voice sounding tremulous, Anna stepped towards him as he collected his jacket.

Luke sucked in a tight breath. He was sorely tempted to say no. But how could he, when he might end up receiving a call from the hospital telling him God only knew what?

'I don't know. Claire might need me,' he said instead. He had no idea how she would get through today. If he hadn't messed everything up, he would have been going to the care home with her. As it was, she'd said she didn't want him there. She would be devastated, going back to that empty house on her own.

'Right. Of course she might. She is your wife, after all. I'm sure you'd rather be with her than here. You go. I'll be fine.'

Oh no… Hearing the quaver in Anna's voice as he headed for the door, Luke's heart slid to the pit of his stomach. 'Anna, don't,' he said, turning back to see her wiping a tear from her cheek. 'I have to go. I have to be there for Ella.'

'Go,' Anna urged him. 'I've said I'll be fine. I don't want you here because you feel responsible for me. That's the absolute last thing I want. I actually thought that we…' She stopped, drawing in a shaky breath. 'Just go, Luke, please. You won't receive any texts from me, I promise.'

Shit. Luke watched helplessly as she hurried to the bedroom. Bracing himself, he followed her, heard a sob catch in her throat as she headed across to the en suite, closing the door behind her.

Now what did he do? Could she not see that he *did* feel responsible? *Don't lock the door.* Swallowing hard, he prayed fervently. There was no way he could walk out of here and leave her if she did. *Please don't lock the door.*

CHAPTER TWELVE

Claire

Stowing the last of her father's bags in the boot of her car, Claire walked around to the driver's door. As she reached to open it, her heart sank. *How on earth did that happen?* There was a long gouge in the paintwork down to almost bare metal, and she silently cursed the driver who must have collided with her car and not even bothered to stop. But… she traced her fingers along it, then ran her gaze over the rest of the car… wouldn't they have taken the wing mirror if they'd driven that close? It might have been a bike, she supposed. She frowned as she realised it was more likely to have been done deliberately. Imagining the malice behind such an act, the sharp implement that must have been used, her heart missed a beat. Who would do such a thing? *Why?*

Drunken idiots, she supposed, reeling home from the pub. She should report it, but she couldn't deal with it now. And alerting her dad to what had happened would only upset him.

Attempting a smile, she braced herself for what lay ahead, and pulled the door open.

'Are we going to the shops?' Bernard asked her as she climbed in.

Claire inhaled deeply. She couldn't meet his gaze for fear he would read what was in her eyes: fury that her suspicions might be right. That his infidelity might have caused that final argument that had robbed her of her mother, her childhood. Robbed her mother of her life.

It might not be true. This Sophie might be some sort of stalker, getting kicks from preying on other people's vulnerabilities. She would have to provide more evidence to convince Claire, more information about herself. There were few details on her Facebook profile. No year on her date of birth, giving no clue to her age. It was clearly a recently added account. But how would she know about his business trips? And if it *was* true? Then her father had a lot to answer for. Except he couldn't, could he? He wasn't capable of answering anything sensibly. Claire bit back her frustration.

'Mummy, Grandad's talking to you.' Ella dragged her attention back to the job in hand.

Attempting to get her rioting emotions in some sort of order, Claire forced her face into a smile. 'Sorry, miles away.' She buckled her seat belt and checked her father's. 'What did you say, Dad?'

'The shops,' Bernard said. 'I wondered if we might be going to the supermarket.'

Claire met his eyes. They were awash with uncertainty and she had no idea how to answer. There was no point repeating what she'd told him: that he was moving into a residential care home. He would only forget halfway there, and she would have to try to explain again once they arrived. Reinforce the fact that there were people there who would look after him, help him to dress, eat and wash, pick him up when he fell. Somehow she had to convince him everything was going to be fine, when it quite obviously wasn't. She was abandoning him, and she had no idea whether he would ever forgive her. No idea how *she* would ever forgive him if the jigsaw pieces fitted together as she suspected they might.

Silently cursing Luke for not being here for his daughter, who shouldn't be involved in any of this, she glanced in the rear-view mirror to offer Ella a reassuring smile, and then tried to focus. She'd known this day would come. It had arrived sooner than she'd planned for, but she had to get through it, get her father through it. Despite his workaholic tendencies, he'd tried to be there for her growing up, and now he needed her to do the same.

'I thought we might stop off at the shops on the way,' she answered carefully. 'Is there anything you fancy?'

Her father pondered. 'Some chocolate digestives would be nice. Or some choux buns.' There was a glint of anticipation of a treat in his eyes as he glanced hopefully at her. 'We could have them for tea and then watch a film together.'

Claire's heart dropped. By teatime he wouldn't remember the choux buns. By teatime he wouldn't be here. Would his one abiding memory be that it was her, his daughter, who'd stolen his home away from him?

'*The Great Escape*'s on, I think,' he went on. 'Have you seen that? It's one of my favourites.'

'We could watch it on your new television, Grandad,' Ella ventured when Claire, trying to collect herself, took a second to answer.

Bernard twisted in his seat to look at her. 'Are we getting a new one then?' he asked, an eyebrow raised curiously.

'You have a new TV in your room, Dad, remember? At the lovely home you'll be staying in,' Claire reminded him, not sure what else to say.

Examining her face, his expression wary, Bernard didn't answer immediately. Then, 'Just for a short while,' he said, with an uncertain nod.

'Yes, just for a short while,' Claire replied emotionally, and then reached to start the engine before her courage failed her. She'd thought she'd prepared herself for this, but all she wanted to do was take him back inside; return to a time when she was tiny and her dad was her hero, not this person she no longer knew, wondered if she'd ever known. A man whose past secrets her instincts told her were about to shatter any illusions she might have had. She swallowed back a tight constriction in her throat. Suddenly, for all her preparedness, she wanted to cry.

Glancing sideways, she noted that his gaze was now fixed on the windscreen.

'And then we'll come home,' he said.

She heard the fear in his voice. It was tangible. She couldn't answer. There was no way to. Blinking away a tear, she checked her wing mirror and readied herself to pull out. Then she noticed a car approaching behind her and breathed a sigh of relief. *Luke. Thank God.* At least now Ella would be spared all this.

Opening her window, she attempted to compose herself as she watched Luke pull up hastily, banging his door open and scrambling out of his car. She wasn't going to demand to know where he'd been. She didn't want to know. She simply wanted him to be here for his daughter when he'd damn well promised to be.

'Sorry,' he said, his expression flustered. 'I got delayed.'

'Daddy!' Ella exclaimed excitedly from the back seat, as Claire looked him over, perturbed. He had a long scratch on his cheek, running almost down to his chin.

'What happened to your face?' she asked him warily.

'Nothing,' he said with an evasive shrug. 'An accident at work.'

'But…' Claire frowned, confused. 'I thought you were still off sick with your ankle?'

'I popped in to see Steve about the property we're refurbing,' Luke supplied. 'Got in a tangle with some barbed wire on one of the perimeter fences.'

Imagining the barbed wire to be old and rusty, and aware of his tendency to ignore cuts and bruises as part of the job, Claire grew concerned. 'Did you get a tetanus jab?'

'Not necessary. I'm up to date.' Shrugging again, Luke looked away, his eyes pivoting towards Ella. 'Hey, pumpkin.' He gave her that special smile he reserved for his daughter, leaving Claire in no doubt how much he loved her. She'd been about to launch into him, reminding him of his fatherly responsibilities, but bit down on her tongue.

'Am I coming with you, Daddy?' Ella was already halfway to unbuckling herself.

'That's the plan,' Luke said. 'I'll take her to the park and then bring her home and get her some dinner, shall I?' he asked, turning back to Claire.

Claire hesitated. Did she want him here, cooking a meal in the kitchen, as he often had in the past when she'd been working? She wasn't sure, but part of her desperately didn't want to come back to an empty house. 'Thanks,' she said, with a small smile. 'I don't know how long I'll be. I'll ring you if—'

'You've arrived then, finally,' Bernard interrupted, leaning forwards to peer past her at Luke.

'Er, yes,' he answered uncertainly. 'Sorry. I'm running late.'

'You really do have to wonder why we bother to pay our water rates.' Shaking his head, Bernard emitted a despairing sigh. 'Well, now you're here, I suppose I'd better let you in.'

'Dad.' Claire stopped him as he reached to unfasten his belt. 'Where are you going?'

He glanced at her, puzzled. 'To let him through to the back. They'll need more than one man for the job, though.' He looked Luke over again, his expression unimpressed. 'The sewage pipe runs the length of the garden, and on through the neighbour's. I suspect it's them who've blocked it up, stuffing God only knows what down the toilet. Nappies probably. The woman has babies like shelling peas, I swear. I said to—'

'Dad.' Claire cut him short. 'The neighbour's children are all grown up now.'

Bernard's expression was blank. 'Are they?'

'They've left home, Dad,' she pointed out, fighting back her frustration. 'And this is Luke.'

Bernard squinted hard at him, but was clearly none the wiser.

'Ella's father,' Claire clarified, weary hopelessness washing through her. 'He's here to take her out for the day so I can come with you; stay with you for a while and make sure you're all settled in.'

Confusion played across his face. Claire could almost see the cogs clunking and grinding as he tried to make sense of what she was saying. 'Settled where, dear?' he asked, a question mark in his eyes.

Claire braced herself. 'Your new home, Dad, the place you're going to be living in,' she said, her stomach tightening as she studied his face, trying to gauge his reaction. 'Do you remember? The one with the lovely views over the grounds? We're going there now.'

'Ah.' Bernard nodded, as if he actually might remember. 'Well, we'd better not dawdle then.' He righted himself in his seat. 'I don't want to keep Ruth waiting too long. She frets, you know, when she doesn't know where I am. Have you met her, my wife?'

Claire felt her heart freeze. She'd told herself she didn't want Luke anywhere near her after what he'd done, but now, aware that her father clearly didn't remember that she was her mother's daughter, *his* daughter, she didn't want him to move an inch away from her. The pressure of his fingertips as he gently squeezed her shoulder was the only thing keeping her from breaking down there and then.

CHAPTER THIRTEEN

Luke

Bolting towards her, Luke scooped Ella off the too-high bar of the climbing frame she was trying to balance on. 'Come on, little monkey,' he said, trying to calm his racing heart. 'We haven't done any of the other stuff yet. What do you fancy, swings, slide or roundabout?'

'Swings!' Ella decided. 'But you have to push me high into the sky.'

'Your wish is my command, ma'am,' Luke said, lowering her carefully to her feet and taking hold of her hand.

'As high as…' Ella glanced upwards, 'those twigs up there.'

Luke squinted to where she was pointing – the top of one of the tall beech trees that populated the park. 'Branches,' he corrected her. 'And maybe not quite that high. You'll end up orbiting the moon.'

Ella contemplated the prospect, and then looked thoughtfully up at him. 'Would I be able to collect Nana's star on the way back for Mummy?' she asked, her expression hopeful.

Luke felt his chest constrict. She was remembering something Claire had told her, he realised. Ella had been having one of those nights where nothing would induce her to sleep. He'd brought her into their bedroom, and she had noticed the framed photograph of the grandmother she'd never met that Claire kept on her bedside table. Undoubtedly sensing Claire's sadness as she'd told her a little about her mum, Ella had asked her whether she missed her.

'I do,' Claire had answered honestly. 'But I still talk to her.'

Ella had looked at her in confusion, and Claire had carried her over to the window and drawn the curtain back. 'She's up there,' she'd said, pointing to the pinpricks of light in the night sky. 'See that twinkling little star? That's Nana. She watches over me, so I never really feel too sad or alone.

She *had* felt alone, though. She had confessed to Luke that there were times in her life when she'd felt the absence of her mother deeply. Luke understood, to a degree. When his dad had taken off, he'd missed him – as a boy misses having a man around, he supposed. But then his old man had only ever been on the periphery of his life, coming and going. Going mostly, to meet other women, he'd learned later. For a young girl to have lost her mother in such a tragic way, though, growing up without her guidance, that must have been so hard for Claire.

Luke had never learned the details of what had happened. Her mother had been drinking a lot, Claire had confided. Luke thought again of the wine glasses he'd seen dotted around, and hoped to God Claire wasn't following in her footsteps. Bernard and Ruth had argued the night of the accident, a bitter argument, apparently. They'd argued often, it seemed. Claire never knew why. Bernard was reluctant to talk about it; Claire suspected that he blamed himself for his wife's death. Having seen Bernard twice in the past checking into the hotel opposite the construction site he'd been working on, each time with a different woman, Luke wondered whether he might have had something to blame himself for. Whether he might have been a womaniser even when he was married.

Had Claire been aware of this? Was she drawing parallels between her mother's life and her own? It might explain why she wasn't prepared to listen to anything Luke had to say. He wished he could make her believe that he bitterly regretted what had happened, that he would never hurt her or risk their daughter's happiness ever again. She'd never looked as alone as she had when Bernard had mentioned Ruth earlier.

'Daddy…' Ella tugged on his hand, reminding him that she was there.

'Sorry, pumpkin.' Realising they'd reached the swings, Luke turned his attention to her and the tricky question of the star. 'Nana's star is a little bit further away than that, sweetheart,' he said softly, bending down to her level. 'She has to be really high up so she can keep an eye on the people she loves. That would be you and Mummy.'

'And you and Grandad,' Ella added, scrutinising him hard.

'Yup, and me and Grandad,' Luke said, a lump rising in his throat as he realised she was trying to hold onto the people close to her. 'Right now, I imagine she'll be watching me to make sure I don't launch you into space.' Smiling, he zipped her coat up. 'Come on, let's see how high we can go without taking off. Which swing do you fancy?'

'The end one,' Ella said, twirling around to set off at a run.

Luke ignored the twinge in his ankle to sprint after her and pluck her out of the path of one of the other swings. He offered the woman pushing her little boy an apologetic smile.

'Check next time, Ella,' he warned her, carrying her onwards as the woman rolled her eyes in empathy. 'I'll have heart failure at this rate.'

Noting that she looked upset as he seated her on the swing, Luke berated himself, thinking his tone had probably been a bit too harsh. 'What is it, sweetheart?' he asked, crouching in front of her. 'Ella?' he urged her when she didn't answer.

She hesitated. 'I don't want you to be a star, Daddy,' she whispered, her little fingers reaching to tentatively trace the scratch on his face.

Christ. Realising what was going through his little girl's mind, Luke felt something crack inside him. 'Hey…' He locked his gaze firmly on hers. Her eyes, wide blue eyes, once crystal clear with the innocence of childhood, were now shot through with heart-wrenching apprehension. 'I'm not going anywhere, pumpkin,' he assured her. 'Mummy and I are not living in the same house, but we're still friends. I'll always be around. It's my job to look after you.'

Still Ella looked doubtful. 'Promise?' she said, her voice filled with uncertainty.

'Cross my heart.' Luke smiled, and made sure he did cross it.

After a second, she nodded. Then, 'Will you be coming back to live with us soon?' she asked him.

Luke had no clue how to answer. 'I don't know, Ella,' he said carefully. 'Mummy and I… we have some things to work out. Lots of things we need to talk about.'

'But you might?' Ella's expression was now filled with hope, and Luke's heart fractured another inch. 'I could ask Mummy to take the baby gates down now that Grandad's going to be safe in his new home. I don't need them because I'm quite big now,' she added, her little face serious as she offered him the incentive she thought he needed.

He realised that she'd witnessed him falling over one of the gates, that she was imagining that was the reason he hadn't come home. He gulped back an overwhelming sense of guilt. He'd lost his temper with Claire. Why the bloody hell had he done that? Yes, he'd been tired, struggling to do his job safely after endless nights of interrupted sleep. Fed up of the constant arguing. Frustrated as they'd lain together in the same bed barely touching. Had he considered the extra stress his attitude was creating for Claire, though? How exhausted she was? He really had been a self-centred bastard.

'I'm honestly not sure yet, Ella.' He answered her evasively. 'Like I say, Mummy and I need to sit down and talk.'

Ella considered that, then, 'Mummy will have time to sit down now,' she said confidently.

Luke couldn't help but smile. You couldn't get much past his daughter. She was obviously well aware that Claire was run ragged.

'Will you miss Grandad?' she asked him, blindsiding him.

'Er…' Not sure how to answer that one either, Luke took a second. 'A bit,' he said eventually.

'Mummy will miss him,' Ella said, nodding sadly. 'Daddy, can I ask you something?' she tacked on before Luke could comment.

'Anything,' he assured her.

'Does keeping secrets mean telling lies?'

He looked at her curiously, wondering where that had come from. 'Possibly,' he said, considering it. 'If you don't tell someone something because you want to keep the truth from them, then I suppose that's kind of a lie.'

Again Ella nodded thoughtfully. 'Grandad's been keeping secrets,' she said, and her gaze flicked down and back again.

CHAPTER FOURTEEN

Claire

Going across to the dresser in the large bay window to place her father's photograph albums in the top drawer, where he could easily find them, Claire glimpsed down at the leafy gardens beyond. The grounds really were beautiful. She did hope he would take up the offer from one of the other residents to explore them with him later. He'd refused point blank to take a stroll outside with her. Straightening the photograph of her mum that she'd placed on top of the dresser – one of several photos she'd brought, along with his bedspread and anything else that might make the place feel homely – she went back to where he was perched on the edge of his bed. She wished he would sit in his armchair. He looked so lost.

'There, I think that's everything,' she said, her voice overly bright as she adjusted the position of his alarm clock on the bedside locker; as if the passing of time would mean anything to him any more, other than to remind him of mealtimes. 'I've put your sweaters on the top shelf of the wardrobe in case it's cold when you go for a walk. And your DVDs are in the cupboard under the TV.'

Bernard looked up at her, his eyes still flecked with the confusion she'd seen there since they'd arrived. 'Are we going home now?' he asked.

Claire gulped back the heavy guilt expanding in her chest. 'No, Dad,' she said gently, sitting down alongside him and taking hold of his hand. 'This is where you live now. This is your new home. We've brought all your things here, see?'

Bernard glanced vaguely around and then back to her. 'So will you be living here too?' he asked, his face so hopeful Claire didn't think she could bear it. He looked more like a child than Ella did.

Struggling to know what to say, she took a breath. 'No, Dad, I won't,' she answered honestly, 'but I'll be coming to see you regularly. And Ella will come with me sometimes. She's already planning to paint you some pictures. That will brighten the place up, won't it?'

Gazing up at the dusky pink and cream walls, Bernard nodded and managed a small smile. Seeing his expression relax a little, Claire debated with herself; then, desperate to find out what she could before she left, tentatively broached the subject.

'Would you like me to pass on your address to Sophie?' she asked him, keeping her tone light whilst mentally crossing her fingers. She was sure she'd seen a flicker of something in his eyes when she'd first asked him about her, and he himself had mentioned her name – though might that have been because he'd retained it for a short while after she'd brought it up?

He eyed her narrowly. 'Who?' he said again.

Noting his now wary expression, Claire immediately regretted her impulsiveness. She shouldn't be bringing this up now, when he was so emotionally muddled. But if not now, when? His memories were slipping away like sand through a timer. If he had even a sliver of recollection, she needed to know. 'I thought you might like her to come and visit,' she continued, pushing it a little.

Bernard's expression was uncomprehending for a second. Then his face darkened. 'I'd like to go home now,' he said abrasively, hauling himself to his feet to stride past her, leaving Claire staring after him bewildered.

'Dad?' Panic tightening her chest, she jumped up. 'Dad, wait.' She caught up with him at the door and placed a hand on his arm. 'Where are you going?'

'I'm sorry, do I know you?' Snatching his arm away, he glared mutinously at her, and then reached to yank the door open and march briskly out into the corridor.

Shocked, Claire waited a second to take stock. Was that hurtful absent-mindedness a deliberate deflection? Uneasy goose bumps prickled her skin as she followed him. 'Dad, please wait.' She struggled to keep up with him as he descended the stairs with remarkable agility and headed across the open hallway into the lounge.

'Afternoon, Mr Harvey.' The resident who'd offered to show him around the grounds greeted him with a cheery smile. 'It's a lovely one, isn't it? Here, take my chair,' he said, levering himself from an armchair by the window. 'I'm just off to telephone my son. Need to stock up on the old supplies.' He tapped the side of his nose conspiratorially. Bernard stared at him as if he were quite mad.

'Some people find that spot quite peaceful,' a carer called across from where she was chatting to another elderly gentleman. 'It has gorgeous views of the grounds.'

Bernard paused to look at her, his expression a combination of irritation and indignation. 'Do I look as if I'm ready to be put out to grass?' he boomed, causing alarmed faces to turn in his direction. 'Idiots,' he muttered, about-facing to walk in the opposite direction. 'Godforsaken fucking mausoleum.'

Wincing at his language, Claire trailed after him. 'Dad, where are you going?' she asked him again, feeling now more than desperate. There was no way she could leave him here in such an agitated state.

Her father glanced back at her, his expression confused once more, then, 'My taxi's here,' he announced, marching on.

Claire caught up and moved around in front of him. 'Dad, it's *not*. You haven't called one.'

Bernard stopped and blinked uncomprehendingly at her. 'Haven't I?' He shook his head in bafflement. 'Well, I should have done. Ruth will be wondering where I am. She gets in a state if I'm not home when I say I will be. You couldn't call one for me, could you, dear?'

'Dad…' Claire's heart sank. Why did he keep mentioning her mother? As if he'd lived his whole life loving her when in fact he'd bloody well *cheated* on her? Inhaling deeply, she tried to quash her sudden anger. She didn't know yet, after all, not for certain.

'I can't seem to locate my phone.' Bernard frowned and patted his pockets anxiously. Must have left it in my glove compartment. I really should call her. She—'

'Dad, Mum's not *at* home,' Claire snapped, despite her best efforts not to. 'She's not wondering where you are. You're not going in a taxi. You're staying here. *This* is your new home. Please try to remember.'

'Ah.' Oddly, he seemed to brighten at that. 'She's here then, is she?' he asked, gazing around expectantly.

Claire's heart plummeted to the pit of her stomach. 'No, Dad, she's not. She…' She trailed off, her voice catching.

His expression now dazed, like that of a child who'd rushed gleefully downstairs at Christmas to find no presents under the tree, Bernard studied her for a long moment, then, 'I think I'd like to go home now,' he said shakily. There was no anger in his voice this time, no cantankerousness; nothing but fear and soul-crushing defeat.

Fighting back her tears, her chest aching with a mixture of frustration and grief, Claire watched helplessly as he peeled his bewildered gaze from her and then walked away. She had no clue what to say to him. Absolutely none.

She felt an arm slide around her shoulders as she stood there wondering what to do next. 'Why don't you slip off?' the carer suggested kindly.

'How?' Claire whispered, her throat hoarse. 'How can I leave him like this?'

'He'll be fine.' The carer gave her a reassuring squeeze. 'This is always the hardest part. I'm on duty for a while, so I'll keep an eye on him, don't worry.'

Claire nodded, a sense of hopelessness washing through her. What about when the woman's shift finished? What then? Would he even try to make friends? Relate to anyone?

'Bernard's going to show me some of his photograph albums, aren't you, Bernard?' the carer called cheerfully across to him.

Bernard said nothing; simply stared out of the window he'd now wandered over to. Gulping back the huge knot in her throat, Claire went across to him. She should leave. She was doing no good here. If anything, she was making things worse. 'I'll come and see you tomorrow, Dad,' she promised.

Bernard glanced from the window down to the hand she'd placed on his arm. 'No need, dear.' His gaze coming back to her face, he scrutinised her intently. 'My daughter will be here soon to take me home. She's a good girl. I expect she'll be here any minute now.'

Checking his watch, he turned back to the window, his expression closed, and Claire felt something break inside her. *Which daughter, Dad?* Studying his profile, wondering if she knew him any better than he seemed to know her, she stepped shakily back, and then turned to walk quietly away.

CHAPTER FIFTEEN

Claire

Tears streaming unchecked down her cheeks, Claire climbed into her car and buried her face in her hands. She shouldn't have asked him. What had she been thinking? He was bound to be highly strung, being shunted off to a bloody care home. Taking a minute to compose herself, she mulled things over, and then picked up her phone and flicked to Messenger.

I need to ask you some things, she sent to Sophie, and drew in a sharp breath.

Sophie replied swiftly, to Claire's surprise. Again, it was almost as if she'd been waiting for her to message. *Ask away. I'll do my best to answer.*

Wary apprehension settling in her chest, Claire hesitated, and then, *Might be better to talk on the phone. Can you send me a number?*

Once more Sophie replied promptly, including a telephone number. *I could ring you, if you like?* she added.

Claire didn't answer, calling the number instead. Her stomach churned with anxiety as she waited. 'Sophie?' she said nervously when she picked up. 'It's Claire.'

'Hi, Claire. Thanks for getting in touch. I wasn't sure you would.' Sophie sounded as nervous as Claire felt.

'I didn't have a lot of choice really, did I?' she responded. She couldn't help herself. She was hardly going to be ecstatic at the prospect of her father having had an affair that had wreaked such utter devastation in her life. That he might have had a child with another woman was soul-destroying. All those times he'd stayed away from home purporting to be on business trips. All the times he'd left Claire to her mother's dark moods. Had her mother known? Claire didn't have all the pieces yet, but she was beginning to form a picture. If Sophie was who she claimed she was and her mother had been aware of the affair, then it was possible she had known about the child, which would explain an awful lot: her drinking, her headaches, the arguments. The image of her mother's limp body flashed graphically again through Claire's mind, and the anger in her chest tightened.

'No, I suppose not,' Sophie agreed, now sounding contrite. 'I'm sorry about that first message I sent. It must have seemed really blunt and impersonal, but I wasn't sure what else to do. I was going to write you a letter, but—'

'You know my father's address, then?' Claire interrupted.

'He kept in touch,' Sophie said, driving home the enormity of Bernard's lies. 'Irregularly, and not for some time, but yes, I know where you live.'

'When did you last see him?' Claire gulped back her hurt. He'd had a whole other life that had excluded her. Why had he done that? He must have realised she might find out. Why hadn't he prepared her? Realised the pain he would cause her?

'Just over a year ago,' Sophie supplied. 'He'd just had his memory assessment test and… To be honest, I think he felt bad that he hadn't been in touch more. Maybe he thought he should let me know because he might not be in future. I'm not really sure.'

Claire's hurt turned to crushing heartache. He hadn't told *her* about the test, not until weeks afterwards. He'd waited until he'd had his MRI scan before breaking the news. That was when Claire had decided she would look after him. They'd moved in with him a month or so later. But how could Sophie know that?

'I wasn't sure how his illness would progress,' Sophie went on. 'And then, when I didn't hear from him…'

'Rapidly,' Claire snapped, fresh tears springing from her eyes. 'It's a cruel, relentless disease. I've just left him in a care home, did you realise that?'

'No. No I didn't. God, I'm so sorry, Claire,' Sophie said sympathetically. 'I wish I'd known.'

'Why?' Claire asked, incredulous. 'What would you have done? Come along to hold his hand?'

Sophie went quiet. Then, 'I know you don't know me, Claire. You might not want to, either, although I would really love to get to know you. I wouldn't blame you if you wanted nothing to do with me, but…' She faltered. 'Yes, I would have come along – to hold *your* hand, though, more than his. It must have been heartbreaking for you.'

Claire closed her eyes. 'It was,' she whispered. 'It's the worst thing I've ever had to do in my life.'

'I can imagine,' Sophie said softly. 'Was your husband with you?'

She knew Claire was married? But then she hadn't hidden the fact on social media. Plus, Bernard would probably have told her. 'No.' Claire took a shaky breath. 'He's looking after our little girl.'

'Ella,' Sophie said. 'She's beautiful. I saw the photos on your Facebook page. Bernard showed me the photographs he had on his phone, too.'

Claire felt her throat close. She felt cheated on, her feelings trampled, just as she had with Luke. She'd obviously meant nothing to the two most important men in her life. Men she'd built her life around. Now she had nothing. And it hurt. Oh God, how it hurt.

'He loves her to bits,' Sophie went on kindly. 'You too, Claire. You mustn't ever doubt that. He's so proud of you. He told me about your job working with special needs children. I must admit I felt a bit jealous. I messed about so much at school, it's a wonder I managed to get a job at all when I left.'

Claire swallowed. She wanted to get to know Sophie too, she reluctantly acknowledged. To have someone in her life where she felt there was now no one. 'What do you do?' she managed, wiping a hand under her nose.

'At the moment, just casual work in one of the cafés on the pavilion,' Sophie answered, almost apologetically, 'but when Bernard told me about your achievements, it did make me think maybe I should try to go back to college and get some qualifications. You're never too old, as they say.'

'So how old are you?' Claire asked, wondering when it was that her father had made the decision that would destroy his marriage and ruin his child's life.

'Thirty-four. My birthday's in September,' Sophie answered, and Claire felt it like another cruel blow. Sophie was a month younger than she herself was. Did that mean there was a possibility her father might not have known her mother was pregnant when Sophie was conceived?

'We could almost be twins,' Sophie went on tentatively.

They could be. How ironic was that? Claire had been lonely even as a small child, more so after her mother died. She'd so longed for a sister or brother she could share her secrets and troubles with.

'Have you always lived near Rhyl?' she probed carefully, thinking it was perhaps time they met. It couldn't hurt, after all; not any more than it already did.

'I have,' Sophie said. 'Hopefully I won't forever.'

'And you say you have no other family?'

'No one.' Sophie sighed. 'I was in a long-term relationship, but he turned out to be a bastard, to be honest – you know, cheating, lying through his teeth – so I kicked him out. The only company I have now is my cat.'

Claire couldn't help feeling sympathetic. Sophie sounded as lonely as she was herself. She hesitated for a moment, deliberating, and then, 'Look, Sophie, I can't pretend I'm happy about any of this. What you've told me has turned my world upside down. To be frank, I was going to ignore you, but now… I think we need to meet up and talk properly. That's if you'd like to.'

'Really?' Sophie sounded surprised. 'I'd love to,' she added quickly. 'I'd need to book a day off and check out the train times, but I could come to you whenever. Tomorrow, if that suits you. I could always take a sickie.'

She didn't drive, then? Possibly couldn't afford a car. 'No, I'll come to you,' Claire offered. She would take Ella with her. She had nothing else to keep her here. She could head off after Ella's check-up at the hospital tomorrow. She would pop in and see her father first thing, but as he didn't appear to know her any more, he might not even miss her. A wave of sadness washed over her.

Agreeing a time with Sophie, she signed off and quickly texted Luke to tell him she was on her way. Surprisingly, she actually felt better for talking to Sophie, realising she was someone she could confide in about how she was feeling. Gemma would always be there for her if she asked her, but conversation about her father's condition wasn't something most people were comfortable with.

He was still at the window when she drove past. Raising a hand, she gave him a wave. He didn't wave back, although she was sure he could see her.

CHAPTER SIXTEEN

Claire

Her chest heavy, Claire drove blindly for a while, random thoughts rushing pell-mell through her head. She was back in Rhyl on that long-ago summer's day, laughing with her father, squealing in delight as the fairground ride they were on plunged, twisted and spun. She pictured him smiling and chatting to the lady with the leopard-print shoes in the pretty village pub. Flirting, that was what he'd been doing. Swallowing, Claire squeezed her eyes closed, and then, feeling the car judder beneath her, snapped them open again in alarm.

What on earth…? The front near-side wheel clunked and dipped as, panic clutching her chest, she struggled to keep the vehicle straight. Did she have a flat tyre? *How?* She'd checked her tyres when she'd last filled up. Pushing her foot hard on the brake, she ground to a halt, sighing with relief when she realised how narrowly she'd avoided veering off the road. The driver behind her didn't help her shattered nerves, blasting his horn as he sailed by. *Idiot.*

Her heart hammering, feeling sick to her stomach as she thought about Ella, her small heart breaking if Mummy didn't come home, Claire climbed out and went to assess the damage. The tyre was flat, as she'd suspected. Punctured, she realised, crouching to run her hand over the tread. By a screw? A brand-new screw, from the look of it. How the hell had that got there? She hadn't been anywhere apart from the care home. She must have picked it up on the road. She tried to convince herself that the succession of odd things happening – the gate she'd thought she'd heard banging and the windows locked when it appeared her father hadn't moved from his armchair – were all just coincidence, the alternative being that someone wished her physical harm; that the person who'd scratched her car had deliberately pushed that screw into her tyre.

Ten minutes later, realising she was as likely to release the nuts on the wheel as fly to the moon, she rang the breakdown service, and then called Luke to tell him she would be delayed.

'Do you want me to drive out to you?' he asked, sounding alarmed. 'I don't like the idea of you being on your own.'

Claire couldn't help but laugh quietly at the irony of that. 'No thanks,' she said shortly, stopping short of caustic. 'I'm perfectly capable of managing, Luke.' With the practical things anyway, she didn't add.

An hour later, approaching her house, she had to admit she felt a huge sense of relief at seeing Luke's car parked outside. She should hate the sight of him, but right now, she craved the familiarity of his physical presence. At the same time, she wanted to hit him. Why had he done it? Treated her so badly when she needed him most? When Ella, with all that was happening around her, needed stability in her life? She couldn't believe that he, of all people, hadn't considered what the consequences would be for his daughter. She remembered him telling her about the sense of failure he'd felt when his own father had abandoned him; the crushing hurt because he hadn't been enough to make him stay; the loneliness. Losing her father and her grandfather in such a short space of time, Ella would be feeling as bereaved as Claire was. It seemed incomprehensible that Luke hadn't thought about that; a man who would sing his baby soft lullabies while gently rocking her back to sleep. Right up until things had started to go wrong, he'd always been sensitive and caring, tactile and loving. Bringing his special girls little gifts: flowers or furry animals – Ella was mad on them. But his feelings had changed, hadn't they? Or else he was never the person Claire had thought he was.

Were all men the same? Unable to see that, in giving in to their primal urges, embarking on their little flings and affairs, they were making the woman they were with question everything that fundamentally made her who she was; her personality, her sexuality. Why had her mother stayed with her father, assuming he had done the unthinkable and had a child with another woman? Would Claire take Luke back if he asked? Try to make a go of it, for Ella's sake? He didn't want her, though, did he? That was the cold fact. But that was okay. Claire swallowed back the pain where her heart should be. She'd made up her mind she would much rather not live a life where she was constantly viewing herself through his eyes and finding herself lacking, as her mother must have done.

Parking up, not even bothering to check her face in the mirror, Claire reached for the door and climbed out. As she walked to the front door, she tried not to notice the unpruned roses her father had tended in lieu of her mother – until he'd forgotten how to.

Letting herself in to be greeted by the aroma of cooking wafting from the kitchen, she faltered, overwhelmed by a crushing sense of homesickness for the little cottage she and Luke had lived in until she'd insisted they move here. Now, though, she had no choice but to get the sale of this house under way if she was going to meet the care home fees. It was possible there wouldn't be anything substantial left over. Whatever happened, she would have to move out. Move somewhere else on her own.

The deep sense of loneliness she'd been feeling multiplied tenfold as Luke stepped from the kitchen into the hall.

'Hi,' he said with a cautious smile. 'You got it sorted, then?'

Claire nodded tiredly and shrugged out of her coat.

'How did it go at the care home?' Luke asked.

What do you care? Claire was tempted to say. She didn't. She didn't want to argue with him. She just hadn't got the energy. 'Awful,' she admitted. 'It was like leaving a child at nursery for the first time.'

Luke's gaze flicked down and back. 'I'm sorry, Claire,' he said, coming towards her.

She wanted to resist, to move away when he placed his arm hesitantly around her, but she was so very weary that she gave in to her urge to rest her head on his shoulder, as she had done many times in the past: when social services had been poking around, believing them capable of harming their child; when Ella had first been diagnosed and their world had come crashing down; when she'd learned about her father's devastating prognosis. Luke had always been there for her then. What had gone so wrong?

He eased her towards him, holding her gently. Claire inhaled hard, trying to force back her tears, to no avail. They came anyway, plopping hotly down her cheeks.

He didn't seem to mind that she was wetting his shirt. One hand stroking her hair, the other softly caressing her back, he waited, and then, 'I'm so sorry, Claire,' he repeated hoarsely. 'For everything.'

She looked up at him, at her husband, the man she'd loved and still loved with her whole heart, the man she'd created a perfect child with – and Ella *was* perfect; her illness made her a little more vulnerable, that was all. His expression was one of heartfelt remorse. He was sorry for the pain he'd caused. It was obvious he was. But if it was forgiveness he was seeking, she couldn't offer him that. She would remain friends with him, for Ella's sake, but she doubted she could ever forgive him.

Wiping a hand across her face, she nodded, and stepped away. She couldn't be this close to him. It was too painful. 'Where's Ella?' she asked, though she knew it was well past her daughter's bedtime.

'Fast asleep,' he supplied. 'She wanted me to read her *Mrs Tiggy-Winkle*, but she was out for the count before I'd finished.

She was worn out from the park and from helping me with dinner. It's soup, by the way, roasted onion with goat's cheese.'

Claire had guessed as much from the smell of caramelised onions. It was one of the special recipes Luke cooked on sick days and winter holidays, because it hit the spot, he said. It was one of her favourites. Tonight, though, she doubted she would be able to swallow it.

'You will have some, won't you?' he asked, his eyes clouding with concern. Honest eyes, Claire had always believed. She'd never thought there would come a day when she would look for the lies there. Had he lied throughout their marriage? Had other affairs? She didn't know. She didn't want to know, couldn't expose herself to more hurt, risk that he might pile lie on top of lie. Her emotions were too raw.

Smiling tiredly, she nodded. 'Maybe later. I'm not very hungry.'

'I didn't think you would be.' Luke followed her as she walked to the kitchen. 'I left the toasts out. I thought you could warm the soup up later.'

'Thanks. I'll do that,' Claire said. He was trying to be thoughtful. She didn't want to shove it back in his face. 'Did Ella have some?'

'Two helpings,' Luke assured her. 'She almost spat it out when I told her she might not have left enough for you.'

Picturing Ella's alarmed face, Claire smiled, and flicked the kettle on, though she didn't really fancy tea either. She wasn't sure what she would do with herself now her father wasn't here. Glancing around the kitchen, it occurred to her that for the first time in a long time, she might have time on her hands. A vast void to be filled, and she wasn't sure she knew how. She would look for a job, she supposed. She would need to now she was a single parent. Not yet, though. She could afford to take a month, maybe two, to think about what she wanted to do.

The snakes and ladders board was still on the table where Ella had left it. Claire wandered across to it. She and her father had played the game often when she was little. What was he doing now? Picturing him at the window, looking as lost and lonely as she felt, she closed her eyes and pulled in a shuddery breath.

She didn't realise Luke was behind her until he placed a hand on her shoulder. 'Do you want me to stay for a while?' he asked gently.

She turned to him to find his eyes searching hers. Anxious eyes, intense blue, they still took her breath away. He was genuinely concerned. He would stay if she asked him to; sleep on the couch, no doubt. She wanted him to – the house already felt so desperately empty – but… *What about the new woman in your life? Would she approve?* she was about to ask, just as his phone rang.

She noticed his guilty expression, the same reluctance to answer it she'd seen once before. She couldn't do this, have him stay here out of pity. She might not have much left in her life, but she still had her pride, just.

'No,' she replied. 'It probably isn't a good idea. It might send the wrong signals to Ella, and we wouldn't want to do that, would we?' The last bit came out sarcastically. She didn't much care. Why should she be treading on eggshells around his feelings? Walking past him, she headed for the fridge. Wine she possibly could manage. Numbing her feelings seemed like a very good idea right now.

'Are you sure?' Luke asked. 'I don't need to rush off.'

Claire pulled out the wine and glanced back at him, her mouth curving into a cynical smile as his phone sounded with an incoming text. 'Are *you* sure?' she asked. 'Someone seems a bit keen to me.'

Luke said nothing, glancing uncomfortably down instead. It *was* her then.

'I'll be fine,' Claire assured him, selecting a large glass from the cupboard and filling it. 'I'm sure I'll sleep after a few of these. Cheers.' Tipping the glass back, she took a huge gulp, which definitely hit the spot, since she'd eaten nothing since lunchtime.

Luke was watching her, his expression troubled. What? Did he disapprove of her drinking alone? That was a pity. She took another swig.

'Go easy on the wine, Claire,' Luke suggested.

Unbelievable! He blew her world apart, destroyed everything they had in one fell swoop, and he actually thought he had the right to tell her what to do?

'I'm having a glass of wine, Luke. After the day I've been through, I think I deserve one, don't you?' she asked, eyeing him levelly. 'Don't worry, I won't sink the whole bottle and do anything rash, like go out and pick up the first available man. Unlike some people, I realise I have responsibilities.'

Accepting the dig with a tired nod, Luke blew out an expansive sigh. 'I'm just concerned, Claire, that's all. I'm bound to be when I find…'

'Find what?' she challenged him. That your wife isn't coping with being alone as well as you'd like her to? What a terrible burden that must be.

'Nothing,' he said, after an awkward pause. 'Can I call you tomorrow?' he asked tentatively.

'About?' Claire topped up her glass.

'Ella.' He shrugged. 'Arrangements. I assume you're staying here for a while? I was just wondering about schools, whether she'll still be going to the local one here, or…'

Again he trailed off. Clearly he'd realised there was no alternative. Claire would have to stay here until the house was sold. She had nowhere else to go. But she didn't want to discuss any of this now. Surely he wasn't so insensitive he wouldn't realise that?

Was he considering his own future arrangements and where his daughter would fit in with those? she wondered. And there she'd been, determined to try to keep things amicable between them, worried about the injury to his ankle, the scratch on his face, the fact that he looked more tired than he ever had. She'd imagined he would still care enough to be concerned about her. She really had misjudged him, hadn't she?

'Call me,' she said shortly, taking another glug of wine and then picking up the bottle. 'But not tomorrow. I'm going to be busy.'

'Doing what?' Luke asked curiously. Then, 'Sorry,' he backtracked, 'I guess it's not really any of my business, is it?'

'Just seeing a friend,' Claire said, and then hesitated. Did it matter if she told him about Sophie? She debated, and decided it didn't. In fact, it wouldn't hurt for him to realise she had someone in her corner. 'Actually, she's a relative,' she added.

'Oh?' Luke's tone was wary.

Claire took a breath and pushed on. 'I think she's my half-sister.'

Stunned silence from Luke. And then, 'Your half-sister?' he said, astonished. 'You *think*?'

'We're just getting to know each other. She lives in—'

'But how…? Who…?' Luke was clearly struggling to digest the information. 'Where did you meet? Did she contact you, or…?'

'She contacted me,' Claire supplied. 'On Facebook. I was dubious at first, but I'm beginning to think—'

'Facebook?' Luke emitted a disbelieving laugh. 'And you just took her word for it?'

'No!' Claire said crossly. 'Of course I didn't. That's why I'm trying to establish whether she is who she says she is.'

'That's bloody nuts, Claire. You should have nothing to do with her. Half-sisters don't just appear out of the ether without you ever having had an inkling they existed. Whose side of the family does she claim to be on?' he demanded.

'I don't have to answer to you, Luke,' Claire pointed out, making a monumental effort to contain her growing anger. 'I'm going to have a bath. You can find your own way out, can't you? You managed it well enough last time.'

'Claire, for Christ's sake…' She heard the desperation in his tone as she headed for the stairs. He could never be as desperate as she felt right now.

Pausing halfway along the landing, she parked the bottle on the floor, leaned against the wall and then slid to her haunches, hugging her knees close to her as she waited for him to go. He seemed to take ages, going back to the kitchen and then loitering in the hall.

When he did finally leave, he closed the front door quietly, but still it sounded like a death knell. And suddenly there was complete silence. No TV blaring out, no agitated shouts or shuffling footsteps. No smoke alarms going off because her father had left the grill on, or the oven, or a saucepan to boil itself dry. No sweeping of palms against walls. Nothing but the too-loud tick of the clock on the landing.

He was meticulous about setting the time when the clocks changed.

Now he didn't know what day it was. Who she was.

Glancing at the ceiling, Claire blinked hard.

After several minutes, she noticed that her dad's bedroom door was ajar. Pulling herself to her feet, she bypassed the bathroom – despite what she'd told Luke, she had no inclination to take a bath – and reached to close it. Then she paused, bracing herself to peer inside. The curtains were still open, the furniture silhouetted by the thin light of the moon through the window. Seeing his bed neatly made up, the one abiding habit he couldn't seem to forget, she felt a stab of grief run through her. Many of his clothes were still there, shirts, trousers and pressed suits hanging in his wardrobe. His shoes, all highly polished. She would need to sort through it all. Take him anything he might want. *Want?* She emitted a laugh, which turned to a sob. He didn't *want* anything, apart from his stolen memories. Her chest heaved as she gulped back a huge breath. She couldn't do this on her own. She just couldn't.

Coming out of the bedroom, she closed the door softly behind her and retrieved the bottle and glass from the landing. Lost in her thoughts, she wandered towards her own room, but stopped short as something glinting on the landing snagged her eye. She walked across to it, her heart skipping a beat as she realised what it was. Broken glass? But how? Her heart almost stopped as she considered what the consequences might have been for Ella if she'd cut herself on it. It was a wine glass. Had her father broken one and she hadn't noticed? Dear God, had Luke been right about how dangerous it was for Ella to be around him? She would never have forgiven herself if…

Making a mental note to vacuum the whole house before Ella set foot out of bed in the morning, Claire placed the bottle and her own glass on a shelf and rushed to check on her. She was sleeping, as Luke had said, her Beatrix Potter First Flopsy toy clutched tightly to her chest. Carefully, Claire pulled back the duvet and crouched to examine the soles of her baby's soft feet, relief crashing through her when she found no evidence of injury there.

Easing the duvet back over her, she looked heavenwards and blinked back her tears. She felt like a child, vulnerable and so alone. But it was Ella who was the child. Ella who was vulnerable, and no doubt feeling every bit as lonely as Claire was. She needed her mummy here in the moment. Not distracted, not constantly tearful. She needed her attention. And starting tomorrow, Claire aimed to make sure she got every bit she deserved.

'Night night, precious angel,' she whispered, tucking one little bare arm under the duvet, then tugging the covers up to her chin and pressing a soft kiss to her cheek. *Mummy will look after you, darling. Mummy will never, ever let anything hurt you, I promise.*

CHAPTER SEVENTEEN

Luke

Tossing his phone onto the dashboard, Luke drove a short way from the house and then slowed. He shouldn't be leaving Claire like this, particularly now she'd told him about the bloody nutter stalking her on Facebook. *Dammit!* Thumping the heel of his hand against the steering wheel, he pulled over, debating whether to go back. And what then? Insist on staying to protect her? She wasn't about to let him do that. She wasn't prepared to hear him out. As far as she was concerned, there was obviously no going back. Luke wished he could. Wished to God he could wind the clock back, but he couldn't. All he could do, he supposed, was try to warn her off.

What the hell he was going to do about Anna, he had no idea. He felt as if he'd been hit by a freight train when she'd eventually emerged from the bathroom, screaming about falling out of one abusive relationship into another and trying to prevent him from leaving. The woman didn't just need counselling, she needed serious help. And, God help him, so did he.

His stomach knotted as his mobile signalled yet another incoming text, one of so many today he'd lost count. Nervously he reached to pick it up. Why was she doing this? What had he done to trigger such a volatile reaction, apart from beg her to come out of the bloody bathroom? Up until recently, he'd felt responsible for her, thinking he'd played a part in her attempt to take her own life. Guilty, that too. Now, he was angry. Furious, in fact. And frightened. He had no idea how this would end, which petrified him. Warily, he selected his messages, expecting yet more demands to know where he was, why he wasn't returning her calls or texts, and was surprised to see the last one was from Steve.

Been trying to ring you, mate, it read. *Anna's been here looking for you. Seemed a bit weird. Everything all right?*

She'd been to Steve's house? Meaning she must have bloody well followed him there, at some point, because he'd certainly never given the address. Christ, the woman really was off the wall.

Yeah, good, he sent back. *Sorry about that. Call you later.*

He took a breath and scrolled down to Anna's number. Even glimpsing the first few words of her last text had him breaking out in a cold sweat. Opening it, he scanned it in growing confusion.

Right, fine. Message understood, she'd sent. *For the record, it's me who's doing the dumping. You should know that I've reported you, by the way.*

Reported him? Luke's heart missed a beat. Bewildered, he flicked to her previous messages.

Why aren't you returning my calls? the first one demanded. *Are you still with her?*

The next was sarcastic. *Have your fingers dropped off? Can you text me back, please? Or are you getting some kick out of this?*

Growing increasingly worried, he scrolled on. *You are, aren't you?*

He could almost feel her mounting rage as he read the next few messages. *Are you dumping me? I mean, not replying to my texts? Really? How juvenile are you?*

You're a bastard, do you know that?

You knew I was vulnerable and you didn't really give a shit, did you? It was all a game, pretending you cared, that you were protecting me. That your poor heart was breaking and that your wife was a frigid, unreasonable bitch. Crying all over my shoulder. All designed to get me into bed.

Nausea twisting his gut, Luke stared hard at his phone. She was completely insane. He hadn't pretended anything. He'd been straight down the line. And there was no way on God's green earth he would ever say anything so derogatory about Claire.

You're just as bad as he is. An abusive bastard! I am NOT some cheap little slut you can just shag and then dump! You do not get to use me and then just walk away!

The last message was a warning. *I'll give you one hour before I pick up the phone. Don't think I won't.*

'Jesus Christ.' Luke checked his watch, rammed the car into gear and drove. Fast.

CHAPTER EIGHTEEN

Luke

Working to control his frustration after repeatedly phoning her and getting no answer, Luke pushed the key she'd insisted he have into the lock and shoved the apartment door open. 'Anna!' he called, heading for the combined lounge and kitchen area.

There was no sign of her, so he went through to the bedroom. 'Anna?' Going warily in, he stopped dead when he noted the closed bathroom door. She wasn't really playing this game again, was she? He'd been on the point of breaking the door down before she'd emerged earlier and all hell had broken loose. He breathed in hard and stepped towards it. 'Anna,' he called more loudly, cold foreboding creeping through him despite his growing anger.

No answer. *Jesus!* Why was she *doing* this? His heartbeat slowing to a dull thud in his chest, he reached for the handle, fearing the worst. Finding the door unlocked, he pushed it open and stepped cautiously in.

The shower curtain was drawn. A pulse of tension tightened in his neck as he stepped further in. His gaze strayed to the wall over the sink, and his legs almost gave way. There were blood spatters on the mirror and the tiles. Gulping back a sick taste in his mouth, he dragged an arm across his forehead. Christ, this couldn't be happening. A petrifying scenario was unfurling in his head as he turned to the bath. His hand visibly shaking, dread snaking the length of his spine, he braced himself to reach for the shower curtain and draw it back.

The tap was dripping, the sound echoing around the room in tandem with his heartbeat. Panic gripped him, turning his insides over. He registered the watery trickle of blood in the base of the bath. No Anna. Where the *hell* was she?

Gulping back the bile rising in his throat, he stepped back, collided with the door frame and almost slid down it. Then he yanked himself upright and headed for the front door. Fumbling his phone from his pocket, wondering who in God's name he was supposed to ring, he pulled the door open, and froze.

'Evening, sir,' said one of the two uniformed officers standing outside it. 'We're responding to an emergency 999 call from this address. Do you mind if we come in?'

'A…' Luke felt the floor shift beneath him. 'What?'

'It might be better if we talk inside, sir.'

Luke nodded confusedly and stood aside. 'Anna's not here,' he said, grappling to understand what was happening as he closed the door behind them and led the way into the living area.

'And you are?' the officer asked. His eyes were steely, unflinching, appraising Luke coolly. His colleague was looking around the apartment, checking out the kitchen area.

'Luke Elliot. A friend,' Luke said. He knew he sounded evasive, but he wasn't sure what else to say.

'And you've been here all evening, have you, sir?' the officer asked.

'No, I've just arrived. I couldn't get hold of her on the phone, and… This call, who…?' Luke shook his head, attempting to unscramble his brain. 'What was it about?'

'A domestic incident, we believe,' the officer supplied. 'Reported approximately fifteen minutes ago. We've also had reports from neighbours of screams coming from this apartment.'

Screams? Luke felt sweat prickle his forehead.

'You're claiming you weren't here when this incident occurred?' the officer asked.

Luke hesitated. 'No. No, I wasn't,' he said, deciding not to mention the argument they'd had earlier unless he had to. 'I would have been on my way here. Before then, I was with my wife.'

The officer raised an eyebrow. 'Wife?'

'We're separated,' Luke explained awkwardly. 'I was looking after my daughter while my wife took her father… Look, is all this relevant? I haven't been here this evening.'

The officer looked him over impassively. 'And your wife can verify where you were, can she?'

'Yes,' Luke said. His stomach clenched as he realised that wasn't strictly true. 'Well, she was taking her father to a care home. I collected my daughter, took her to the park and then waited at my father-in-law's house until Claire came back.'

'And how old is your daughter, Mr Elliot?'

Luke's heart dropped. 'Four,' he said, guessing that Ella's account of his movements might not be enough to verify what he was saying. Feeling sicker by the minute, he knew he had to tell it as it was. 'There's something you need to know,' he said guardedly.

'Which is?' The officer waited.

'Anna, she's…' *What?* He could hardly tell them she was a nutjob without sounding as if he was looking to defend himself. 'Unstable,' he settled for, only to realise from the meaningful glances the two men exchanged that that didn't sound much better. He drew in a breath. 'She was seeing her GP,' he added.

'Unstable how?' the second officer asked, shoving his hands in his pockets and tipping his head to one side. His eyes were narrowed, Luke noticed, a new wave of panic twisting his stomach.

'She… attempted suicide.' He forced the words out. 'Just after we met. She was attacked by her former boyfriend.'

'I see.' The man frowned pensively. 'And can you supply the name of this former boyfriend?'

'I, er…' Luke realised he couldn't. She'd talked about the man often, but she'd never mentioned a name. 'No, I'm afraid not. I saw him once in a nightclub, witnessed him being abusive.'

'Go on,' the officer said, his expression dubious at best.

A cold knot of fear tightening inside him, Luke continued. 'She was pretty down after her suicide attempt. Depressed, I think. Since then, I've hardly dared leave her alone. The thing is, she won't let me go out. She…' Suspecting that what he was about to say might well make *him* sound like the nutjob, he faltered.

'You were saying?' the first officer picked up.

Luke kneaded his temples. 'We did argue,' he admitted, his heart sinking further as he realised he had no choice. 'But not this evening. Earlier.'

'And this would account for the injury to your face, would it, sir?' the officer enquired, his suspicion now blatantly obvious.

'No,' Luke said quickly. 'I… fell.'

Now the guy looked sceptical. 'Fell,' he repeated, his tone unconvinced. 'Against what?'

'Barbed wire,' Luke supplied. 'Old stuff, on a perimeter fence. I work in construction. We're refurbing a property. I was on site and I slipped, and—'

'You fell,' the officer cut in, with a short nod of his head. 'This argument,' he resumed, his expression now communicating that he didn't believe a word Luke had said, 'would you like to tell me about it?'

Luke's gut churned as he guessed where this might be leading. 'She… tried to stop me leaving,' he said reluctantly. 'The situation got…'

'Out of hand?' the officer suggested.

'Heated,' Luke corrected. 'She followed me to the front door. When I tried to go, she freaked out.'

'So, things got physical then?'

'No,' Luke stated categorically, and then backtracked. 'That is…' He noticed the second officer heading towards the bedroom. 'I pushed her away. Nothing more. Then I left. I haven't been—'

'Jack!' the other officer shouted.

Luke pressed his hand against his forehead, swallowed hard and prayed.

CHAPTER NINETEEN

Claire

Having checked on Google Maps, Claire realised Sophie's flat was within walking distance of Rhyl promenade and beach. Now all she had to do was actually find it. Her sat nav seemed to be sending her around in circles. Driving along the parade, she felt a painful stab of melancholic nostalgia as she passed the places she'd visited with her father. The SeaQuarium, viewed from the road rather than the waterfront, looked almost sad and lonely on a wet, grey April day. Or maybe that was just the way she was feeling inside.

'Can we go and see the fish, Mummy?' Ella asked enthusiastically as Claire pointed the building out.

'Ooh, I should think so.' Claire smiled at her in the rear-view mirror. 'But not today. We have to see Mummy's friend, remember? And then we have to go to the hotel and unpack our things and find somewhere to have dinner.'

'McDonald's!' Ella suggested excitedly.

'Hmm?' Claire eyed her knowingly. Aware that being on holiday meant the mood was relaxed, her daughter was taking advantage, she suspected. 'Maybe. We'll see,' she said.

'Happy Meal Veggie Wrap.' Ella nodded, the decision clearly already made.

Claire couldn't help but laugh. Her daughter was a shrewd little operator. Claire had no doubt her mind was more on the free toy than on eating sensibly. 'Veggie Wrap it is then.'

Claire had booked a room at the Travelodge, fancying that the hotel on the seafront where she'd stayed with her dad might bring back memories that would be too difficult to deal with in light of what she now knew. Though in reality she didn't know anything, other than what Sophie had told her. That was the whole point of her being here, she reminded herself, to establish whether her dad was the man she'd thought he was, or whether there was a whole other side to him he'd kept hidden from her. As Luke had. Realising she didn't know anything about Sophie other than what she'd told her, she'd wondered whether it was wise to bring Ella along with her, after all, and had tried to contact her husband several times this morning. She'd hoped he might take Ella for the day, in which case, she would have driven back this evening. Once again, he'd chosen to ignore her texts and calls, meaning he was ignoring not just her, but Ella too. This was a side of Luke she once would have struggled to believe existed. She'd just have to learn to manage without him, wouldn't she? Suppressing the sudden overwhelming wave of sadness that crashed through her, she attempted to steel her resolve.

'Will we be able to swim in the sea, Mummy?' Ella asked, her eyes wide as she took in the sights. She was definitely getting into the holiday spirit.

Claire smiled. 'It might be a teeny bit cold for swimming in the sea, sweetheart, but maybe we'll go to the swimming pool, if we have time.'

'Yippee!' Ella clapped her hands in delight, and Claire marvelled at how easily pleased her little girl was, even now, with all that was going on. She should be counting her blessings. She would be, were it not for this complete sense of failure she couldn't shake off. She knew deep down that she wasn't to blame for anything Luke or her father had done, but still she felt that she was. That she really was lacking in some way. She'd driven Luke away, after all. But then, he'd undoubtedly wanted to go. She couldn't help wondering now whether her father might have wanted to leave too, whether he might have stayed with her mother out of a sense of duty when in his heart it was Sophie's mother he'd wanted to be with. And, ultimately, Sophie.

Stop. Gripping the wheel hard, she warned herself not to make assumptions that were breaking her heart as surely as Luke had. She had no real proof yet that Sophie was who she said she was. Her spirits dipped at the prospect of meeting her, and then lifted a little as she realised she'd finally located the right road.

'Are we nearly there yet, Mummy?' Ella asked the inevitable question.

'We are, sweetheart,' Claire assured her, squinting at house numbers as she drove by, and then pulling up outside the one she was looking for: a three-storey red-brick Victorian terrace.

Hoping she hadn't made a huge mistake coming here, she braced herself to climb out. 'Got Flopsy, lovely?' she asked Ella, turning off the engine.

'Got her,' Ella said, straining to grab her precious rabbit soft toy from the seat next to her and hugging it to her chest.

'Good girl.' Claire collected up her bag and reached for the door handle, then stopped as her phone rang. Pulling it from her bag, she checked the number. It wasn't one she recognised. She debated for a second, and then, thinking it might be something to do with her dad, accepted the call.

'Claire, it's me,' Luke said. 'I haven't got my phone. I'm sorry, I…'

'Was otherwise engaged?' Claire suggested as he trailed off. She didn't want his apologies.

'I'm in trouble, Claire,' he continued, sounding choked, which immediately sent a prickle of apprehension through her. 'I'm at the police station. They're letting me go, for now, but… Something's happened…'

Claire glanced quickly at Ella. 'What?'

He didn't answer, igniting a new wave of panic inside her. 'Luke?' She clutched her phone tighter to her ear.

'Is it Daddy?' Ella asked, her wide blue eyes hopeful. 'Can I speak to him?'

'Luke, are you there?' Claire pressed a finger to her lips, shushing Ella. 'Luke? You're scaring me. Talk to me. What's happened?'

'I don't know. I…' Luke faltered, his voice catching. 'Anna, she…'

Anna? Claire tried to get her head around the situation as Luke broke off again. The woman he was cheating on her with, presumably. Did he seriously think she wanted to hear about anything to do with his relationship with her? She might have laughed, but for the fact that he was clearly distraught. Something was very wrong.

'Mummy, I want to talk to Daddy,' Ella insisted.

'She's gone.' Luke's tone was ragged. 'She wasn't there when I went to her flat. The police arrived five minutes after I did. They—'

'*Mummeee…*'

'Ella, *quiet*,' Claire snapped. 'The police? But why? Who called them? I don't understand. Luke, you need to slow down.'

Clearly trying to compose himself, Luke took a long breath. 'The neighbours called them,' he went on, sounding no less fraught. 'We argued, yesterday, before I came over to you. She didn't report it until later. It wasn't—'

'Report it?' Claire's stomach flipped over. She pictured the livid scratch running the length of his cheek, his closed expression when she'd asked him about it, the evasiveness in his eyes, and felt her heart settle like ice in her chest. They'd fought, obviously. How bad had it been that the police were involved?

'There was blood… in the bathroom,' Luke said, shocking her to the core. 'She's not answering her phone. If they don't find her…'

Dear God! Instinctively, Claire glanced again in Ella's direction, and her heart lurched. Her daughter was crying. Because Claire had snapped at her. Because she could hear all of this and she was scared too. Her soft toy clutched to her face, she was quietly sobbing, because of her bloody, bloody father and his *mistress.*

'Claire, are you still there?' Luke asked.

She could hear his fear. It was palpable. Cautioning herself not to do or say anything else that might upset her daughter, she tried frantically to make sense of what had happened. What did he mean, *if they don't find her*? People didn't just disappear. Not unless they had reason to; that reason being that they were frightened. Or, God forbid, unless they were made to.

'Claire…' Luke's voice was strained. 'I have no idea what to do.'

Claire's pulse raced. Luke wasn't violent. He'd never been aggressive. He'd slammed the front door that morning he'd fallen over the baby gate; he'd been furious then. But he'd had every right to be after being attacked the night before by her father. Hadn't he? Her mind whirled with confusion. Did she know him? Really? This man who'd cheated on her. Had she ever? 'I have to go,' she said quickly. 'Ella…'

'Right. Of course.' Luke sucked in another sharp breath. 'Can I come and see you?' he asked. 'At the house? I need to explain, Claire. About everything. Will you give me a chance to?'

'I can't.' Her stomach twisting with anxiety, Claire reached for door handle again. 'I'm not there. I'm away.'

'Away where?' Luke's response was one of alarm.

'I'm meeting someone, I told you,' Claire reminded him. But she didn't want to go into all that now. 'Luke, I have to go.' Ella would need reassuring. God, how much more reassuring would she need before this nightmare her own father had turned her world into was over?

'Can I call you?' Luke asked.

Claire hesitated.

'Claire, *please*,' he begged. 'You've every right to tell me to piss off, but… I'm desperate.'

Pushing her door open, Claire deliberated. She couldn't not speak to him. For their daughter's sake, she had to know what was going on. 'I'll call you,' she said. 'As soon as I can.'

Ending the call, she opened the door, unbuckled Ella and lifted her out. Setting her down on the pavement, she crouched down to her. 'What's the matter, sweetheart?' she asked, brushing Ella's hair back and silently cursing both herself and Luke for bringing such emotional trauma into their child's life.

Ella pressed Flopsy to her chin. She was holding her breath. Claire's throat constricted. 'Ella?' she urged her.

'That woman is staring at me, Mummy,' Ella said tremulously, looking upwards over her shoulder. 'She's watching me out of the window.'

Her heart flipping over, Claire twisted to follow her gaze. 'What woman, sweetheart?' she asked. Whoever had been at the window had disappeared.

CHAPTER TWENTY

Claire

'Claire, hi. I'm so glad you could make it.' A woman Claire assumed to be Sophie pulled the front door of the house open almost before she'd rung the buzzer. 'Come in, come in,' she beamed, stepping back to hold the door wide.

Claire offered her a tentative smile back and guided Ella in before her.

'And you must be Ella?' Sophie smiled down at her as Ella stopped uncertainly in the hall.

Ella answered with a small nod. 'Yes,' she said quietly, her expression nervous and her eyes still watery with tears.

'Oh dear.' Sophie laughed kindly. 'You look as though you've lost a shilling and found sixpence.'

Her heart skittering, Claire stared at her, dumbfounded. That was one of her dad's sayings. Whenever she'd looked grumpy, he would come out with that quip and tweak her nose, the tip of his thumb protruding between his forefinger and middle finger as he pulled his hand away, as if he'd plucked her nose from her face. It was silly, particularly as she'd grown older, but it had usually cajoled her out of her moodiness. Sophie couldn't have known about that, unless she'd known him.

Dismissing that painful recollection, Claire explained Ella's sad mood as best she could. 'She's a bit tired and upset. I'm sure she'll feel better when she's had a little cuddle and a nap, hey, sweetheart?'

'Oh no. Poor thing.' Sophie looked from Ella to Claire, her eyes sympathetic. Rich brown eyes, Claire noticed, searching for any resemblance to her father's. They were definitely similar. But then, wasn't brown the world's most common eye colour? She was very pretty, her delicate features set off by her short hair, which was cut in a cute pixie style. Also dark brown – again similar to her father's – it had subtle auburn tones running through it. Aware of her own mad straggle of frizzy red hair, Claire felt acutely self-conscious. She was sure that the fact she hadn't had time to pimp and preen was one of the reasons Luke had been tempted elsewhere. She'd wished fervently that he would suffer for what he'd done, that it would all blow up in his face, but after receiving that phone call, she was truly worried for him.

What on earth had happened? How did there come to be blood in the bathroom? Recalling the fear in his voice, Claire felt her eyes fill with tears. She fought them back. The last thing she wanted to do was end up blubbing in front of Sophie.

'Claire?' Sophie stepped towards her, her brow creasing into a concerned frown. 'Is something wrong? Is it Bernard?'

Claire shook her head. 'No,' she managed, working on all her usual tactics to keep the tears at bay, but no matter how deeply she breathed, how long she held it, it didn't seem to be working.

Sophie searched her face, her eyes flecked with worry, and then pressed a hand gently to her arm. She didn't speak, but took hold of Ella's hand instead. 'Come on, little one,' she said, leading her to the stairs. 'Come with Auntie Sophie and we'll get you something lovely to drink. What do you fancy? I have fruit juice or Coke. Or I have milkshake: chocolate and vanilla flavour, bought for really special guests.'

Pausing before they mounted the stairs, Ella, who adored milkshake, looked hesitantly up at her. 'Am *I* special?' she asked, her little face hopeful.

'Very.' Sophie squeezed her hand, and led her on up. 'And once we've got you a drink and maybe a biscuit if Mummy agrees, we'll download you a fab film to watch while I get Mummy a cup of tea and we have a catch-up. How does that sound?'

'*Peppa Pig*?' Ella sounded ever more hopeful. 'Or *Paddington 2*?'

'Ooh, I think we can manage one of those, providing your mummy's okay with it,' Sophie said, heading on up the second flight of stairs.

Claire followed, feeling slightly bewildered. She had reservations about this woman until questions were answered. But with her emotions in turmoil and in danger of spilling over, she was glad of her timely intervention.

Ten minutes later, she watched awestruck as Sophie settled Ella on the sofa with her cat Cinder and Flopsy the rabbit, Paddington Bear ready to play on the TV. The woman seemed to be a natural with children, and Ella was clearly taken with her.

'Feeling better?' Sophie asked, relieving Ella of her beaker once she'd slurped back the last of her milkshake.

Nodding, Ella wiped her mouth and wriggled down under the faux-fur throw Sophie had fetched from her bedroom.

'Right, Mummy and I will be just through there in the kitchen.' Sophie pointed to the doorway. 'You sure you won't be lonely?'

Ella's eyes flickered down and back. 'A little bit,' she said sadly, squeezing Flopsy closer to her chest. 'Daddy usually watches films with me.'

Sophie glanced in Claire's direction, her expression curious. 'Well, I'm betting this one will be worth watching twice,' she said, tucking the throw more tightly around Ella. 'You can ask Daddy to download it when you get home.'

Ella immediately looked crestfallen. 'Daddy doesn't live at home,' she whispered, dropping her gaze.

'Ah.' Sophie's eyes pivoted towards Claire again. 'Sorry,' she mouthed, and then to Ella, 'In which case, you can get Mummy to organise a viewing evening with him and tell him to get the milkshake and popcorn in. Sound like a plan?'

Ella thought about it, and then answered with a contented nod.

'Good girl,' Sophie said, smoothing a stray strand of hair behind Ella's ear, and then pressing the back of her hand affectionately to her cheek. 'We'll be just next door. Shout if you need anything.'

Pressing play, she handed Ella the remote control and then led the way to the kitchen.

'Try not to notice the decor,' she said, visibly shuddering as she indicated the badly painted sage-green walls. 'It's worse in here than it is in the lounge, if that's possible. I'm saving up my pennies to give the place a makeover.'

Picking up the kettle, she shook it to check for water and then filled it up and switched it on. 'So…' She turned from the work surface, clapping her hands nervously together. 'I'm not sure where to start.'

'No, me neither,' Claire said. She had questions, reams of questions, but after the shocking news Luke had delivered, she wasn't sure she was in an emotionally strong enough place to hear the answers.

Sophie came across to her. 'I'm really sorry if I put my foot in it regarding Ella's dad,' she offered. 'I know it's none of my business and you might not want to talk about it, but I just wanted you to know, if you do need to talk, I have an ear. Two, actually.'

She smiled apprehensively, and Claire just hadn't got the heart to demand her whole life story here and now, as she'd intended to do. 'It's nothing,' she said, heaving out a shaky sigh.

Sophie nodded, but she looked far from convinced. 'A big nothing,' she said softly. 'To have reduced you and your little girl to tears.'

Hearing the kindness in her voice, Claire felt a lump rise in her throat. So much for the in-control person she'd intended to be when she met her. 'I had a call from him as we arrived,' she admitted, then wavered. As desperate as she felt to confide in someone, this woman whose agenda she didn't yet know possibly wasn't the right someone. 'You've obviously gathered that we've split up?' she went on.

Sophie smiled sadly. 'I did.'

'Ella's coping quite well, but she is upset, naturally, and hopes he'll come back.' She stopped. Imagining what was going on in her little girl's mind brought the tears once again too close to the surface.

'Oh Claire, I'm so sorry.' Stepping towards her, Sophie hesitated, then reached to pull her into a hug, which almost proved fatal. Claire managed not to cry, but it took a monumental amount of effort. After a second or two, Sophie eased back. 'And are *you* coping, what with everything else you've got going on?'

Claire shrugged dejectedly. 'Just,' she said, with a wan smile. 'I don't have a lot of choice, do I?'

'Not when you have a child who needs you to be strong,' Sophie agreed. 'You really do wonder what goes on in men's heads sometimes.'

Claire sighed. She'd thought she'd known what went on in Luke's head, but she hadn't, clearly.

Sophie went back to the kettle. 'Tell me to mind my own business if you want to. I don't mind, honestly,' she said, busying herself with making the tea. 'But was it because of the situation with Bernard? You having to devote your time to looking after him, I mean? I imagine that couldn't have been easy on any of you.'

Noting her understanding expression, Claire nodded, and seated herself tiredly at the little kitchen table. 'He was feeling neglected, so he went in search of comfort elsewhere,' she said, and then felt immediately guilty. Even after everything Luke had done, her natural instinct was still to defend him.

'Couldn't have things his own way, so he went off in a sulk. Typical.' Sophie sighed despairingly. 'That's exactly what my loving partner did,' she added.

Claire eyed her curiously.

'I nursed my gran for a while before she died,' Sophie went on.

'Oh. I'm sorry. That must have been difficult for you.' Claire felt for her. 'Did you… Were you close?' she asked, digging a little for her history.

'She brought me up after Mum died.' Sophie smiled sadly. 'So yes, it was difficult. Made more so by my now-ex throwing a wobbly. He didn't like the fact that I wasn't accessible twenty-four/seven, so off he went, shagging some cheap little trollop to prove a point. Point being, he could have any woman he fancied. He thought I would be desperate, begging him to come back. He got the surprise of his life when I dumped his stuff out of the flat window.'

From three floors up? Claire boggled at that. 'You didn't?'

'Afraid so.' Sophie shrugged indifferently. 'I'm not sure his vinyl record collection fared too well, but he got the message.'

'Oh God.' Claire laughed. She couldn't help but admire the other woman's nerve.

Sophie's mouth curved into a conspiratorial smile. 'Served him right,' she said, coming across with the tea. The man was a complete control freak. Sounds like your husband is much the same.'

Claire furrowed her brow and took a sip of her tea. 'Luke's not controlling,' she said.

'It's controlling behaviour, Claire,' Sophie pointed out gently. 'Think about it. You obviously weren't dancing to his tune, so he decided to play with someone else.'

Claire's frown deepened. She took another pensive sip of her tea.

'I'm assuming he wasn't happy about living with Bernard?'

That was true, Claire had to concede. Luke couldn't have been any unhappier when he'd stormed out the morning after the incident with her father on the landing. 'He wasn't, but… How did you know we were living there?' she asked her. Hadn't she said the last time she'd seen her father was before they moved in?

'I spoke on the phone with Bernard. Only briefly. We lost touch after that,' Sophie explained, looking pensive. 'You can't blame your husband for being unhappy about the situation, I suppose,' she continued. 'It couldn't have been easy for him, but pressurising you to put his needs first was hardly going to help, was it?'

Again Claire wanted to defend him, but she couldn't, because she *had* felt under pressure. Trying to care for everyone and juggle everything just wasn't possible.

'Did you really want to put Bernard into care?' Sophie asked. 'I mean, I know you would have had to eventually, for his sake, as well as your own and little Ella's, but were you really ready to go that route when you did?'

Feeling slightly disorientated by the turn of the conversation, Claire hesitated. 'Yes,' she said, after a pause, but even she could hear the lack of conviction in her voice. She hadn't been ready. She really had thought she would have more time when she'd set out to care for him. That she would be by his side at the end, easing his struggle. 'No,' she backtracked. 'I needed Luke to be there for me, not fighting me.' Running the rim of her finger around her mug, she failed to suppress a tear.

Sophie was quiet for a second, then, 'I'm here for you, Claire,' she reached to squeeze her hand, 'if you want me to be.'

Claire looked up from her tea. 'What is it you want, Sophie?' she asked. She had to know. 'Why get in touch now?'

Glancing down, Sophie appeared to think about it. 'To be part of your family,' she said, looking up hopefully. 'For you to know I'll always be there, wherever you are.'

CHAPTER TWENTY-ONE

Claire

'Can I ask you something, Sophie?' Claire said, pausing before going into the lounge to collect Ella, who was stirring after falling asleep. The little girl was obviously exhausted. Claire had to get her settled in her bed for the night, but first there was something she was desperate to know. 'Your mother, what happened? How did she…?' Noting Sophie's eyes filling up as she glanced quickly away, she stopped, concerned.

'Sorry.' Sophie smiled apologetically and rubbed a hand over her eyes 'It's, um… it's pretty awful, to be honest, Claire. I get upset every time I think about it, let alone talk about it.'

Claire nodded. She got that completely. 'I understand,' she said. 'Probably better than you'd realise. It's just…'

'You want to know more about how I came to be,' Sophie finished, with a knowing smile. 'Of course you would. It's a long story, and I have to gear myself up for it, but I'd be happy to tell you all you need to know. Maybe when Ella's a little less tired, though?' She nodded towards the sofa.

She was right. Now wasn't the time to get into a prolonged conversation that was bound to be painful for both of them.

Claire smiled and scooped Ella up. 'Come on, sleepy head, time to go.'

'Are you sure you won't stay?' Sophie asked. 'The spare room's on a par with the rest of the place decor-wise, but it's clean and the bed's comfortable.'

Setting Ella down, Claire eased the hand she was kneading her eyes with away from her face and fed it into her coat sleeve. 'Thanks, but I've promised Ella a McDonald's, and after that she'll definitely be ready for bed. We're probably best having a bath and an early night at the hotel, aren't we, sweetheart?'

'That's understandable, after all the excitement today,' Sophie said sympathetically. 'Maybe we could get together tomorrow?'

'Maybe.' Claire buttoned Ella's coat. She hadn't thought that far ahead yet.

'Can Auntie Sophie come to McDonald's, Mummy?' Ella asked, glancing hopefully at her and then back to Sophie.

Caught off guard, Claire wasn't sure how to answer. She needed a little space, time to go over things.

Coming back from the sofa with Flopsy, Sophie evidently caught her hesitant expression. 'That's a nice thought, Ella, and I'd love to, but I've already eaten. As well as which, I think Flopsy's tired too, aren't you, Flopsy? She's yawning, see?' Turning the stuffed rabbit towards her, Sophie studied its face. 'Oh my gosh, that was a *huge* yawn.' She looked wide-eyed back to Ella. 'I think you'd better get her tucked up in bed as soon as possible, otherwise she'll be too exhausted to enjoy her holiday.'

Smiling, she crouched to pass the toy to Ella and then opened her arms and invited her into a hug. Without hesitation, Ella locked her hands around Sophie's neck and hugged her firmly back.

'Bye, Ella.' Sophie kissed her cheek. 'Be good for your mummy.'

'I will,' Ella promised, planting a kiss on Sophie's cheek in turn before unlatching herself. 'Bye Auntie Sophie.'

Her smile now a little on the sad side, Sophie straightened up. 'Shall I ring you?' she asked, her expression uncertain as she glanced in Claire's direction.

'Do that.' Claire extended her hand for Ella. 'We'll catch up whenever you're free.'

'Brilliant.' Sophie looked pleased. 'I've actually got a day off tomorrow. Why don't we meet up early? I could show you the sights and we could have lunch and then do something afterwards. Children's Village, possibly? It has some fun rides and a bouncy castle. Ella would love it. What do you think?'

Noting Ella's eyes popping with delight at the prospect, Claire dithered. She'd didn't want to be seen as a spoilsport, particularly having snapped at Ella earlier, but nor did she want to let her guard down too quickly with Sophie. On the surface she seemed fine, friendly and open, but she didn't know her that well yet.

'Can we, Mummy?' Ella asked, now wearing her best beseeching expression. 'Flopsy loves bouncy castles.'

Realising she was outvoted, Claire relented. 'As long as you promise to be on your absolute best behaviour,' she said, smiling tolerantly.

'*Yippee*.' Ella jumped gleefully.

'And only if you eat up all your dinner and go straight to sleep tonight,' Claire added, making sure to give her a no-nonsense look.

Ella missed it, already twirling around to practically drag her to the door. Claire certainly wouldn't have any trouble getting her to go to bed tonight. Whether she would actually sleep was a whole other matter. 'I'll ring you after breakfast,' she said to Sophie. 'Thanks for downloading the film, and for the tea and the ear.'

'No problem,' Sophie assured her. 'Ooh, hang on a sec. I have a new phone. My old one died a death, so I had to upgrade it. Let me give you my number.' Turning to the coffee table, she picked up her mobile and scrolled through it. 'Here we go…' She reeled off the number, and Claire keyed it into her own phone, noting as she did so that she'd received a text from an unknown caller.

'Talk tomorrow,' she said, following Ella into the hall and checking the text in case it was anything to do with her father. As she approached the front door, she slowed, and then stopped and stared at her phone screen, confounded.

You don't know me, but I just wanted to let you know your husband is a bastard, the message started.

Realising that the sender must be this Anna person, she felt the hairs rise over the entire surface of her skin.

Just so you know, he said you were separated. When I asked him jokingly whether it was because he was so moody, he lost his temper, the text went on. *He got violent and—*

'Mummy, Flopsy's hungry,' Ella said, jiggling impatiently by the door.

Claire looked at her, flustered. 'Coming, sweetheart,' she said, her throat tight.

'Problem?' Sophie asked behind her.

'No. Just a sales thing.' Claire snapped her phone case shut and counselled herself to stay calm. The woman hadn't disappeared then, but she was clearly deranged. 'See you tomorrow, Sophie,' she said, attempting to gather herself as she opened the door.

'Careful how you drive,' Sophie called after her, a curious edge to her voice, as Claire plucked Ella up into her arms and hurried down the stairs.

Once Ella was safely buckled into her seat, she pulled the message back up.

He got violent and he hit me, it continued. *He's volatile and aggressive, especially when he's been drinking. I'm assuming you know this. You were right to throw him out. I would never let him near a child of mine.*

Was she completely mad? Queasiness churning her stomach, her hands visibly shaking, Claire tried to make sense of it. There *was* no sense. Luke had been going out with his mates more lately, but he didn't generally drink that much. He never drank in the house, and even when he had been out with friends, he'd never come home rolling drunk. Tipsy sometimes, but never totally inebriated. He certainly wasn't volatile. Bad-tempered, yes, over the last few months. Growing more so recently because of the situation with her father. And yes, there had been the slamming door incident, but that wasn't enough to label a man…

There was blood in the bathroom. She recalled again what Luke had told her, the terror in his voice. It couldn't be true. Could it? She'd never imagined him capable of violence. But then she'd never imagined he would cheat on her either.

CHAPTER TWENTY-TWO

Claire

'Why are you scared of Daddy, Mummy?' Ella asked as Claire pulled the duvet up over her.

Claire felt her heart drop. 'I'm not, sweetheart,' she quickly assured her, reaching for Flopsy from the foot of the bed and tucking it in with her. 'I was just a bit scared when there was a funny noise on the phone and I couldn't hear him talking, that's all.' The wary look in her daughter's eyes told her Ella knew that was a lie. She'd hoped she might forget all about the phone call, but clearly she hadn't. Aware that her mummy and daddy weren't living together, her radar was on red alert whenever there was any conversation between them. She'd skirted around the subject several times over their meal, asking if she could talk to her daddy when they next spoke, whether he could come with them the next time they went on holiday, which caused Claire's chest to constrict. Her little girl was worrying, and she felt powerless to reassure her.

Her wide blue eyes never leaving Claire's, Ella studied her quietly for a second, and then, 'Were you worried he might have turned into a star, like Nana?' she asked.

Swallowing back a stab of pain, Claire took a second to answer. 'No, darling, I wasn't,' she said softly, reaching to brush her daughter's fringe from her furrowed little brow. 'I knew he was still there. I just panicked because I thought we'd got cut off, that's all.'

Nodding, Ella lowered her eyelashes and then looked thoughtfully back at her. 'Will we see Daddy soon, Mummy?' was her next question.

'We will,' Claire promised, breathing out a breath she hadn't realised she was holding. Another lie, she thought. As things were, she had no idea when they would next see Luke. Whether it would be wise for Ella to have any contact with him right now, given the circumstances.

'When we go home?' Ella pushed, her expression hopeful and uncertain all at once.

'Soon after,' Claire answered vaguely. 'We'll ring him and have a chat with him when we get back, okay?' She'd been going to call him tonight – tell him about the disturbing text she'd received – but with Ella in the same room, there was no way to do that.

'Okay.' Ella nodded, somewhat appeased.

'Good.' Claire gave her a reassuring smile. 'Now come on, little madam, sleep, or no Children's Village tomorrow.'

Ella's eyes widened delightedly. 'Are we really going to go?'

'We are.' Claire guessed there was no way to deny her daughter. 'But only if we stay asleep in the morning until the clock shows…?'

'A seven, a three and an O,' Ella supplied confidently.

'Seven thirty. Correct,' Claire said, and kicked off her shoes.

'Are you sleeping with me?' Ella blinked, surprised, as she hitched up the duvet.

'I am,' Claire confirmed, sliding into the bed alongside her. 'Shuffle round and we'll snuggle. You can be my hot-water bottle.'

Ella looked pleased at that, dutifully wriggling onto her side. 'But you're not to squish me,' she said, as Claire curled her body around the little girl, desperate to keep her safe, emotionally as well as physically.

Claire drew her closer. 'You like Auntie Sophie, don't you?' she asked carefully.

'Uh huh. I didn't like her when I first saw her staring at me through the window, I thought she was mean, but I like her now. She's fun.' Ella yawned and snuggled closer. 'Night night, Mummy.'

'Night, precious girl.' Claire kissed her hair and breathed in the special scent of her, then winced as her mobile signalled a text. Ella hardly stirred, though, thank goodness. Luke? she wondered. Or the deranged girlfriend? *Was* she deranged, though? Was it possible, however incredible or unpalatable, that she might be telling the truth? Claire felt goose bumps prickle over her flesh, even under the duvet.

Giving Ella another few minutes to drift into a deep sleep, she eased herself carefully away from her and padded across the room to fetch her phone from her bag. She was relieved to find it was Luke who'd texted.

Hi. Just checking all okay with you, he'd sent.

Not exactly hunky-dory, Claire thought reproachfully. Sighing, she replied, *Not great under the circumstances. Can't talk now. Ella sleeping. Will call tomorrow.*

OK. Thanks, Claire, Luke sent back. *Kiss my baby for me.*

Claire's heart ached at that. For Ella. For herself. For him. How must he be feeling, after being interviewed by the police? Did they even know the woman hadn't disappeared? Did he?

She hesitated, and then, *She texted me*, she sent. *Anna.*

There was a beat before Luke replied. *Thank God*, he sent back. *What did she say?*

Claire was perturbed. Clearly he *hadn't* known she wasn't missing. *You should let the police know. Will talk to you tomorrow*, she responded. She had no wish to prolong this tonight. She wasn't just tired; she felt bone-weary. She couldn't deal with any more now. Her one consolation was that her father had seemed more accepting of his surroundings at the care home when she'd last seen him.

Whatever that madwoman had said, she was sure Luke could never have done the things she'd said he had. Could he? *The scratch.*

The incontrovertible evidence that something had happened between them popped jarringly into her mind once again.

Could she be sure? Really? Could she allow Luke access to Ella until she knew absolutely that she wasn't placing her daughter in a volatile situation?

CHAPTER TWENTY-THREE

Luke

Feeling impatient at the man's lack of urgency, Luke repeated to Detective Sergeant Myers what he'd already told the officer at the front desk: that Anna had surfaced and been in touch with Claire. He bit back his agitation as Myers raised his eyebrows in surprise. *What?* Did he think he was lying? Or that Claire was?

'The evidence will be on her phone,' he pointed out, praying that Claire hadn't deleted the text. But then the police had ways of retrieving deleted messages, didn't they? He was sure they could request data, including calls and text messages, from the service provider. Curtailing his frustration, he waited while the guy wrote down the information he'd given him, irritatingly slowly.

'And this was yesterday?' Myers asked, his expression now openly suspicious as he glanced up at Luke.

'I think so, yes,' Luke confirmed, trying to quieten the panic that had been churning in his gut ever since the police officers who'd come to Anna's apartment had invited him to accompany them to the station, where DS Myers had as good as accused him of being violent towards her, if not worse. 'People don't just disappear, Mr Elliot,' he'd said. His expression had been bland, but the look in his eyes had been one of quiet contempt. He'd clearly thought Luke capable of being physically abusive, particularly when Luke hadn't helped his case by losing his temper when they'd suggested a feasible scenario. She'd been winding him up, they'd implied, pressing his buttons. 'You hit her, maybe in the heat of the moment. That's understandable. Panicked when she lost consciousness. Why don't you help yourself now by helping us, Luke?'

'Ask your wife to come to the station. We'll need a statement,' Myers said now. Luke noted the weary look on his face, as if he might even be disappointed that he hadn't got a juicy murder case on his hands.

'She can't.' He attempted to keep his tone calm. 'She's away.'

Myers raised his eyebrows again. 'Away where?'

Luke sighed inside. Half of him wanted Anna to reappear, the other half dreaded it, because he knew there was no way she *wouldn't* claim he'd been violent. 'I'm not sure,' he admitted with a disconsolate shrug. Why, he wondered, had Claire chosen now of all times to go away? And why hadn't she told him where she was? He had no idea where this woman who was claiming to be her half-sister lived. He hoped to God she wasn't getting too involved with her. Christ, he needed to speak to her.

'Another missing person then?' Myers commented drily.

His agitation rising rapidly, Luke erred on the side of caution and said nothing.

'And her mobile number is?' His pen poised, Myers looked at him dispassionately. 'I'm assuming you know that much?'

Luke tugged in a terse breath and reeled off Claire's number.

'We'll need the number of the sender of the text. Perhaps you could let your wife know, assuming you can communicate with her?' Luke didn't miss the sarcasm in the man's voice.

'What about if it's a pay-as-you-go phone?' he asked. He was guessing it was, since the number he had for Anna was no longer in service.

'Providing we have the number, even without the phone itself, we can apply for data from the service provider: details of calls made and received, texts sent and received and voicemail messages,'

Myers confirmed. 'We can also possibly identify when and where the phone was first activated or used, which may provide us with additional evidence as to the identity of the user.'

Luke blew out a sigh of considerable relief. 'I'll let Claire know.'

'Let's hope she's not too pissed off with you, hey?' Myers said, shooting him yet another unimpressed look as he got to his feet to walk past Luke to the interview room door. The same interview room he'd been questioned in for hours, after being cautioned and booked in, fingerprinted and stripped of his belongings: the clothes he was wearing, his phone. He'd been cautioned again once they'd brought him in here; told he could be kept for up to thirty-six hours, longer if they applied to the magistrates' court for an extension, which the seriousness of the suspected crime might warrant. His solicitor had confirmed they could actually do that. It had been a living nightmare. With no evidence, and no mention of him by name in the call they'd received reporting the domestic, they weren't charging him yet, they'd said, but Luke had been terrified. With no clue how far Anna might take this, he was still terrified.

'You do realise that until we've proved the text exists, we'll still be treating Anna Checkley's disappearance as suspicious?' Myers said as Luke heaved himself to his feet and followed him. He'd obviously taken up enough of his valuable time.

Luke answered with a tired nod. 'Have you spoken to the ex-boyfriend yet?'

'We have,' Myers supplied. 'He's not her ex. Denies having seen her either before or after the incident at the nightclub. His story checks out. He's in the armed forces; has been posted abroad since the morning after the alleged incident took place.'

'Alleged?' Luke stared at him, incredulous. 'There was a stand-up argument between them. He was well out of order. There must be CCTV footage, surely?'

'We've been through it,' Myers informed him, with forced patience. 'It's clear an incident took place. The thing is, it doesn't give us any more than you and him arguing. There's nothing to tell us who instigated the argument, or what it was about.'

'Great.' Luke swallowed back a sick taste in his mouth as he realised the implication: that it could have been him who'd started it. 'What about witness statements?' he asked, his hope fading fast.

'Likewise. Witnesses corroborate there was an argument, but they can't provide sufficient detail to back up your story.' Myers looked almost apologetic as he banged another nail into Luke's coffin.

'And the guy who owns the apartment she was living in; have you established whether she's been in touch with him?' Luke asked wearily. He wasn't sure what difference it would make now, but he needed to know more about the woman he'd become so disastrously involved with. She wasn't renting the apartment, it had turned out. One of the other coppers had told Luke they'd made some enquiries and the neighbours had said she was flat-sitting while the owner was working away. It made sense. Luke had wondered how she could afford to live there. He'd doubted her wage from working behind a bar would have covered the rent on a city-centre apartment, albeit a small one.

'Not yet, no,' Myers supplied. 'He's working on some water and sanitation project in deepest Ghana, apparently. We're still trying to track him down.'

Track him down? Luke squinted at the detective quizzically. He was in Africa, not on Mars. The man had to have a contact number, surely?

Myers clearly noted the look. 'We'll keep you posted. We're as keen to locate Anna as you are,' he said as he nodded Luke towards the corridor. 'Establish that she's okay after finding evidence that she might have been injured,' he added with an acerbic smile.

'Right. Thanks.' Luke smiled flatly back. *For nothing.* Averting his unimpressed gaze, he strode angrily towards the exit. He very much doubted they were as keen to locate Anna as he was – to establish why the fuck she would want to ruin his life.

CHAPTER TWENTY-FOUR

Claire

After a strenuous workout on the water-walker ride, Claire was about to pass on the bouncy castle, thinking she would let Sophie leap about like a loony with Ella instead. As Sophie scooped her up onto it, though, she thought better of it. Though she and Luke had wanted to protect their daughter when they'd first received her diagnosis, they'd soon realised that letting Ella find her own boundaries, within limits, was essential for building her self-confidence. She wasn't sure yet that she could entirely trust Sophie, however, even though she'd told her about her condition. Risking her child's safety with someone she didn't really know would be nothing short of negligent. Quickly removing her shoes, she stepped up onto the castle, shouting, 'Make room for me,' and boinging across to join them as Ella and Sophie bounced into what appeared to be a leopard's mouth.

'Yay! Mummy's coming, too,' Ella whooped. She flopped down on her bottom and then sprang up again, righting herself remarkably quickly. Claire wished she had half her energy and agility.

'Coming where?' she called after her, as Ella bounded onwards to disappear into the leopard's throat.

'Down the slide.' Sophie nodded across to the leopard's rear end, from which protruded a long plastic chute.

Claire eyed it with trepidation. 'Oh God, not another one. I think I must have turned into a lightweight. The helter skelter scared me to death.'

'It was a bit hairy, wasn't it?' Sophie said, as the two of them bounced onwards to where Ella was now positioned at the top of the chute. 'I could have sworn I'd ripped my knickers coming down it that last time. That would have stopped the guy who was moving in on you in his tracks.'

Claire laughed. She couldn't help herself. 'Moving in on *you*, you mean.'

'Uh uh, it was definitely you he was after,' Sophie assured her. 'You're much prettier than I am. Ella, wait for us!' she called. 'We're coming down with you.'

Claire was surprised at the compliment, but also quietly flattered. Glancing at Sophie's shapely rear end, shown off to maximum advantage in leggings, she felt fairly certain about the object of the man's attention. Still, with Luke preferring the attractions of another woman, the comment about her looks had done her ego no harm – even if it wasn't true. Sophie was very pretty, and this was without a scrap of make-up.

Reminded that she hadn't yet rung Luke, Claire felt a touch guilty. She'd meant to, but she wasn't sure she was in the right frame of mind to process what he might say. She couldn't avoid speaking to him, as evidenced by the several times he'd already texted her this morning. He was Ella's father. She would have to know all the unsavoury details at some point. This wasn't the place to talk to him, though, with fairground music blaring in the background and Ella and Sophie in earshot. She would brace herself and call him later. Sophie had been so good with Ella, Claire was sure she wouldn't mind keeping her occupied for a few minutes.

'Mummy, I want to go down on my own,' Ella insisted when she reached her, her eyes shiny with excitement.

Claire wasn't so sure about that. Trying her best to stay upright, which Ella and Sophie seemed to achieve with ease, she eyed the slide in front of them doubtfully.

'It's only a little one, Mummy. Please…' Ella cajoled, wearing her best beguiling eyes.

It was true that it wasn't a long chute, but still the plastic looked a bit flimsy. Claire didn't want Ella crash-landing at the bottom of it.

'Mummy, there are other people coming,' Ella pointed out urgently.

'Go on then,' Claire reluctantly relented. 'But be careful.'

'*Yes!*' Ella whooped. 'You and Auntie Sophie can hold hands.'

Claire definitely wasn't sure about that, but she found her hand snatched before she could verbalise her objections. Tugged unceremoniously down onto her hindquarters, she had no choice but to start the downward journey, unfortunately rather faster than she'd expected.

'*Ouch!*' She winced, cracking heads with Sophie as they landed in a muddled heap at the foot of the chute.

'God, sorry, Claire.' Scrambling to her feet, Sophie reached to help her up. 'That was a really stupid thing for me to do. Are you all right?'

Managing to find her balance, Claire rubbed her head and met Sophie's gaze. Her huge brown eyes were so wide with shock and worry, she looked like a startled deer. 'I'm fine,' she assured her. 'We were probably both being a bit overzeal—'

'Whoops.' Cutting her short, Sophie tore her gaze away and dived to hoist Ella out of harm's way as another little body whooshed down the slide. Setting the little girl down, she took hold of her hand. 'Disaster averted,' she said, rolling her eyes with relief as she looked back at Claire.

Thank God. Imagining what might have happened, Claire sagged with relief.

'Do you think we should make a discreet exit now that we've caused pandemonium?' Sophie suggested, her gaze gliding towards the way out.

'Good idea,' said a man standing just beyond the exit. 'Do you two idiots have eyes, or what?' He indicated a sign behind him that stated: *Strictly No Adults Allowed.*

'We do, actually.' Sophie gave him a sweet smile. 'It's a pity you don't have any manners, though.' She led Ella through the exit, giving the man another bright smile and muttering 'Moron' under her breath as they passed him.

'Sophie…' Claire glanced back over her shoulder, hoping he hadn't heard.

'Well, he is,' Sophie said. 'A rude one into the bargain. Why would he want to spoil a child's fun, especially when he hasn't got a clue why we would be bouncing with her?'

She had a point, Claire supposed, surprised and touched that Sophie felt so protective of Ella.

'Right, what do we fancy next then, girls? Mini golf or beach?' Sophie asked.

'Beach!' Ella squealed. 'Can we, Mummy. Can we?' She turned to Claire, jiggling enthusiastically. 'You promised we could.'

'I don't know.' Despite her determination not to let Ella's condition impact on her life, Claire was reticent. 'It's not that warm today, Ella.'

'Please, Mummy, please,' Ella begged. 'I want to build a sandcastle.'

'She does have her jelly sandals on,' Sophie pointed out.

She was right, but still Claire couldn't help feeling worried. The beach might be strewn with all sorts of litter.

'Mummy?' Ella looked up at her hopefully.

'I suppose,' Claire relented, since it seemed she was outvoted. 'You have to be very careful though, Ella.'

'Yay!' Clearly delighted, Ella grabbed hold of Sophie's hand and tugged her forward. Sophie smiled down at her indulgently and they set off, chatting excitedly.

Watching the two of them together, Claire wondered again whether she should trust Sophie. She was possibly being oversensitive, but should she be letting someone into their lives who she didn't yet know very well; someone who already seemed to have a big influence over her daughter?

CHAPTER TWENTY-FIVE

Claire

Nostalgia swirling inside her once more, Claire walked along the beach a yard or two behind Ella and Sophie. It was quite clean and just as she remembered it, stretching on forever – a long expanse of gritty golden sand. Gulping back a mouthful of sharp, salty air, she caught her breath as she recalled how her dad had carried her to the sea high on his shoulders. He'd placed her down carefully, and then, taking a firm hold of her hand, his business suit trousers rolled up to his knees, waded out with her.

He'd laughed and called her his brave Claire Bear as she'd forgotten her fear of jellified things and grown more assured in the water. They'd laughed a lot that day.

Swallowing back her sadness, she glanced ahead of her to check on Ella. Seeing that Sophie had a firm hold of her hand as they picked their way carefully through the shingle that hugged the shoreline in search of seashells, she relaxed a little. Ella had definitely bonded with Sophie, she acknowledged, still not sure whether that was a good thing. She needed to talk more to the woman. Hopefully, after the day's adventures, Ella would take a nap and she would be able to do that. For the moment, Ella had Sophie's undivided attention – and that was no bad thing with her mum being so distracted.

She needed to ring Luke. She couldn't leave it any longer. Taking a fortifying breath, she pulled her phone from her bag and flicked through her texts. There were several from Luke wondering how she was. How Ella was. Where they were. When they would return home.

Her heart jolted, her tummy twisting with anger and confusion, as she noted another text from his girlfriend. Warily she read it.

Don't believe a word he says, was all it said.

Why was she doing this? She stared at it, bewildered. What in God's name *had* Luke done? Bracing herself, she selected his number and hit call.

It barely rang out before he answered. 'Claire, hi,' he said, tangible relief in his voice. 'Thanks for calling back.'

'I'm sorry I didn't call sooner. I didn't want to talk with Ella in earshot,' Claire replied, forgoing the niceties.

'Is she not there with you then?' Luke asked, concerned.

'Of course she is,' Claire said, irked by the fact that he thought she wouldn't be. 'I'd hardly just abandon her, would I?' *Unlike some people*, she was very tempted to add. 'In any case, I don't have anyone to leave her with,' she reminded him pointedly.

'No, sorry,' Luke said, now sounding contrite. 'I'm not thinking straight. How is she?'

Claire paused before answering. He would know how she was: confused, obviously. 'Coping,' she said eventually. 'What happened, Luke?' she asked him, turning around to take a few more steps away from where Ella and Sophie were crouched down, poking in rock pools. 'Why did the neighbours feel it necessary to call the police?'

She heard his tight intake of breath. 'We argued,' he said, repeating what he'd already told her.

'Loudly, presumably?' she surmised.

'Yes,' Luke admitted awkwardly.

'Violently?'

Luke drew in another sharp breath. 'I… She wouldn't let me leave,' he said, breathing out long and hard. 'She tried to stop me, blocked the door, grabbed hold of my arm. I—'

'Did you hit her?' Claire got bluntly to the point. She had to. She had to know, assuming he didn't lie. *Don't believe a word he says*: the woman's texted warning loomed large in her head.

'No. No way,' Luke refuted vehemently. 'I pushed her away, that was all. I swear. I could never do anything like that, Claire. Surely you know me well enough to know that?'

Claire hesitated. 'I thought I did,' she said quietly. Then, 'It sounds like a pretty toxic relationship to me,' she went on, before he could answer.

'It wasn't a relationship,' Luke said jadedly. 'It was just…'

'A one-night stand,' Claire supplied, as he trailed off. 'Which meant nothing.'

'Not that either, though I know you won't believe me.' Luke sighed. Then, 'Did she say I hit her?' he asked worriedly. 'In the text she sent you, is that what she's claiming I did?'

'Amongst other things, yes,' Claire answered, a chill settling in her chest as she tried to imagine what possible reason this woman would have for sharing all this with her. Revenge, she assumed. Was her aim to shock her, make sure she refused to have anything to do with Luke? Alienate him from his daughter?

'Other things, as in…?' Luke asked.

Claire noted the sudden agitation in his tone, and didn't much like it. Had he always been like this? Lately, he had been, she reminded herself; before they'd separated. 'She said you were volatile and aggressive,' she supplied carefully, 'especially when you'd been drinking.'

'Drinking?' Luke laughed, disbelieving. 'I don't drink in the house, Claire. You know I don't.'

'But you do drink when you're out with your mates.'

'Yes, but—'

'You would have been the worse for wear when you came back.' Claire resisted reminding him about the incident on the landing with her father that had set this bloody nightmare in motion.

'It's bullshit,' Luke countered angrily. 'She's insane, a complete fantasist.'

'In your opinion,' Claire pointed out.

'Yes, in *my* opinion,' Luke snapped. 'For Christ's sake, Claire, you don't really believe any of this, do you?' he asked, incredulous. 'It's *her* who's volatile. She's off the bloody wall. Always demanding to know where I am. Calling me and texting me day and night. She tried to commit suicide. The night I—'

Claire felt her heart flip. 'That doesn't make her insane,' she cut in angrily. She'd been low enough herself with all that had happened to have considered killing herself. Only briefly, though; she'd soon thought of Ella. She couldn't believe that he would label a person insane because they felt so depressed they couldn't see a future. He really wasn't the man she'd thought he was, was he?

'I know. I…' Luke stopped and blew out a heavy sigh.

'Why did you continue to see her? If she's as off the wall as you say she is, why did you have anything to do with her?'

'Because…' Luke faltered, 'I was scared. I didn't know what to do.'

'Scared?' Claire struggled with that. 'Of her?'

'Of what she might do. I thought she might try it again,' he confessed gruffly. 'She didn't want to be alone. I was too frightened to leave her. I know it sounds nuts, but I almost felt as if I was being stalked in the end. I wasn't sure how to handle it.'

Dumbfounded, Claire didn't answer.

'I know you'll probably find it laughable, but I swear to God it's the truth, Claire.'

Claire didn't find it laughable. Far from it; she found it chilling. That she didn't know whether this really was the truth made it all the more so. 'What do the police say?' she asked him shakily. 'Are they going to charge you with anything?'

'Not once they establish she's okay, and assuming she doesn't take it any further.' Luke sighed again, tiredly. 'I'm not sure they believe my side of the story.'

Claire said nothing, probably communicating that she wasn't sure what to believe either.

'They want you to make a statement,' Luke said. 'They'll need to see the text, too. When you get back, obviously. Or maybe you could forward it. I don't know. I'll ask, assuming you're okay with that?'

Claire paused before answering. 'You obviously don't know me very well, do you, Luke, if you honestly think that I wouldn't be?'

Luke went quiet. 'Thanks,' he said gratefully after a second.

'Did they take your phone?' she asked him. 'Is that why you have a new number?'

'Yep,' Luke answered despairingly. 'It didn't help my case much that she'd sent reams of messages accusing me of being exactly what they thought I was, an abusive bastard. *Jesus.* Where are you, Claire?' he asked, a desperate edge now to his voice. 'When will you be back?'

'Rhyl,' Claire told him.

'Rhyl? Is that where she lives, the woman who contacted you on Facebook?' Luke asked.

'Yes. I thought it was time we met.'

'And you took Ella? Christ, Claire? Don't you think that was a bit impetuous?'

'Me, impetuous?' Claire laughed disdainfully. He was standing in judgement on *her*? Unbelievable. 'Yes, I took Ella,' she hissed. 'As I've already said, I didn't have a lot of choice, since her father was apparently being detained by the—'

'But you don't know who she *is*.' Luke's voice was tight with anger. 'She could be anybody.

'She's not anybody,' Claire countered. 'I've told you, I'm—'

'Do you realise what could happen if social services got hold of this?'

Fear gripped Claire's stomach. 'Of *what*?' Was that some kind of threat?

'You're putting Ella at risk, Claire.'

'What *risk*?' Icy panic climbed her chest. What was he *talking* about?

'Your father, for one,' Luke pointed out.

Claire felt as if he'd punched her. 'He's in a care home!' *You absolute…*

'Exposing her to someone who *claims* to be your half-sister,' Luke continued, soul-crushingly.

'I am not *exposing* her to *anything*.' Claire choked the words out. 'Why are you—'

'How much are you drinking, Claire?' Luke asked bluntly.

What? Claire was utterly stunned. She drank occasionally. More frequently just lately, but did he really wonder at that? 'You self-righteous bastard,' she said, swiping a tear from her chin. 'How *dare* you? I have the odd glass of wine. That's *not* a crime, Luke,' she reminded him pointedly. 'I'm perfectly capable of looking after my child, unlike some people who end up so drunk they—'

'You left a wine glass on the floor of her fucking bedroom!' Luke shouted furiously.

Claire felt her stomach turn over. The broken glass. *He'd* picked it up. Why hadn't he mentioned it? Why leave it on the landing? To make her feel guilty?

'I didn't. I have no idea how… It wasn't *mine*!' She hadn't left a glass there. She didn't take glasses of wine into Ella's bedroom. She wouldn't take a glass of anything in there. Ella only ever had drinks in her room in a plastic tumbler. Why was he doing this?

'Bernard doesn't drink, Claire,' Luke pointed out flatly. 'You told me he stopped when your mother died. Or are you going to try to convince me he took it up again because of his illness?'

'Yes. No… I don't know,' she stammered. She *hadn't* left it there. But if her father hadn't either, then who?

Not Luke, surely? Was it *him* who'd unlocked the gate; locked the windows? The scratch on her car, her tyre mysteriously picking up a brand-new screw; was he playing some sick psychological game with her? Trying to erode her confidence more than he already had? Make her believe she was a bad mother? Well, it was working. She was beginning to think she was as insane as he claimed his girlfriend was. Was she, though? Was anything he was telling her the truth? 'I'm going,' she said, now truly scared.

'Claire, wait!' Luke said, clearly panicked. 'I'm sorry. I'm just worried, that's all. I didn't mean to—'

A loud scream from behind her cut the conversation dead. 'Ella!' Sophie's voice was filled with terror. 'Come back!'

CHAPTER TWENTY-SIX

Claire

'Ella!' Claire screamed, lunging forward as her baby slipped under the unforgiving waves. 'Ella!'

God, please don't do this. Please… don't do this! Her blood turning to ice in her veins, oblivious to broken seashells and sharp gravel biting spitefully into the soles of her feet, she ran.

Sophie was faster. Racing towards Ella from the opposite side, bounding across the white froth towards her, she reached her, plunging into the waves as the little girl surfaced and then went under again, causing Claire to almost drop to her knees.

A split second later, Sophie reappeared, swooping Ella high into her arms and whirling around. 'I've got her!' she shouted, making her way back towards the shore. 'I've got her,' she repeated, her face deathly pale, as Claire stumbled the last yard between them.

Her heart pumping with shock and anger, Claire snatched Ella from her, hugging her daughter tight and rubbing her back as she spluttered and spat seawater from her mouth. 'What the bloody hell were you doing?' Her voice shrill, her anger building, rising red hot inside her, she stared horrified at the woman, her supposed half-sister, who'd risked her child's *life*.

'I'm sorry,' Sophie whispered, as if that could fix it, as if that could possibly excuse what she'd done.

'She could have *died*!'

'Mummy…' Ella wriggled, wet and cold in her arms.

'What were you thinking?' Claire exploded, continuing to stare furiously at Sophie. 'She's four years old, for God's sake! And you let her—'

'Mummy, don't!' Ella cried. 'Sophie told me not to. I went to fetch some water in my bucket so she could fill the moat we were making. She told me not to move. She did, Mummy. Please don't shout at her.'

Claire's anger, born of dread at what might have happened – what very nearly *had* happened – refocused on her daughter. 'You *never* go in the sea on your own, Ella. Not *ever.* Do you—' She stopped, terror now gripping her heart like a vice as she noticed rich droplets of blood bleeding into the little girl's blonde curls.

'Oh God, no. Ella, what have you done?' She felt herself reel as her world shifted off kilter. *Any injury to the head, face or neck needs immediate treatment and should be assessed at hospital.* Her heart squeezed painfully as she recalled the consultant's advice with jarring clarity. *Bleeding into the brain is uncommon, but…*

'I'm sorry, Mummy.' Her face crumpling as she noted Claire's obvious distress, Ella sobbed in earnest.

'It's okay, baby. It's just a little cut. The doctors will soon fix it,' Claire murmured, hugging her close. 'We need to get her to the hospital,' she told Sophie, trying to communicate the seriousness of the situation with her eyes rather than her voice, not wanting to upset Ella further.

'Shh, sweetheart,' she tried to reassure her daughter as she hurried back the way they'd come. 'It's okay. It's no one's fault. Mummy was frightened, that was all. I didn't mean to shout at you, darling.'

But she *had* shouted. And Ella was hurt. And it was Claire's fault. She should have been watching her. *She* was responsible, not Sophie. Luke was right. She'd risked her baby's life.

'Should I call an ambulance?' Sophie asked, jolting herself out of her shocked stupor and running ahead.

Claire nodded, tried to stay focused and calm. Ella would be all right. They would give her an injection of clotting factor concentrate and she would be fine. Why had she allowed herself to be persuaded to come here? she asked herself, her heart barely functioning. Why hadn't she brought her fucking *car*?

They waited up on the seafront for the ambulance, Claire hugging Ella tight, talking reassuringly to her. 'Where *is* it?' she cried wretchedly as she noticed her baby's blood now bleeding into her shirt like an ink stain.

'It's all right, Mummy,' Ella said, pressing the palm of her hand to Claire's cheek.

Claire looked into her earnest eyes and felt like weeping. 'I know it is, baby.' She smiled, stifling a sob. 'I know.'

'Stuff this,' Sophie growled, heading for the kerb, where she tried unsuccessfully to flag down a taxi. And another. 'What is the *matter* with everyone?' she seethed, running a hand through her short crop of hair in frustration. 'Will someone please just… Stop!' she shouted.

Claire's heart turned over as she launched herself from the pavement into the path of an oncoming car.

CHAPTER TWENTY-SEVEN

Claire

'There we go. Someone's a very brave girl,' said the doctor who'd administered the injection of clotting factor concentrate.

'Daddy says I'm brave.' Ella peered at her over the warming blanket she was cocooned in. 'He usually pulls a face to make me laugh when I have to have a needle.'

'Does he indeed.' The doctor smiled. 'He sounds like a nice dad.'

'He is,' Ella assured her. 'He didn't come on holiday, but him and Mummy are still friends, aren't you, Mummy?'

'Well, that's excellent. Mummies and daddies should always stay friends.' Giving Ella another reassuring smile, the doctor turned to Claire. 'You're separated, I take it?' she asked quietly as Sophie sat down next to Ella.

Claire nodded, and prayed she didn't put that information on Ella's file. Parents did separate, that was a fact, but with so much going on, the thought of social services contacting her to check on Ella's home situation petrified her. What Luke had said had petrified her too. But what petrified her most was that, instead of listening to her instinct, she'd done exactly what he'd accused her of and put Ella at risk. The fact that the cut hadn't needed stitching hadn't made her feel any better.

'We have some issues to deal with. We're meeting up tomorrow, when I get back. Hopefully we can sort things out,' she lied.

There was no way to sort any of this out. Her world seemed to be spiralling out of control, one catastrophe after another hitting her and absolutely no one to turn to. She glanced at Sophie. She was as white as a ghost, plainly shocked and upset. Guilty, too; that had been obvious in her eyes. Yet at the end of the day, she had been there, literally stopping traffic to get Ella to hospital, thus averting the disaster that might have transpired.

'I hope so.' The doctor looked sympathetic. 'One way or another, I hope it's amicable, for your little girl's sake.'

Her guilt now almost choking her, Claire nodded and swallowed. She couldn't see how that could happen either. She was beginning to hate Luke for what he'd done. She was so angry with him. Yet now it was her who had to be on the defensive. He would be furious with her, and rightly so, to a degree. He'd barraged her with so many texts since their interrupted phone call. She'd replied briefly, assuring him that Ella was okay. She knew he'd be worried but she had no idea what to tell him. Not yet. She couldn't think straight.

'The CT scan's clear and there's no sign of concussion,' the doctor went on, referring to her notes.

Claire glanced again at Sophie, who wiped her eyes, a shudder of relief running visibly through her.

'One infusion should be enough to stop the bleed, and you know to keep an eye out for side effects: headache, nausea, drowsiness,' the doctor said, giving her a reassuring smile. 'I'll pop a note on her file, and you can leave as soon as she has the okay from one of my colleagues. Take her to your local hospital for a check-up once you're back home, and get in touch with us meanwhile if you're worried about anything. Bye Ella.' She gave her a wave and disappeared into the corridor.

A myriad of emotions now coursing through her – confusion, relief, most of all guilt – Claire walked across to Ella and pressed a kiss to her cheek, then glanced up at Sophie, whose complexion was still the colour of chalk. She'd been beside herself with worry as they'd travelled here, blaming herself.

'Sorry,' Sophie mouthed, her huge brown eyes glassy with tears and filled with something close to torture.

Claire tugged in a tight breath. 'Don't worry. She'll be fine,' she managed, though it took a huge amount of effort. 'I just need to keep an eye on her.'

'I really am so sorry, Claire,' Sophie said again, wrapping her arms about herself, clearly distraught. 'I only looked away for a second, I swear. One minute she was there, and the next…'

'I should have been watching her,' Claire admitted. 'Let's get you home, and then I can concentrate my attention on Ella, hey, sweetheart?'

'Sophie needs some attention too,' Ella piped up, her little face serious. 'She's feeling sad.'

Claire's phone rang as they neared the taxi. Luke, she guessed. She didn't answer it, climbing into the back with Ella instead. She still had no idea what she would say to him.

The phone beeped an incoming text as Sophie got in after them. With Ella now on her lap, Claire fumbled the phone from her coat pocket and handed it to Sophie. 'Can you send a brief text for me?' she asked her. 'It's Luke, I imagine.'

'Can I speak to him, Mummy?' Ella looked up hopefully.

'Not now, sweetheart.' Claire kissed the top of her head. 'I think Daddy's at work.'

'What would you like me to say?' Sophie asked.

Claire thought about it. 'Just tell him Ella slipped over,' she said. 'That she's been checked over at the hospital and is fine, and that I'll get her to text him tomorrow.'

Sophie nodded. She took a second to read Luke's text, and then keyed in a reply.

'It *was* him then?' Claire glanced worriedly at her.

Sophie answered with a nod.

'What did he say?'

'He wanted to know what happened,' Sophie supplied. 'There are a few, um, expletives in there too,' she added, her eyes gliding towards Ella.

Claire got the gist and was grateful. Furious texts from her father were the very last thing she wanted Ella to see.

CHAPTER TWENTY-EIGHT

Claire

Claire couldn't believe it. Had she done something awful in another life? Was she being punished for some reason?

'I thought it looked a bit flat when I came out this morning,' Sophie said, following her bewildered gaze to the deflated tyre on her car, this time on the driver's side.

'It's not a *bit* flat,' Claire said, working to control her emotion in front of Ella. 'It's been slashed.' She could see the gaping gap in the rubber above the wheel rim from three feet away.

'Kids. The little…' Sophie stopped herself short. 'They tore the wing mirrors off a car just up the road a couple of weeks ago.'

Her mouth dry, Claire nodded. She guessed Sophie must be right, but why did these things keep happening? 'Hell, I've let the taxi go now.' She glanced despairingly after it as it turned the corner.

'Come in and have some tea, and I'll call you another one,' Sophie offered. 'Or you could stay. I know you'd probably rather not now, but the least I can do is look after you and Ella after all the upset I've caused you.'

'Can we, Mummy?' Ella asked, that hopeful glint in her eyes, and Claire knew that, once again, she couldn't say no.

*

'Is she all right?' Sophie looked worriedly up from the drinks she was making, as Claire came back to the kitchen after settling Ella down.

Claire nodded and went to seat herself at the table. 'Asleep at last,' she assured her. She hadn't been sure whether to take up Sophie's offer to stay over, but Ella had been thrilled at the prospect of spending the night and the promise of a film of her choice being downloaded in the morning. The fur throw and hot-water bottle had been immensely appreciated, and the tinned tomato soup Sophie had prepared for Ella had hit the spot, as Luke would have said. Sighing wearily inside, Claire wondered what his reaction would be when she spoke to him. She couldn't face that conversation tonight.

'Hot chocolate,' Sophie said, carrying two steaming mugs across to the table. 'It's only the instant stuff, but it will warm us up.'

'Thanks.' Claire wrapped her hands gratefully around her mug and took a soothing sip. Sophie was still worried to death, trying to do all she could to help.

'Are you all right?' Claire asked her. She certainly looked better after the hot shower she'd taken while Claire lay with Ella until she drifted off. She finally had some colour to her cheeks, and her eyes were less tormented. Sitting here in her small, sparsely furnished kitchen, dressed in teal-coloured flowery pyjamas rather than the black leggings and fitted black shirt that had showed off her sleek figure to perfection, she looked more like a vulnerable child than an adult.

'I'm fine.' Sophie gave her a wan smile. 'I'm really sorry, Claire,' she blurted, reaching to catch hold of her hand. 'I can't believe I took my eyes off her. I don't know what I would have done if anything had happened to her. Killed myself probably. I'm so bloody *stupid*.'

There were fresh tears welling in her eyes, Claire saw, her initial anger giving way to compassion. She must have apologised a thousand times. 'You're not stupid, Sophie,' she said, giving her hand a gentle squeeze. She above all people knew the impossibility of keeping eyes on an impulsive four-year-old every minute of every day. And it had only taken a moment, she imagined, for Ella to cross the short distance from where they were to the sea. 'Ella can be very headstrong. I need eyes in the back of my head to keep up with her sometimes.'

Sophie smiled again, tremulously. She didn't look convinced.

'It might have ended in disaster but for your quick reaction,' Claire reminded her, a shudder running through her as she imagined again what might have happened. Ella could swim, but only with her armbands. The current had been strong. She would have been disorientated, flailing about, lost and terrified under the swirling water. From where Claire had been, some way up the beach, she would never have reached her in time. And then Sophie had made sure they got to the hospital. She could have been run over in the process. 'Children are resilient,' Claire assured her, although she hadn't been thinking that way herself earlier. 'She'll be fine.'

'I suppose,' Sophie said with a weak smile. 'I know I was as a child. When anything bad happened, I always came back stronger. I still do.' She met Claire's gaze, holding it for a second, and then looked away.

Claire couldn't quite read what was in her eyes. It was as if they'd glazed over, as her father's sometimes did. Her past was obviously painful. What she'd just said about killing herself had jarred her. She was still clearly wretched with guilt and utterly miserable. 'It was my fault, Sophie, not yours,' she told her firmly. 'I should have been watching her. I was so busy with the problems between her father and me, I forgot about our child. I wouldn't have been able to live with myself if anything had happened to her. She's my heartbeat, everything I have in the world. If not for you, she might have...' She trailed off, unable to speak the word.

Sophie squeezed her hand hard in return. 'We'll both have to be extra vigilant next time,' she said, smiling kindly. 'That's assuming you ever want to see me again. I don't think I'd blame you if you didn't.'

Claire studied her thoughtfully, noting the immense sadness now in her eyes, as if she fully expected Claire to return to her own life and have nothing to do with her in future. But she couldn't just ignore Sophie's existence. She actually liked her, despite everything that had happened. Sophie didn't appear to have anyone else in the world either. No one she'd mentioned anyway.

'Do you want children some day?' Claire asked her carefully. Aware that Sophie was not long out of a bad relationship, she didn't want to venture too clumsily onto sensitive ground. She did want to know more about who she was, though. Did she long to create a family of her own, as Claire had? To have people around her to fill the void in her heart left by the loss of her mother?

Sophie reached for her mug, swishing the contents around it as she pondered. 'I do,' she said, 'very much. I'd have to find a man who's half-decent first, though, wouldn't I?'

Claire felt for her. 'You will,' she said encouragingly. She was absolutely sure Sophie would meet someone else soon. She couldn't fail to notice heads turning in her direction while they were out. She really was extremely pretty.

'Maybe.' Sophie pondered. 'I thought my ex was, you know, The One. I even came off the pill for a while. Thank God I didn't get pregnant,' she said with a relieved roll of her eyes. 'I would have been left bringing a child up on my own with absolutely no support whatso— Oh God.' She stopped, cringing at her obvious faux pas. 'Me and my runaway mouth. I am *so* sorry, Claire. That was really crass.'

Claire couldn't help but be touched by her mortified expression. 'It's fine. I'm getting used to the idea now.' She forced a smile, and buried the feelings of isolation and loneliness that immediately assailed her. She wasn't getting used to the idea. The cold reality of her complete aloneness still hit her in soul-crushing waves. 'I think I'd rather be on my own, to be honest, than with a man who doesn't have his child's best interests at heart.'

'Do you think Luke doesn't then?' Sophie asked, her expression troubled.

'Honestly,' Claire took a breath, 'I'm not sure.' She jumped as her phone beeped between them. Another text from him, no doubt. One of many since they'd got back, all of which she'd ignored in favour of seeing to Ella and then giving herself some breathing space. Why was he doing this? She'd already sent another text confirming that Ella was fine.

Sighing despairingly, she picked up the phone and switched it to silent. She didn't want to speak to Luke until she could think what to do about his ongoing contact with Ella. She certainly didn't want her anywhere near some bitter lunatic ex-girlfriend. Assuming he was telling the truth and that was what the woman was. It was him who'd sounded irrational, and given the seriousness of what he was being accused of, she wasn't sure she was happy with him having access to Ella at all. At least not until she knew for sure.

Sophie glanced at the phone as Claire placed it back on the table. 'He's a bit persistent, isn't he?' she suggested hesitantly.

'Very.' Claire emitted another heavy sigh. 'I'll call him tomorrow,' she said, absent-mindedly twirling her mug around on the table. 'I just can't face talking to him yet.'

'I know that feeling,' Sophie empathised. 'My ex used to barrage me with calls,' she explained, when Claire glanced at her curiously. 'He did it before we broke up, always wanting to know where I was and who I was with, but after… he almost drove me insane. Texting and ringing at all hours, calling round uninvited. I swear he didn't want me to have a life. He does the cheating and then he's jealous? I mean, how does that work?' She looked at Claire in bafflement.

'I doubt Luke's jealous, given he was so ready to throw our marriage away. He's bound to be worried, though. He is Ella's father, after all.' Claire found herself defending Luke again, and had no idea why.

Sophie raised her eyebrows at that. 'I suppose,' she conceded, not looking very convinced. 'I still think his text was a bit aggressive, though, demanding to know where you were and when you would be back home.' She paused, glancing at Claire guardedly. 'And he's very fond of the F word, isn't he? Did he not consider that Ella might see it?'

Claire felt it again, a tug of fear and confusion at the mention of Luke as aggressive. 'That's just it,' she dropped her gaze, 'I'm not sure he's considering anything right now. Least of all Ella.'

'Do you want to talk about it?' Sophie offered kindly. 'It might help.'

Claire looked back at her, and was met with such sincerity in her eyes she felt like bursting into tears. Inhaling a shuddery breath, she managed not to, just. 'Who did you confide in?' she asked. 'After your mum died?'

'My gran.' Sophie smiled, heart-wrenchingly. 'She still had all her faculties almost right up until the end. She didn't like my ex. Said he was bad news, warned me off him. I didn't listen, of course. We're our own worst enemies sometimes, aren't we? After that, no one. Well, no one I could trust, anyway.'

Which might explain why she was suddenly so desperate to find her family, Claire realised.

'I might not be able to do much, Claire, but I'm a good listener,' Sophie assured her.

Claire debated with herself, then took another deep breath. 'He was arrested,' she confided, 'Luke…'

Sophie looked shocked and worried in turn. 'What for?' she asked.

Claire hesitated, feeling unaccountably like a traitor. *But it's Luke who's the traitor*, said an angry little voice in her head. And now he was accusing her of being a bad mother. Despite what had happened today, Claire was sure he was wrong about that. She loved her little girl so much it hurt. Starting tonight, she'd sworn off the wine. She only ever had the odd glass, he knew that. It had helped her to get to sleep, but perhaps made her sleep a little too heavily, she now realised. She would do without it in future. She wouldn't give him ammunition against her.

Glancing back at Sophie, she spoke falteringly. 'His girlfriend went missing… under suspicious circumstances.'

Sophie's look turned to astonishment. 'Bloody hell, Claire.'

'She turned up,' Claire added quickly. 'That is, she texted me. That's what I was talking to him about on the beach. The police need me to go in and make a statement, apparently.'

'Blimey.' Sophie ran a hand through her hair. 'No wonder you were distracted.'

Her heart fluttering with uncertainty, Claire scanned the other woman's eyes as she looked back at her. There was no judgement there, only sympathy.

'So what were the suspicious circumstances?' Sophie asked.

Again Claire hesitated. 'Blood in the bathroom,' she answered eventually, icy cold spreading through her as she imagined the scene. 'Luke denied there was any violence on his part, but he did admit they'd argued.'

She wasn't comfortable sharing things about Luke after the security of her marriage, where she'd thought he was the only one she could ever truly trust, but as Sophie continued to listen without judging, the words came tumbling out, and soon Claire had told her everything. About Luke's ultimatum. His moodiness. How he'd stormed out and cheated on her that very night. Her heart growing heavier, she told her about the scratch on his cheek, his evasiveness when she'd asked him about it. His explanation, which she didn't know whether to believe. She had to summon up the courage to tell her what they'd argued about earlier. 'He made out I was a bad mother,' she said, her guilt resurfacing. 'That I was drinking too much, putting Ella at risk.'

'*You* putting Ella at risk?' Sophie laughed incredulously. 'He's got some nerve, hasn't he, after what he's done?'

Claire answered with an unsure nod. 'The thing is, he's right, isn't he?' She wiped an errant tear from her eye. 'I'm scared he's trying to take her away from me.'

'What?' Now Sophie looked flabbergasted. '*Why?*'

'I don't know…' Claire faltered. 'I live in fear of losing her, Sophie. I have done since social services started asking questions before she was diagnosed. If they started poking around again, I swear I would run away with her.'

Sophie nodded thoughtfully at that. 'I see,' she said. 'Well, rest assured, Claire, he wouldn't stand a snowball in hell's chance of getting custody of her, not with this on his police record, and it will be, trust me. As for you being a bad mother, that's bollocks, excuse my French. I haven't known you long, admittedly, but even without what Bernard told me – which was that you're a kind, caring person – I can see that you're a damn good mother. If I were you, I would ignore him. He's obviously trying to get your attention.'

'He's got it.' Claire smiled shakily. 'He said she was insane,' she went on, after a second. 'Anna, I mean. He said she was volatile, violent. I'm not sure whether to believe that either.'

Picking up her phone, she scrolled to her texts and selected the one the woman had sent her. 'What do you think?' she asked, passing the phone to Sophie.

Reading it in silence, her forehead furrowed pensively, Sophie took a moment to answer. Then, 'Truthfully?' she said, her eyes holding a warning as she glanced back at her. 'It's not my place to tell you how to bring up your daughter, Claire, but you can't let this poison seep into Ella's life. He's obviously involved in a very toxic relationship. I can't see how it can end amicably… assuming it does end.'

'Of course it's going to end.' Claire laughed. 'It's already ended. He's been accused of attacking her, for God's sake.'

'Which he says he didn't,' Sophie pointed out. 'Claiming she's volatile, violent, insane… Say he is telling the truth.' She studied Claire carefully. 'What do you think would have attracted him to a woman like that?'

Claire scanned her face in turn. She had no idea how to answer. The thrill of a night of illicit sex to salve his ego, she'd thought initially.

'Precisely those qualities.' Sophie's next comment stunned her. 'She would have been quirky, teasing, intriguing. Volatile. Who's to say he'll be able to resist if she lures him back with promises of sex – sadomasochistic sex probably; it sounds to me as if that's the sort of thing she's into. If it were me, Claire, I'd have nothing to do with him.'

CHAPTER TWENTY-NINE

Claire

'Hi, sleepyhead.' Sophie smiled brightly as Claire wandered bleary-eyed into the kitchen the next morning.

'God, what time is it?' Claire blinked around, disorientated. Despite the lack of wine, she'd slept heavily, dreams of her mother haunting her as they always did. Normally she dreamed of her mother smiling and happy, crouching beside her as she pointed out the pretty birds in the garden – greenfinches, robins and fat wood pigeons – then immediately unsmiling and angry. This time, though, it had been different. Like a thin wisp of smoke on the air, it was already escaping her. She remembered one bit of it: her mother's expression when she'd fallen. Her eyes had been pleading, her face ridden with guilt as she lay broken at the foot of the stairs. *I'm sorry, my darling*, she'd whispered. *I tried to stop him.* To stop him doing what? Claire tried to make sense of it.

'Nine forty,' Sophie supplied, snapping her from her reverie. 'I take it you slept well?'

'Like a log.' Claire stifled a yawn. 'I could have slept the clock round.'

'That will be the shock catching up with you.' Sophie glanced at her sympathetically from where she was sliding a baking tray into the oven. 'You've had an awful lot to deal with. You're bound to be exhausted.'

'I must have been.' Claire stretched and massaged the back of her neck. 'Thanks for the bed for the night, Sophie, and for the shoulder. I think it did me good to talk about things.'

'No problem,' Sophie assured her, reaching for the kettle to pour water into two mugs. 'That's what sisters are for. Where's Ella?'

Claire noted the sisters reference and decided she didn't mind. She felt stronger having someone on her side. 'In the lounge, snuggling Cinder. I've a feeling someone might be mithering me for a cat when we get back.'

'Uh oh, sorry.' Sophie winced apologetically.

'Not your fault. She loves furry things. All the more so if they're *live* furry things.' Claire smiled. 'I might consider getting her one once I know what I'm doing. It will be company for her, and better than a dog, which I suspect she was hankering after. That's not really feasible now I'm on my own. I'll probably have to go back to work sooner rather than later.'

'I can see a dog would be a problem, having to leave it.' Sophie's eyes flicked downwards as she carried the coffee to the table. Placing the mugs down, she looked up again. 'You do have me,' she said with a hesitant smile. 'If you need help with anything, I mean. I'd be more than happy to help out if I can.'

Claire studied her for second. She looked so hopeful, it was heart-rending. 'I know you would,' she said, giving her another small smile. 'Something smells scrummy.' Nodding towards the oven, she changed the subject.

'Fresh croissants,' Sophie said, now looking pleased. 'I nipped out while you were sleeping. They're warm, but they need another minute. Grab a seat and I'll bring them over.'

'You don't need to wait on me, Sophie,' Claire said, though actually she was quite enjoying it. It was usually her running around after everyone else.

'Make the most of it,' Sophie insisted. 'I think you've earned it, don't you?'

Claire plonked herself gratefully down. She *had* earned it, she supposed. 'I was wondering…' she said hesitantly as Sophie pulled the croissants from the oven.

'About?' Sophie slid the pastries onto a plate and glanced across to her.

'Your mother,' Claire went on cautiously, aware how painful the subject was.

Sophie nodded, her expression telling Claire she'd expected her to ask again. 'She died in a car accident,' she said, walking across to place the croissants on the table and then going back for smaller plates. 'A motorbike came straight at her. Mum skidded to avoid it, the car flipped and…' Shrugging sadly, she came back to the table. 'The driver of the motorbike was drunk, apparently. Some people thought he did it deliberately, but… I don't suppose we'll ever know.'

'Deliberately?' Claire felt a chill of trepidation run through her, and her mind went immediately to her dad's old BSA sitting in his garage.

'He was an ex-boyfriend.' Sophie's eyes were full of pain and sadness. 'They say he was jealous of her involvement with…' Trailing off, she glanced at Claire worriedly.

'Bernard?' Clare finished, her throat thick.

Nodding cautiously, Sophie pulled out a chair and sat down. 'Mum saw him for years off and on. I think she was very much in love with him.' She paused, appearing to take stock, while Claire thought of her own mother, how she could have borne it; how either of the women could.

'The car caught fire. Mum didn't stand a chance,' Sophie continued, swallowing emotionally. 'The ex-boyfriend went to prison, but he's out now. You do wonder, don't you, about the justice of him having a life when my mother was so cruelly robbed of hers.'

'Oh my God, Sophie…' Shocked to the core, Claire stared at her. She had no idea what to say. 'That's terrible. I'm so sorry.' She reached for the hand Sophie was absent-mindedly dusting crumbs from the table with. 'Did he plead guilty?'

Sophie shook her head. 'He denied it. He was there that night, in the pub where Mum worked. Witnesses said he was there most nights, hanging around her; that he often said she would regret the day she finished with him. The landlord said he'd been drinking steadily and that he'd overheard them arguing.' She stopped and pulled in a shuddery breath.

'There wasn't much evidence, I gather,' she went on quietly after a second. 'The tyre tracks were inconclusive, but there was part of a number plate that the police were able to match to his bike. He said he used that road often and that he'd skidded there once before. A witness from a cottage just past where it happened said they saw him riding off at speed after the car caught fire, though, so…'

Claire gulped back a hard lump in her throat. 'Oh Sophie, that must have been so awful for you,' she said, horrified and aching with hurt for her. Yet also relieved. For a second, she'd imagined… She wasn't sure what she'd imagined, but her own mother's words – *What happened was because of you, Bernard Harvey! Live with the consequences. I have to* – her drinking, her deteriorating mental health had come petrifyingly to mind.

'It was.' Sophie smiled sadly. 'They're going to be pulling the pub down soon,' she added, almost as an afterthought. 'It's already half demolished. I find that quite upsetting too, to be honest. I spent most of my early childhood in that place. It was lovely in the summer. The gardens at the back were really pretty. Not so much in the winter. It was cosy, but a bit gloomy.'

Claire remembered it well. And the woman with the red-painted lips and the leopard-print shoes. Sophie's mother. Her father's lover. She swallowed heavily.

'I went there a few times after it closed. I even stayed there for a couple of weeks before I got this place,' Sophie went on.

'On your own?' Claire looked at her, surprised. 'Didn't you find that a bit… haunting?'

'Not really.' Sophie shrugged, unperturbed. 'I suppose some people would, but it made me feel closer to her somehow. I swear I could hear her laughing from behind the bar sometimes. She had a nice laugh, bubbly,' she added sadly, and then pressed a finger to her lips and nodded towards the door.

Claire followed her gaze to see Ella standing there with her arms full of cat. A remarkably patient cat, considering that its bottom half was dangling precariously floorwards and its top half was in danger of being hugged to death.

'*Mummeee…*' The little girl's voice was her best wheedling one, and her eyes were in beguiling mode as she leaned her cheek to nuzzle the bewildered-looking animal.

'We'll see,' Claire said.

Ella looked up, her eyes wide with surprise. 'How did you know what I was going to say?' she asked.

'I'm a mind-reader,' Claire told her with a smile. 'I'm also sensing you're hungry. Come on.' Exchanging amused glances with Sophie, she patted the chair next to her. 'Come and have some chocolate croissants. No, not the cat,' she added as Ella pondered how to scramble up with her arms wrapped around it. 'Pop Cinder down, sweetheart. You can have another cuddle with him before we leave.'

'It's a *her*, Mummy.' Ella sighed despairingly and bent to plop the cat down. Cinder immediately made a sharp exit to the lounge.

'Better go and wash your hands, lovely,' Sophie suggested. 'Cats are cute, but they do catch mice. Better not swallow any germs with your croissant.'

'Oops.' Ella dutifully about-faced to the bathroom, leaving Claire thinking that Sophie was more proficient at parenting than she was.

Her hands duly washed, but still dripping wet, Ella returned to have them quickly dried by Sophie on some kitchen towel.

'Can I talk to Daddy today, Mummy?' she asked, as Claire hoisted her up onto the chair, and then fetched her some juice.

Heck. She'd forgotten to turn her sound back on. 'When we've finished breakfast,' she promised, ferreting her phone from the pocket of the dressing gown Sophie had kindly offered her the use of. Checking it, she found several texts and missed calls from Luke. He'd obviously been desperate to get hold of her.

'Everything okay?' Sophie enquired, noting her worried expression.

'Yes, fine,' Claire said, smiling as Ella's shrewd gaze slid between them. Immediately the phone rang again. 'I'd better take this,' she said, pushing her chair back and getting to her feet.

'Claire? Where the bloody hell have you been?' Luke demanded as soon as she accepted the call.

Claire was tempted to hang up there and then, but restrained herself with Ella looking on. 'I've told you where I am, Luke,' she said, politely but tightly. 'Is there a problem?'

He emitted an incredulous laugh. 'Yes, there's a problem,' he growled, making no attempt to hide his agitation. 'I hear you screaming Ella's name, then the phone goes dead. I text you to be told she's been to the *hospital*. I call you and text you at least another thousand times and get a short reply telling me nothing except to basically piss off and stop bothering you. So yes, I'd say there's definitely a problem, wouldn't you?'

Her heartbeat ratcheting up, Claire cautioned herself to stay calm. 'Did you want something, Luke?' she asked him.

'Yes, Claire,' he grated, 'I would quite like to know how my daughter is, if that's okay with you.'

'She's fine, as I mentioned in my text.' Claire kept her tone civil, though she wasn't sure how. 'Would you like to have a quick word with her?'

'If it's not too inconvenient for you, yes,' Luke answered caustically.

Claire ignored him, going to Ella instead. 'Daddy wants to say hello, sweetheart. Don't be too long, though. We have to get washed and dressed, don't we?' Handing Ella the phone, she turned away, her teeth gritted as she tried to quash the anger blooming in her chest. Why was he behaving this way? What did he possibly hope to gain by practically hounding her?

Calming herself with several slow breaths, she cocked an ear to glean what she could from Ella's side of the conversation.

'No, we were sleepy, so we stayed in bed,' Ella said, from which Claire gathered he'd commented about her not being dressed yet.

Silence followed as Ella listened. Then, 'I fell in the sea,' she said, and Claire inwardly flinched. She had no idea how he would interpret that.

'No, I didn't have my armbands with me,' she went on. 'I was all right, though,' she quickly assured him. 'Auntie Sophie came and got me.'

Claire went back to her. 'Say goodbye now, sweetheart. Mummy needs to get on.'

Ella looked up from the phone, her wide blue eyes cloudy with confusion. Also a touch of resentment, which did nothing to improve Claire's mood. This was so unfair – on Ella and her. She hadn't caused this situation. Luke was the one who'd cheated. Yet his aggressive attitude was making her feel that she was in the wrong.

'When will I see you, Daddy?' Ella asked, causing Claire's heart to twist. 'Promise?' she added, her voice small. Plainly, she was reluctant to let him go.

'Say bye-bye, sweetheart,' Claire encouraged her.

'Bye, Daddy,' Ella obliged, her eyes now brimming with tears. 'Love you too.'

Standing up, Claire pressed the phone to her ear. She was grateful when Sophie came to the rescue, taking Ella's hand and signalling towards the lounge.

'Thanks,' Claire mouthed, and waited for them to disappear before turning her attention to the questions Luke was now firing at her. She was glad Sophie had been considerate enough of Ella's feelings to put the TV on, thus drowning out the conversation she was about to have.

'Claire, this is ludicrous,' Luke was saying, his tone now a mixture of agitation and frustration. 'You shouldn't be taking anything that woman says at face value.'

'It's none of your business,' Claire snapped, feeling tearful already. What right did he have to question her?

'Do you have any proof she is who she says she is?' Luke went on. 'Have you checked her out? Properly, I mean, before allowing her access to Ella? What's her full name?'

'Obviously I have,' Claire lied. That was what she was doing here. But she wasn't answerable to him.

'I'm driving over there,' Luke announced.

'Don't you *dare*!' Claire hissed furiously. 'What are you, my keeper? I'm Ella's mother. I'm perfectly capable of looking after her.'

'And I'm her father,' Luke shot back. 'And I have every right to know what the *hell* is going on.'

Claire clenched her free hand so hard her fingernails dug into her flesh. 'Yes, and a very caring one,' she pointed out, growing more angry and disbelieving by the second.

Luke sucked in a breath. 'That's not fair, Claire,' he said, more quietly. 'I didn't want any of this to happen.'

Claire almost laughed at that. 'No, you just wanted a quick shag.'

'Claire, don't. I didn't… Nothing *happened*. Why won't you listen to me?'

Did he really expect her to believe that, given all that was happening now? Claire's mind boggled. Could she have been more wrong about him? She'd scoffed when Sophie had compared him to her abusive ex, but now… This was manipulation, pure and simple. What did he want from her? 'A one-night stand,' she went on, her voice quavering, though she was trying hard to control it. 'Sums up how you feel about women, doesn't it?'

'Could we just stop this please, Claire?' Luke asked, after a charged pause. 'Can we not just talk properly?'

Claire noted his more conciliatory tone. It had probably occurred to him that she had something he wanted. The text that would save his bacon. 'I'm hanging up,' she said, her own tone flat. Her emotions flat. She couldn't do this. She simply didn't have the energy.

'Claire, *wait…*' There it was, the desperate edge to his voice.

'No, Luke. We have nothing else to discuss. Please stop texting me and calling me and threatening me. I—'

'*Threatening?*' He laughed, astonished. 'Come on, Claire. I'm concerned about Ella, that's all. You too. I just—'

'I'm going,' Claire repeated firmly. 'And don't worry, I'll go to the police station – but only because I care about my daughter and what the impact might be on her if I don't.' She ended the call without saying goodbye. She felt as if her heart was tearing apart inside her.

She didn't realise Sophie had come back into the kitchen until she slipped an arm around her shoulders. 'Okay, lovely?' she asked her softly.

Working hard to hold back her tears, Claire answered with a short nod.

'I heard… some of it,' Sophie said, then tensed as Claire's phone rang again. 'Do you want me to take it?'

Claire nodded a second time. She couldn't trust herself to speak. If she did, the tears would come. Ella was safely in front of the TV, but still she couldn't take the chance she might wander in and find her mother sobbing her heart out.

Sophie turned slightly away as she answered. 'She doesn't want to talk to you,' she said bluntly, and cut the call. Then she turned back, her eyes full of concern. 'I'm sure he'll ring again if he has any genuine concerns about Ella, but it's your choice whether you want to speak to him, Claire, and when. Just a suggestion,' she added, 'but maybe you should send him a text telling him you'll change your number if he keeps messaging you. Sometimes you have to meet threats with threats. At least then he'll know you mean it.'

Claire wrapped her arms about herself, feeling inexplicably cold suddenly. 'Thanks, Sophie,' she said, now immensely glad to have her in her corner.

'Mummy,' Ella called from the lounge.

'Coming, sweetheart,' Claire called back. 'Could I ask you a favour, Sophie?'

'Anything,' Sophie assured her.

'The texts Luke sent.' She nodded towards the phone Sophie was still holding. 'Would you mind deleting them?' She didn't want Ella reading them, but neither did she want to have to look at them herself. She didn't want anything to do with him right now.

What she needed to do was get her tyre fixed, go home, and learn how to live on her own. If Sophie could do it, she could. And at least she did have Sophie now.

CHAPTER THIRTY

Luke

'Evening. And who are we today, the plumber or the deliveryman?' The carer he'd met before greeted Luke with a wry smile as he walked into the day room.

Luke smiled tiredly back. 'God knows. The villain of the piece, I've no doubt.'

'It's a wonder you don't have an identity crisis.' The woman's smile was now sympathetic.

'Yeah.' Luke sighed. After the things he'd been accused of, the things he'd done that he'd never imagined he was capable of, he definitely had one of those. 'Is it all right if I go up?' he asked, noting that Bernard didn't appear to be around.

'Feel free.' The carer nodded him on. 'I hope you get a better reception than you did last time.

Luke doubted he would. Whoever Bernard got it into his head he was, he didn't rate him. He never really had; more tolerated him because his daughter had foolishly fallen in love with him. Would he be glad they'd split up, if he was capable of understanding? Probably not, for Claire's sake, but Luke suspected he wouldn't have lost any sleep over it.

Knocking on Bernard's door, he waited a minute and then went on in. Unusually, Bernard wasn't in his armchair. Instead, he was standing in the bay window, gazing out at nothing. It was pitch black outside.

'Hi, Bernard.' Luke offered him a smile as the older man turned to face him. 'How are you doing?'

'Have you come to replace the bulb in the bathroom?' Bernard asked, narrowing his eyes as he ran his gaze over him. 'Because if you have, you can inform your manager that I'll be registering a complaint. It's been two days since I reported it, and it's just not good enough.'

Luke blew out a weary breath. 'No, Bernard, I haven't. I'm not the electrician. I'm Luke, Claire's husband. Remember?'

Bernard frowned, his face etched with confusion.

'Though possibly not for much longer,' Luke went on hesitantly as Bernard walked past him, still eyeing him suspiciously, and lowered himself into his armchair. 'We, er… She thinks I'm having an affair.'

Bernard's frown only deepened. He didn't answer, reaching for his remote control instead.

'I was wondering whether you might have some advice you could offer me. As a man of the world, I mean,' Luke pushed on, hoping that Bernard might dredge up some scrap of information from his past that would give him a clue what was going on. 'I imagine you've probably had the odd fling, and I—'

'I've done no such thing!' Bernard blustered, rising from his armchair so fast, Luke took a step back. 'How *dare* you come in here and make such accusations. Who do you work for?'

'Whoa.' Luke held his hands out in an attempt to placate him as Bernard advanced towards him. 'I'm not making accusations, Bernard. I just wanted to chat, man to man. 'It's just that Claire mentioned—'

'Claire? Claire who?' Bernard demanded, his face puce. 'One of the staff, I suppose. Nothing better to do with her time than spread malicious gossip. Where is she?'

'Bernard, wait.' Luke circumnavigated him as he whirled around to stride towards the door. 'She's not here,' he said, massaging his forehead in frustration. This was hopeless. He wondered what the hell he'd been thinking. He was desperate to establish if there was any truth in this half-sister thing, his gut instinct telling him that Claire might be in danger of some sort. Bernard, though, didn't know what bloody day it was, let alone who his daughter was. Or daughters. If he had had an affair, he would probably take that secret with him to the grave.

The older man looked confounded now, his eyes downcast as he grappled for his memories. Luke couldn't help thinking he would be better off out of his misery than live a life like this. He supposed the one consolation was that he didn't have to live with the consequences of his actions and the misery he might have caused other people.

'She doesn't want you,' Bernard said suddenly, his eyes hardening. 'She never did. So why don't you just piss off.' He stepped threateningly towards Luke.

'Don't, Bernard,' Luke warned, reaching for the door behind him, his shoulders tensed. 'Just back off, okay.'

Who didn't want him? he wondered, bewildered. Had Bernard been talking about Claire? Or was this someone from his past he'd clearly thought was worth fighting over?

CHAPTER THIRTY-ONE

Claire

Two days later

Arriving back at her father's house after a clothes shopping trip for Ella – with a new soft toy thrown in as a bit of a treat – Claire felt a familiar sense of desolation run through her as she stepped into the empty hall. Would her life always be full of loss? she wondered.

'Come on, sweetheart, let's get you a snack,' she said, dropping her bags in the hall and making herself smile for her little girl's sake as she steered her towards the kitchen. Ella could probably use a nap, but they hadn't had much for lunch and Claire doubted she'd sleep on an empty tummy. 'What do you fancy?'

'Oreos,' Ella said with a decisive nod. They were her favourite biscuits in the whole world, and she would eat a whole packet if Claire didn't keep an eye on her.

'One Oreo,' Claire said, determined not to be influenced by her daughter's petulantly protruding bottom lip as she took the biscuits from the cupboard. 'Then how about you make us both some peanut butter apple slices while Mummy takes our shopping upstairs?'

Ella brightened at that. It would be messy, but worth it. She loved helping out in the kitchen, and the peanut butter snacks would provide her with some protein as well as keeping her occupied, for a short while at least.

Claire sliced up an apple, then poured a glass of milk and opened up the peanut butter. 'Won't be long, sweetheart,' she said. Smiling as Ella dipped the spoon in the jar, no doubt to be licked clean in between dolloping the contents onto the apple, she headed back to the door, and then stopped, her nerves jarring as her mobile rang. She checked it before answering – she really had been feeling besieged by Luke's constant texting – and then, relieved, accepted Sophie's call.

'I'm not stalking you, don't worry,' Sophie said quickly. 'I just rang to make sure you're okay. I won't become a nuisance caller, I promise.'

'It's not you who's the nuisance, Sophie,' Claire assured her, smiling wanly.

'Hello, Auntie Sophie,' Ella called, waving a peanut-butter-encrusted spoon. 'I'm making Mummy some snacks,' she informed her, going importantly back to her task.

'Peanut butter and apple slices,' Claire provided. 'There'll probably be more peanut butter in her hair and on the table than on the apple, though.' She smiled indulgently.

'She's a lucky little girl to have such a hands-on mum,' Sophie said, giving her ego a small boost. 'Some mothers wouldn't bother.'

'I'm not so sure she'd agree when I snap at her,' Claire said, glancing back at Ella, whose welfare she'd promised herself would be her number one priority from now on.

'That's normal, Claire,' Sophie pointed out. 'It's what harassed mums do when their patience is stretched thin. It's called being human, and it's perfectly acceptable.'

'Maybe,' Claire said, still feeling bad that she'd been so short-tempered with Ella when she was already bewildered by the things happening around her.

'Definitely,' Sophie chastised her gently. 'So, how have you been?'

'Okay… ish. You know.' Claire sighed. The truth was, she was worried. About her dad. About Luke. About Ella. When and where she should start looking for a job. Whether she should. She desperately didn't want to leave her daughter with people she couldn't trust implicitly, who weren't trained to know what to do in an emergency. She'd found the perfect nursery where they'd lived in Herefordshire, but nothing suitable here. She didn't really have a choice, however. Without her carer's allowance, she would have to work. And though she felt guilty – again – even thinking about it, there would be little money left in the pot now that the house needed to be sold to meet the care home fees.

'You sound a bit fed up.' Sophie cut through her thoughts. 'Luke hasn't been harassing you again, has he?'

'No,' Claire assured her, her heart growing heavier as she acknowledged that that was indeed what Luke had been doing. She'd never have believed him capable once. Was that such a short time ago? She'd gone to the station regarding the text. Made it her first priority on the way back from Rhyl. She had wondered why she cared enough to, when he no longer seemed to care for her. But then if he'd been no more than a friend to her, she would have gone. Whatever he'd done, she could never allow him to suffer any more interrogation at the hands of the police, possibly even face charges about the woman's disappearance. She wasn't happy with the suspicious way she'd been treated though, particularly when she'd realised that Sophie had accidentally deleted the text from Anna along with Luke's messages. Fortunately, they could retrieve the deleted texts. Claire had a distinct feeling the police had thought she had something to do with the whole sordid mess.

Checking again that Ella was occupied, she took the phone through to the hall. 'It's just things in general,' she said, picking up a handful of bags and heading up the stairs. 'Things I need to sort out and have no clue where to even start with.'

'You have a lot on your plate,' Sophie sympathised. 'Look, it's just a suggestion, but would you like me to come over? It would be no trouble, and you sound as if you could use some company.'

She could, Claire had to concede. She felt as if she were rattling around in the house, but surely Sophie couldn't just drop everything and leave? 'What about your job?'

'Not a problem,' Sophie assured her with an expansive sigh. 'I wasn't going to say anything when you already have so much to deal with, but I apparently no longer have one.'

'Oh no. Why?' Dumping her bags on the bed, Claire went back to the landing.

'Because my boss is a tosspot,' Sophie supplied bluntly. 'A groper, to be more precise. We had words when I was last in. I didn't quite tell him where to stuff his job, because I needed the money. Looks like he took exception to me telling him to keep his grubby paws to himself, though, so… Taking an extra day off when you were here didn't help, but I wasn't about to leave you two after the awful ordeal you'd had.'

'But that's terrible.' Claire was shocked. 'He can't get away with that, surely?'

'He can, apparently. I was only casual, cash in hand, so I have no rights as such. In any case, I can't prove anything.'

'What an absolute b—' Claire clamped her mouth shut before the word fell out.

'My thoughts entirely,' Sophie concurred. 'What really upsets me is that I'll probably lose my flat now as well. The landlord doesn't let to people on benefits. I'm guessing anything I might be entitled to would take ages to come through anyhow, and I already owe a month's rent, thanks to the pittance I was being paid.'

'God, Sophie.' Claire felt bad for her. 'If there's anything I can do…'

'Thanks,' Sophie said gratefully. 'There isn't really. I'll go into town tomorrow. Some of the shops will be hiring, with the summer season coming up. Don't worry, I'll get something sorted. I usually do.' She paused. 'So, would you like me to come over? I won't be offended if you'd rather I didn't, but the offer's there.'

Claire thought about it. She hadn't wanted her here at first. Couldn't imagine she ever would, but now… Ella would love it. She adored Sophie, and Sophie was so good with her. Luke's comment about allowing her access to Ella came to mind, and she hesitated. And then stopped dead, her heart freezing as her gaze fell on something on the landing windowsill. Something that had most definitely *not* been there when she'd gone out earlier this morning.

She stepped towards the half-full wine glass as if it might bite her. Either she was losing her mind, or… Her stomach turned over. 'Yes,' she said, suddenly petrified at being here on her own. 'Please come.'

CHAPTER THIRTY-TWO

Sophie

'We're not homeless after all, Cinder. At least not for a while.' Finishing her call with Claire, Sophie bent to stroke the cat's sleek back as it came into the kitchen to weave its way around her ankles. 'But then *you* never were, were you?' Cinder was obviously a wherever-I-lay-my-hat sort of cat – something they had in common, which was why Sophie had been happy to accept her aloofness and allow her to come and go as she pleased. The cat had actually been extremely useful, portraying Sophie as a big-hearted animal-loving type, which had gone some way to winning Claire over. She'd certainly won little Ella over. Sophie was glad she'd gone to the trouble of feeding the animal now.

Going to the fridge, she took out the milk and topped up Cinder's dish as a reward, then pulled her phone from her pocket to check her texts, of which there were several, all from Peter, the latest man in her life. She'd avoided any contact with him while Claire was here. She'd desperately wanted to bond with her, and a man lurking in the background, she suspected, might give the impression she wasn't as traumatised by her ex's controlling behaviour as she'd claimed to be.

He was obviously getting desperate. Sophie's mouth curved into a smile as she read the last text he'd sent: *You're driving me insane. Can't stop thinking about you. Hope it was as good for you as it was for me? Need to catch up with you. Text me back. Please.*

She debated whether to keep him waiting, thereby keeping him keen, but then decided against. Experience told her he was the kind of man who was likely to move on if he wasn't getting what he wanted. *What's it worth?* she sent back.

Takeaway picnic? he replied swiftly. Clearly he'd been eagerly checking his phone, awaiting her response. *Your choice.*

Picnic in bed, he meant. Sophie wasn't sure she was up for that. He was definitely into kinky stuff – and she'd been left with the cleaning bill for the duvet the last time he was here. But then it wasn't his money she was after, though running his own financial services company in Birmingham, he had plenty of it.

Thai, she typed back. *From the posh place.*

I'm ready to fulfil your every desire, he sent back, with a winking emoji.

Sophie sighed inwardly. *And wine. Dry. White.*

Fuck me like you did last time and you can have champagne, he assured her.

Sophie rolled her eyes. It was strange how some men thought flaunting their wallets, along with their imagined macho physiques, would impress a woman. *When?* she sent.

Today? I'm in the area. Could make it about 8.

Definitely keen. Evidently he didn't intend going home to his wife and baby tonight. Sophie curled her lip in disgust. The child was barely a month old. Some men really were complete bastards. *Make the champers the good stuff*, she replied.

Nothing but the best for you, my sexy little temptress, he responded, reinforcing the fact that she would never be anything more to him than a convenient shag while his wife recovered from giving birth to his child.

She supposed she should take herself to the bathroom to titivate. This would be the last time, she'd already decided, and she wanted it to be unforgettable. She needed him to remember it – every intimate, sordid detail – when she offered him her proposition: her silence in exchange for his services.

CHAPTER THIRTY-THREE

Claire

Her father was eating his evening meal in the dining room when Claire arrived to visit. Or rather, pushing the food around his plate. Had he lost weight? It was hard to tell, since he appeared to have dressed for dinner in a jacket and tie.

She hovered at the dining room door holding onto Ella's hand and wondering whether she should go in. The carer who'd taken him under her wing when he'd first arrived spotted her and came over.

'Is he eating?' Claire asked her.

The carer, Julia, nodded. 'He's fine,' she said. 'Just a bit grumpy.' She lowered her voice. 'He got the hump because we had to gently persuade him that the motorbike belonging to one of our visitors that he was trying to drive off on wasn't his.'

Claire caught her breath as, out of nowhere, an image of Sophie's mother appeared: the pretty woman in the leopard-print shoes, her petrified face blistering and burning, her eyes… Clamping her own eyes shut, she tried to block it out, her chest expanding painfully as she felt a sense of the woman's abject terror.

'Mummy…' Ella tugged on her hand, bringing her sharply back to this place, this time, this man she no longer felt certain how to approach. 'Why did Grandad try to drive off on a motorbike?' she asked, her expression one of worried confusion.

Claire swallowed, and found her voice. 'I don't know, sweetheart,' she answered with a shaky smile. 'He must have got a bit confused. He does sometimes, doesn't he?'

Her forehead knitted in consternation, Ella nodded slowly before looking back at her grandad. Then she let out a gasp, her eyes springing wide, as Bernard yelled, 'Get your bloody hands off!'

Claire turned to see her dad on his feet, his face puce with rage and one of his hands clamped over that of the man sitting beside him, who appeared to be stealing the food from his plate. It was the hand her father was waving his fork about with that was concerning Claire, though. 'Dad!' She stepped instinctively forward.

'I'll sort it,' Julia said, stepping smartly in front of her.

Claire watched as, her tone jolly, Julia placated her father, relieving him gently of the fork as she did so, and easing his other hand away from the sheepish-looking resident beside him. She was obviously used to such volatile situations.

'Back to your own dinner, Raymond,' she said, then, placing an arm around Bernard's shoulders, she encouraged him away from the table. 'Why don't we go and get your pudding, Bernard?' she suggested cheerily. 'It's apple pie and custard tonight.'

His face still flushed with indignation, Bernard looked her over. Claire could almost see the wheels going round as he scrambled for the thoughts in his head. Then, 'I detest apple pie and custard,' he said, his chin jutting, his gaze now fixed forward and his expression unimpressed.

Claire's heart dipped helplessly. That wasn't true. Apple pie and custard had always been one of his favourites. She so wanted to talk to him. After two days trying to pluck up the courage, that was her main reason for coming here tonight, but seeing how he was, how could she hope to get any sense out of him?

'In which case, I'll have it,' Julia responded, unperturbed. Giving his shoulders a squeeze, she smiled reassuringly back at Claire, and then dropped her gaze to Ella. 'There are some jigsaw puzzles in the day room you might like,' she said kindly. 'There's a Thomas the Tank Engine one I've been dying to have a go at. I'll be on my break in five minutes. Fancy helping me with it?'

Ella nodded timidly. 'Uh huh,' she said, looking as if she would far prefer Thomas the Tank Engine to a visit with her grandad.

Immensely grateful, Claire smiled back, then squeezed Ella's hand and led her along the corridor to the day room. She wouldn't bring her again, she decided, her heart swelling with an overwhelming sense of loss for the man she'd once thought her dad was. She didn't know him at all any more. She'd possibly never truly known him. That was her stark reality. He might not have physically pushed her mother, but he'd driven her to her death, Claire was growing certain of that. He must have known that by cheating on her, destroying their marriage, eroding her self-confidence, he was slowly killing her.

Pushing down the crushing hurt churning inside her, she fixed her smile in place as she chatted to Ella about the exciting prospect of Auntie Sophie coming to stay and helped her search through the various boxed games and jigsaws stored on the bookcase in the day room.

Five minutes later, Thomas the Tank Engine located, the pieces emptied onto the table and two of the four corners found, Julia came in. 'Crisis averted,' she assured Claire with a bright smile. 'He's in his room watching his favourite DVD. The one with Steve McQueen escaping from the Germans on a motorbike.'

'*The Great Escape*,' Claire supplied. She'd watched that film over and over with him. 'Do you think that's why he was trying to borrow the motorbike?' Julia rolled her eyes in amusement.

'Probably.' Claire smiled weakly. 'I'll just pop and say hello to Grandad,' she said to Ella. 'Will you be all right, sweetheart?'

'We'll be fine, won't we?' Julia said, settling herself in the chair Claire had just vacated. 'Ooh, look another corner.' She picked up a jigsaw piece delightedly. 'How many more do we need?'

'One,' Ella said decisively, and proceeded to palm through the rest of the pieces. 'I bet I find it first.'

Glad to leave her in Julia's capable hands, Claire headed on out and up the stairs to her father's room. His door was open a fraction. She tapped on it; pointlessly, she realised. Sitting in his chair, his hands resting on the wooden arms and his eyes glued to the TV, Bernard didn't even glance in her direction.

'Dad…' Claire approached him tentatively. 'How are you?'

No response. His gaze – glazed over, almost – was still fixed on the screen. Claire wondered if he was seeing what he was watching, or whether his mind had drifted off to some other place. 'I'm sorry I couldn't visit before,' she said, summoning up a smile. 'I took Ella away to spend some time with her.'

Bernard blinked. Other than that, he barely acknowledged her, but Claire was sure she saw a flicker of recognition cross his face. 'We went to Rhyl,' she announced, then took a deep breath. 'To see Sophie,' she added nervously.

Bernard's attention was still firmly on the TV, but the slight shift in his gaze told her something had registered.

'Do you remember her, Dad?' she asked. Mentally crossing her fingers, she pushed on. 'Sophie?'

This time, Bernard stiffened visibly. A deep furrow forming in his brow, he pulled himself more erect in his chair. Still he didn't acknowledge her. It was as if he was determined not to.

Don't do this, Dad. Please look at me. Claire had put this recent behaviour down to the disease, imagining his mind had wandered off to some place in his distant past. Now, she was sure that it had – to the very place she was so desperate to find out about – and that he could probably recall every detail. Determined to get through to him, to have him admit what he'd done, if nothing else, she crouched down in front of him, obscuring his view.

'Do you remember Cathy?' she asked him, her tone firm but, she hoped, not threatening. He couldn't leave her with so many unanswered questions. She needed to know he cared. That somewhere along the path he'd chosen to take, deceiving people, destroying lives, he'd considered the consequences.

He didn't reply; merely tightened his grip on the arms of his chair, a sure sign that he was agitated.

Cautioning herself to tread carefully, Claire placed a hand over one of his. She didn't want to panic him. 'Catherine Tyson. Do you remember her, Dad?'

She watched him carefully. He didn't react, but the two bright spots blooming on his cheeks told her he was hearing her. That on some level, what she was saying was having an impact.

'Did you know her well?' she forged on.

Bernard didn't answer, snatching up the TV remote from the table beside him instead.

'Dad!' Claire gritted her teeth as he pointed the remote around her and turned up the volume. '*Please* talk to me. I have to know.'

His expression that of a recalcitrant child, he increased the volume another notch and stared mutely ahead.

'Was it her that you and Mum argued about?' Frustration mounting, Claire almost shouted over the motorbike on the TV, which was revving too loudly in her head. 'Was Mum jealous?'

Though he seemed to resolutely ignore her, she was sure he understood her. There was something in his eyes. A spark of rebelliousness? Anger? Claire couldn't tell, but every instinct was screaming at her. He'd been lying, hiding the truth from her all these years. 'Was Mum jealous of Cathy? I need to *know*, Dad.' she implored him. 'You have to tell—'

Bernard yanked his hand from under hers, and stood abruptly, sending her sprawling back on her haunches. Momentarily stunned, she gathered herself and scrambled to her feet. He'd gone over to the window. His body tense, shoulders stiff, he stared out at the garden beyond.

'Dad…' She took a step towards him, stopping as he about-faced. His cheeks were ruddy, his expression thunderous. Claire took a faltering step back.

Bernard glowered at her for an interminably long minute, and then seemed to deflate where he stood, his tension dissipating to give way to what appeared to be a mixture of guilt and regret – and in that moment, Claire knew. Fear gripped her chest, her heart pumping inside it with shock and raw anger. Acrid grief kicked in fiercely – for the mother she hadn't been able to grieve the loss of properly because she'd blamed her; been angry with her for turning to alcohol as a crutch to help her through whatever she was suffering, for being so drunk she'd been unable to stop herself falling. Nausea swirling inside her, she heard it again and again, the wretched accusation that plagued her dreams: *It's your fault, you bastard. You drove me to it.* The dull *thud… thud… thud* of her mother's body bouncing off each step of the stairs, her limp figure lying twisted at the foot of them, her eyes fixed, pleading for the nightmare to end. For him to *stop.*

The strange yelp of fear, she heard that too, and the short loaded silence that followed it. She was back in the hall, her seven-year-old-self, holding her breath, holding the tears in; straining to listen, to see. And now she did see, with crystal clarity. The dream she'd had, the one that had been different: her mother's face ridden with guilt as she lay broken and still in the hall; the words she'd whispered: *I'm sorry, my darling. I tried to stop him.*

To stop his affair, Claire had thought, trying to interpret it when she'd woken. But what if she was wrong? She hadn't established exactly when Sophie's mother had died; whether it was before or after her own mother. What if was before? If her mother had succeeded in persuading him to end it, might he have been involved somehow in the tragedy that had befallen Sophie's mother?

But he *had* been involved. Hadn't Sophie said her mother's ex-boyfriend had been consumed with jealousy? That he might have killed her deliberately. She'd died because of Bernard. Her own mother had died because of him too. He had blood on his hands. Claire felt a surge of raw anger rise hotly inside her. It was an inescapable fact. Had he hit her before she fell, she wondered now; lashed out in the heat of the argument?

Her mother had been scared. Claire hadn't seen her teetering at the top of the stairs, but she'd heard her fear. She'd felt it. Her heart felt as if it might explode inside her as she stared hard at her father. He looked back at her, his expression one that she'd come to know and dread: bewilderment as he struggled to understand where he was in time and space, to recognise the people standing in front of him. Was it genuine? In this moment, was this his reality? Or was he hiding behind his illness to disguise his guilt? Because if he was, that was beyond cruelty.

'I did love her,' he said suddenly.

An icy shiver running through her, Claire narrowed her eyes. 'Who?' she managed, past the tight lump in her throat.

'Ruth,' he said. It was as if he'd heard every thought in her head.

Claire swallowed back the sour taste of her own fear. 'Did you hurt her?' she asked, holding his gaze.

Bernard didn't answer for a second. Then, 'I don't remember,' he said, the look in his eyes that of a frightened child.

'I have to go.' Claire could barely get the words out.

She was almost through the door when he asked, 'Will you come to see me again?'

She didn't answer this time. She couldn't.

'I thought you were my friend,' Bernard said, his tone forlorn, as she fled.

CHAPTER THIRTY-FOUR

Bernard

Bernard ignored the knock on his door, hoping that whoever it was would go away. Why was it they always insisted on spoiling the best bit of what he was watching? Sighing irritably, he dragged his eyes away from the TV screen as his caller pushed the door open and came in anyway. A member of staff, presumably. He noted the uniform as the woman passed by his armchair.

'Just me, Julia,' she said, going across to draw his curtains. 'Everything all right, Bernard?'

Had he seen her before? He tried to place her as she turned back to face him. He must have done, he supposed, since she was addressing him by name.

'Yes, thank you, dear. My daughter will be here soon,' he assured her, lest she settle down and start talking to him. They meant well, he was sure, popping in for a chat, but he would much rather watch the end of the film. It was good, gripping, reminding him of an event in his past he couldn't quite grasp.

'The one with the little girl, do you mean?' the woman asked him. 'She's just been, Bernard. She needed to go home and get her daughter to bed.'

Bernard arched an eyebrow curiously. *Little girl?* She was mistaken. Getting her confused with someone else. 'She doesn't have any children,' he said, and went back to the TV.

'Ah, you mean the other daughter,' the woman went on. Bernard really wished she wouldn't. He was struggling to concentrate. 'She seems a nice girl. Always ready with a cheery smile. It's a shame she wasn't able to help her sister out more. But then she does live quite a way away, I suppose. She's obviously making up for lost time now.'

'Yes.' Bernard frowned and tried to recall where it was she lived. Hearing the distinct chink of beer glasses, a peal of bubbly female laughter; seeing fleetingly in his mind's eye the salty froth of seawater lapping thirstily at the sand, he thought he'd pinpointed it, but it slipped away from him, as his recollections so often did.

'I was going to marry her,' he said nostalgically, his gaze drifting back to the woman, who paused in her bed-straightening to eye him interestedly.

'Her mother, do you mean?' she asked him, her look now one of surprise.

'It would have to have been a quiet wedding,' Bernard continued, guilt settling heavily inside him as pictures of a white wedding, bells chiming, confetti falling, Ruth smiling, played like an old movie reel through his mind. A different clip then, another woman, not smiling, no bubbly laughter. His chest constricted as her face came to him, her huge autumn-coloured eyes glassy with tears. 'It doesn't have to be a fancy affair, Bernie,' she said, wiping a trail of mascara from her cheek as she blinked hopefully at him. 'The registry office will do. Just me and you.'

'Two witnesses and a quiet lunch afterwards,' he added gruffly as he reminisced. 'She wouldn't have minded that. She was never greedy for material things. It was my company she wanted. Security, that was all.'

CHAPTER THIRTY-FIVE

Luke

Hearing Steve and Lauren arguing downstairs as he came out of the spare room, Luke guessed he'd outstayed his welcome. It was clear that it was him they were arguing about. He should go, though where to, he had no idea. His mother would put him up for a while if he asked her, but that was the last thing he wanted to do. He didn't get on with her partner. The bloke was a loser, treating her like a skivvy, sponging off her and boozing away her money. The way he was feeling, Luke doubted he could hold his temper for long around him.

He'd have to try to find somewhere else. A room to rent near Bernard's house, hopefully. He wanted to stay close to Ella. Desperately wanted to see her, check how she was and reassure her he would always be there for her. That day in the park when she'd got it into her head he might go away forever had almost torn him apart. He also needed to see Claire, try to talk to her. She was ignoring his texts, refusing to answer his calls. Why? His stomach twisted with anger and frustration. She was obviously taking Anna's word over his about the crap she'd texted her, and considered him some kind of threat.

He couldn't help thinking she was being influenced by someone. Gemma, maybe, who was probably her closest friend? The half-sister she'd found – a development Luke couldn't get his head around? Where the hell had she popped up from? Had Claire had some kind of previous contact with her? If she had, Luke had no idea how or when. She'd been caring for her father twenty-four hours a day recently. He had no idea what was going on.

His heart heavy with despair, he heaved out a sigh as the argument escalated downstairs, Lauren's agitated tones drifting up from the kitchen: 'We're newly married and we have an uninvited lodger in the house,' she pointed out tetchily. She was attempting to keep her voice down, but Luke could hear it as plain as day.

'Not uninvited, Lauren. *I* invited him,' Steve said, in Luke's defence.

'Yes, *before* asking *me*,' Lauren hissed.

'I asked you before I brought him in,' Steve argued, exasperated. 'You could have said no.'

'*How?* He was standing right outside the front door.' Lauren's voice went up an octave.

Steve didn't answer. There wasn't a lot he could say to that. Luke had indeed been standing outside the door. Lauren had been put on the spot.

'Three's a crowd, Steve.' Lauren now sounded utterly pissed off. 'We don't have any privacy. We can't talk. We can't even have *sex* without worrying about him overhearing. It's uncomfortable. *I'm* uncomfortable with him being here after what he's done, especially if he's here when you're not around.'

That hit Luke like a low blow to the stomach.

A loaded silence followed, then, 'He hasn't done anything, Lauren,' Steve said tightly. 'I've known Luke for ages. He's just not that type.'

'Right,' Lauren sounded unconvinced. 'And this is why he was questioned for hours at the police station? His girlfriend went missing! Running scared of him, no doubt.'

'It's bullshit,' Steve countered angrily. 'I'm telling you, Lauren, whatever this nutjob is accusing him of, it's all lies. I *know* Luke.'

'You don't know who he is behind closed doors. There's no smoke without fire, Steve. Something bloody well happened if the police were that involved.'

'He hasn't been charged with anything,' Steve reminded her wearily. 'They were questioning him, that's all.'

'*Exactly*. Why would they do that unless they thought he'd got something to answer for?' Lauren asked. Luke supposed she had a point. 'You have to tell him to leave,' she went on, finally getting to the crux of the argument. 'I know he's your best mate, but I just can't do this. If he doesn't go, then I will. I'll stay at Mum's or something. At least until he's gone.'

Time to make an exit, Luke decided, feeling sick to his gut as he descended the stairs. He couldn't just walk out without telling them he was going, though. That wouldn't be fair on Steve, who'd tried to be there for him.

'Today, Steve,' Lauren called after him as Steve came out of the kitchen to answer the landline in the hall, which had rung twice over the last ten minutes.

'All right. I've got the message, Lauren. I'll tell him,' Steve said over his shoulder, and then stopped, his face flushing with embarrassment, as he almost walked into Luke. 'Sorry, mate,' he mumbled, reaching for the phone. 'She doesn't mean anything by it. She just…'

'Wants her space back,' Luke supplied as Steve tailed off awkwardly. 'It's okay. I get it.' He forced a smile. 'I was going to let you know I'd decided to crash at my mother's for a while anyway.'

He did get it. Mud stuck. He was learning that fast. As far as Lauren was concerned, he was an abusive excuse of a man and she didn't want him anywhere near her.

Steve looked relieved as he pressed the phone to his ear. Then troubled. 'Who wants him?' he asked, his gaze gliding warily in Luke's direction.

A second later, he handed Luke the phone. 'I think it's her,' he said, shooting him a warning glance as he turned to walk back into the kitchen.

Luke didn't have time to speak before a female voice growled, 'Serves you right, you bastard.' And then she was gone. Anna. Undoubtedly her. Ringing for what purpose other than to fucking well torment him? She'd destroyed his marriage. She was trying to destroy *him*. Alienating him from everyone around him.

Claire. Luke felt his blood run cold. Why was Anna contacting her? Solely for the purpose of poisoning her mind against him? Or was there more to this?

'That was quick,' Steve said, coming back from the kitchen, plainly thinking he needed some support. 'Was it her?'

'It was her,' Luke confirmed, biting back the fury rising inside him. 'Did her details come up on the caller display?' he asked, praying that they had. He had tried to contact her repeatedly, but she had clearly ditched the phone he'd had the number for. The only hope he had of proving she was alive and well and making his life hell was the text she'd sent Claire, and that depended on the police being able to prove it had come from Anna.

Steve shook his head. 'Number withheld,' he said.

Luke clenched his jaw hard. 'I need to go,' he said, swinging back up the stairs to grab his stuff. He had to see Claire, whether she wanted to see him or not. If she wouldn't take his calls, wasn't at the house, then he'd go to the care home. She had to turn up somewhere sooner or later. He'd wait in the car until she did. He *had* to make her listen.

CHAPTER THIRTY-SIX

Claire

Claire's heart thudded as she crept down the stairs, wondering who would be knocking on the door at gone eleven thirty at night. Reaching the hall, she glanced worriedly back up the stairs, her mind on Ella. She was very aware that she was the only thing between her little girl and anyone intent on causing her harm. She would kill to protect her, instinctively, as any mother would, but she would be no match for some weapon-wielding maniac.

Might it be Luke? She hadn't answered any of his calls or texts, hoping he would get the message and give her some space, so he was probably bound to come looking. She wasn't sure she felt any more relieved at that thought.

Whoever it was knocked again as she deliberated whether to answer, causing her to almost part company with her skin. Hardly daring to breathe, she stepped hesitantly towards the front door, thanking God for the security chain and peephole her dad had installed and insisted she use. Guardedly, she peered out, and then gasped in disbelief.

Sophie? What on earth…? She hurriedly unhitched the chain and opened the door.

'I got the last train,' Sophie said tearfully. 'I'm so sorry, Claire. I couldn't stay there. I didn't know where else to go.'

Claire stepped out to usher her in. 'What happened?' she asked, shocked as she took in Sophie's bedraggled appearance, the bruising to her face, which had been obvious even in the dim glow of the security light.

'I... went out. With a man I know,' Sophie said haltingly. 'I've been out with him once before. We went back to my flat. He must have thought... but I didn't want to...' She stopped, her chest heaving as she gulped back a sob. 'I fought him, tried to run, but...'

'Oh God, Sophie.' Claire wrapped her arms around the other woman, allowing her to rest her head on her shoulder. 'Did he...?' she asked softly, as another sob racked Sophie's body.

Sophie shook her head. 'No, but...' She eased away to look at her. 'He caught up with me at the front door. He was so angry. I thought... I can't go back there, Claire,' she said, her voice trembling, her eyes shot through with fear. 'I have no idea what I'm going to do.'

'You can stay here. Ella's in with me tonight, so you can have her room,' Claire said decisively, placing an arm around Sophie's shoulders and steering her into the lounge. The spare room was full of bits and pieces from the cottage, and she wasn't sure Sophie would be comfortable in her father's bed, under the circumstances. She'd have to sort it out, make some space for her, at least for a while.

'But what about my flat? The neighbours will feed Cinder, but there's all my things.' Sophie seemed bewildered. 'And then there's the rent I owe.'

'There's no need to worry about all that now,' Claire assured her. 'We can sort it out later. Have you informed the police?'

Sophie shook her head, hard. 'I know I should, but... I can't, Claire. I'm so confused and scared. I just can't face it.'

Bastard. Claire felt fury bubble up inside her. That a man could do this to a woman was inconceivable. What went through their minds? She would try to persuade Sophie to report him, but from the look on her face, it wasn't going to be easy. She needed to rest, though Claire doubted very much she would sleep.

For now, though… Sophie had said she wanted to be part of Claire's family. Claire could make that happen; be there for her as Sophie had said she would be for Claire.

'I understand,' she said with a reassuring smile. 'Let's just get you tucked up in bed for tonight. We'll face the rest tomorrow. I'll have to have a reshuffle bedroom-wise, but there's plenty of room now that my father's not here.'

'Thanks, Claire.' Looking hugely relieved, Sophie managed a shaky smile. 'How is Bernard?' she asked, wincing slightly as she wiped a hand over her bruised face.

'Confused, but as well as he can be,' Claire answered honestly.

Sophie nodded, looking contemplative. 'Do you think I could go and visit him?' she asked. 'Tomorrow, maybe? It's been so long since I last saw him.'

Claire was hesitant. 'I'm not sure that's a good idea yet, to be honest. He might find it too upsetting. He doesn't recognise people any more. I honestly don't think he's likely to remember who you are,' she explained carefully.

Sophie searched her face, her huge brown eyes uncomprehending for a second, and then she looked tearful all over again.

'Leave it for a little while, I would,' Claire suggested kindly. 'I'm thinking it might be upsetting for you too. Why don't you see how you feel in a day or—'

She stopped, her heart almost leaping out of her mouth as she heard a noise from the hall that sounded like the front door hitting the chain. Panic clutching her stomach, she looked at Sophie.

'Luke?' Sophie asked, clearly also alarmed.

'It must be; he's the only one with a key.' Steeling herself for what was bound to be a fraught conversation, Claire turned for the hall.

'Let me go,' Sophie whispered behind her. 'I'll get rid of him.'

Claire doubted she would do that, given Luke's overreaction when she'd mentioned Sophie's existence. He'd be bound to demand to come in if he saw she was here. And judging by the fact that he'd used his key, evidently he thought he was entitled to come in. *Uh uh. Not on, Luke.* He'd made his bed and now he could lie in it, with or without the sexually exciting company he preferred.

'No, I don't want him bombarding me with questions if he sees you,' Claire whispered back. 'You stay here. Don't worry; if there's a problem, I won't hesitate to call the police.' Giving Sophie a reassuring nod, she headed into the hall.

'*Shit!*' She heard Luke curse from behind the door as he tried it again. 'Claire?' he called, at least making some attempt to keep his voice down. He'd remembered his daughter would be in bed, then.

'What are you doing here, Luke?' Claire hissed through the gap between door and frame. 'Have you been drinking?'

'No, I have not. I wouldn't come here drunk, for Christ's sake. What do you take me for?'

Apart from a cheat and a liar and a manipulator? 'Asks the man who had a drunken fight with a defenceless old man right outside his daughter's bedroom door.'

Luke shook his head. 'That's not fair, Claire, and you know it.'

'It's *midnight*,' Claire said, exasperated. 'Gone midnight. You'll wake—'

'I *know* what time it is,' Luke cut in. 'What the hell do you expect me to do? You won't answer my texts or calls. I drive over, you're not here. I've been to the care home. I've been going out of my mind with—'

'The care home? At this time of night?' Claire eyed him quizzically.

'Let me in, Claire,' Luke said with a heavy sigh. 'I need to talk to you.'

She looked at him apprehensively. 'About?'

'Anna,' Luke announced, stunning her. 'I need to talk to you properly, face to face. I'm worried—'

'No,' Claire said adamantly. Did he really think she wanted to discuss *her*? What did he want? Advice? A shoulder to cry on? The man was mad. 'You need to go, Luke,' she warned him. 'If you don't, I'll call the police.'

'For fu—' Luke sucked in a terse breath. Holding it, he glanced skywards, and then looked back at her, his expression now one of weary disappointment. 'Please let me in,' he said, his tone quieter. 'It's urgent. I wouldn't be here otherwise.'

'Urgent, as in you need to make sure I go to the station and give a statement?' Claire asked him. She had no doubt he would be concerned about that.

'No!' he exclaimed.

'Don't worry, I've already been,' she informed him. 'I went as soon as I got back from Rhyl in the hope that you would stop bothering me.'

'Bothering you?' Luke baulked.

'Bothering me, yes. So now you've established that I've done what you wanted, you can stop, can't you?' Claire looked him over, disillusioned. How could she have lived with this man and never truly known him? Given what she'd now learned about her father, she was plainly a rubbish judge of character.

'Jesus!' Luke ran a hand agitatedly over his face. 'My being here has nothing to do with that. This is stupid, Claire. Can we not just talk inside?'

Liar. 'Go, Luke.' She made to close the door, but he moved faster, catching her unawares as he stepped forward to block it with his foot.

Her heart jumping, Claire met his gaze, and what she saw there shook her. She could feel the heat from his eyes as they drilled angrily into hers. 'I need to talk to you,' he repeated, his tone now worryingly quiet. 'Please let me in.'

Swallowing back a knot of fear, she scrambled for a way to make him leave. And then closed her eyes with relief as the downstairs loo flushed behind her. *Well done, Sophie.* 'You need to go, Luke,' she reiterated forcefully. 'I have someone here.'

Luke's look turned to one of shock, then he narrowed his eyes. 'Who?'

'A friend.' She summoned her courage, and prayed fervently that this wouldn't turn ugly. 'A male friend. You really should go now. I don't want Ella upset again.'

'A…?' He stepped back from the door. 'You're… seeing someone?' he asked, his expression incredulous.

'Yes.' Her nerves jangling, Claire waited. Prayed harder.

'I see.' Luke nodded slowly, and then emitted a cynical laugh. 'Didn't take you long, did it? Not that devastated about what I *supposedly* did then? Seems to me you couldn't wait to get shot of me. Is that why you moved your father into the care home so fast, I wonder, so you could move that bastard in?'

Claire felt anger explode inside her. 'Piss off, Luke. *Now!*'

'Don't worry, I'm going,' he assured her. 'Do me a favour. Don't fuck him in the bed I couldn't get near you in, hey?' Dragging a disdainful gaze over her, he turned and stormed away.

CHAPTER THIRTY-SEVEN

Sophie

'You are sure your mum likes scrambled eggs?' Sophie asked Ella early the next morning.

Pulling the bowl from the microwave, she examined the contents uncertainly. It didn't look appetising. She was going to have to brush up on her cooking skills if she was going to impress Claire. She desperately wanted to do that; prove she could be helpful and gain her complete trust. She needed to gain her trust where Bernard was concerned, too. She was sure Claire had only had everyone's best interests at heart advising her not to see him, but she'd actually found that a bit hurtful. She'd decided not to say anything. Claire had been his sole carer, after all. She would hate her to think she was challenging her.

'Uh huh.' Ella nodded across from the table, where she was busily arranging the breakfast tray. She'd been thrilled at the idea of allowing her overworked mummy an extra hour in bed while she and Sophie cooked breakfast together to take up to her. She'd even insisted on going out into the garden to pluck a barely open rose for her. She was a pleasant little thing. The two of them would get along fine.

'I'm not sure she'll like mine.' Sophie sighed, thinking her efforts looked more like egg soup.

'You just have to give it a few more minutes, like Mummy does,' Ella informed her knowledgeably, leaving Sophie feeling a bit deflated. Was it her fault she'd had nobody interested enough in her to show her the basics in the kitchen? Her gran's idea of haute cuisine was to pour curry sauce on her chips.

Whamming the bowl back in and setting the timer, she tried to resign all that to history. It only ever upset her to think about it.

'Did you stir it?' Ella asked, pausing in her folding of kitchen towel into napkins.

'Drat. No, I didn't. Thank God for someone who knows what they're doing.' Sophie indulged her, rolling her eyes theatrically and pulling the microwave door open.

She was about to dip the spoon into the bowl when Ella piped up, 'You have to use a fork. Mummy says it fluffs it up better.'

Does it indeed. Well, pardon me. Suppressing another sigh, Sophie ditched the spoon and grabbed a fork. Plainly Ella's mother was competent in all areas. An art therapist, helping special needs children to express their emotions through their art, doting daughter, loving mother loved by her own doting daughter. Not so great at holding on to her husband, though. But then she was well shot of him. Men were all the same in Sophie's experience. What was utterly incomprehensible to her was that they imagined they had a right to abuse women. Even when you indulged their warped little fetishes, they had to push the boundaries. Peter had ignored her safe word. It had been bloody infuriating, even if the resultant bruising had worked in her favour.

Dutifully stirring the eggs – possibly a little too aggressively – she beamed Ella a smile, then bunged them back in. After wiping up the slimy gunk that had spilled onto the work surface and popping the bread in the toaster, she was about to make the coffee when someone knocked on the front door. *Hell.* Sophie froze. She hoped it wasn't Luke come to harass Claire again.

Heading tentatively for the hall, she was wondering what do when she saw Claire padding barefoot down the stairs.

'Was that the door?' Claire blinked groggily. God, she looked exhausted, as if she'd slept the sleep of the dead, pale and disorientated, her hair sticking out at all angles. It was a great colour: scorching red. The cut, not so great. It would look good short. Sophie might suggest it.

She'd thought Claire would sleep well. She'd been yawning her head off last night after their chat about Bernard, during which she had asked a few questions Sophie suspected might have been designed to test her. She knew enough about him to allay any lingering suspicions, of course: when he'd started his job as regional sales manager, what colour suits he liked to wear. Telling her he'd hated the endless lonely road trips he'd had to undertake had clinched it. Claire had agreed with that, confiding that he sometimes took her along with him for company.

Sophie herself hadn't slept. She rarely did. The second she began to drift off, it would emblazon itself on her mind: her mother's body, suspended in petrified limbo for an instant before the fireball consumed her, eating her whole, flames licking and spitting and peeling the flesh from her body. Her scream of pure primal fear resonated through her, causing her blood to thrum through her body, her throat to constrict and the air to be snatched from her lungs. Her Sindy doll was the worst. Sophie could see herself as a child standing over it in her gran's kitchen. It had been with her mother's effects. Her gran had kept it in a shoebox, which she'd left out one day. Sophie had never been sure why she'd done that. Why she would do that to a child. Sindy's beautiful blonde hair had been scorched to a crisp, one side of her flawless face blackened and blistered and melted.

With those images haunting her, she'd had no hope of finding solace in sleep last night. She'd slipped out of bed in the end, once she was sure Claire was asleep, and taken the opportunity to familiarise herself with her surroundings. She'd found some of Claire's concealer in the bathroom. That had been useful. She hadn't wanted to scare little Ella with her bruised face. Her search of Bernard's office had definitely been fruitful.

'I was just going to answer it,' Sophie glanced from Claire towards the door, as whoever was out there tapped on it again, 'but I wasn't sure whether you wanted me to with...' She paused, shrugging awkwardly. 'You know, the situation with your husband.'

'It's fine.' Claire gave her a reassuring smile. 'It's just Gemma.'

Oh yes? And who's Gemma? Sophie strained to peer past her as Claire pulled the door open and a woman with blonde, bouncy hair and a glowing complexion stepped in to pull her into a hug. A friend then, presumably.

'Sorry I couldn't get over sooner,' the woman said, stepping back after a second. 'I've been up to my eyes with wedding arrangements. How are you, sweetheart?' she asked, her face creasing into a concerned frown as she looked Claire over. 'I can't believe you've had such a shitty time.'

Not a very caring friend, Sophie decided. Too busy plucking and preening and spending a fortune on silly wedding dresses to keep in touch.

'I'm fine.' Claire smiled stoically. 'Coping.'

'Bullshit. You look absolutely drained,' Gemma said. She was clearly not one to mince her words – and clearly also totally thoughtless. Who wanted to hear that, for God's sake? 'Come on, tell me all about it.' Hooking an arm through one of Claire's, she all but dragged her in the direction of the lounge.

Sophie, who was loitering outside the kitchen door at the end of the hall, almost stepped back out of sight, but decided to stay where she was. She was entitled to be here, after all. Just because she'd spent most of her life feeling unwanted didn't mean she was now.

'Oh.' Noticing her, Gemma stopped and blinked, surprised.

'This is Sophie, my half-sister,' Claire introduced her, smiling in Sophie's direction.

'Ah,' said Gemma, her gaze immediately travelling judgementally over her, which did nothing to impress Sophie. 'Pleased to meet you, Sophie.' She manufactured a smile and extended a hand. 'Gemma, Claire's best friend. You don't mind if we have a private chat, do you?'

'No, not at all.' Shaking her hand, Sophie smiled brightly. 'I'll keep an eye on Ella. She's making you breakfast.' Hoping that would hurry her up, she offered Claire a smile back and then took her leave.

Once inside the kitchen, she waited for the lounge door to close, as she'd guessed it would, and then went over to Ella. 'Mummy's friend's here,' she whispered, gesturing towards the lounge wall. 'Do you fancy playing a game on my iPad until she's gone?'

Ella's eyes widened in delight. Sophie took that as a yes. 'Do you have Disney Crossy Road?' she asked, abandoning the breakfast tray and scrambling down from the table.

'Do you know how to play it?' Sophie asked.

'Yes.' Ella skipped excitedly alongside her as Sophie led her to the stairs. 'My friend has it. It's a bit like Froggy. You have to make sure you don't fall in the river or get flattened by a train.'

'Sounds delightful.' Sophie smiled, relieved. That should keep her occupied for a while. 'Let's see if we can download it, shall we?'

Minutes later, the app downloaded and Ella sitting happily on her bed with the iPad, Sophie dashed back downstairs to eavesdrop – in Claire's best interests, of course. She wasn't sure a friend who couldn't be arsed to be there for her would truly have her well-being at heart.

Which obviously she hadn't. Standing outside the lounge door, ready to bolt back to the kitchen if it opened, Sophie bristled with indignation as she listened to Gemma's advice. 'Just be careful is all I'm saying. You don't know that much about her, after all.' The woman, who was plainly jealous, was already trying to turn Claire against her.

'She's okay,' Claire assured her. 'I don't know her that well yet, admittedly, but she's great with Ella. She probably saved her life. I can't imagine a woman who would instinctively throw herself into the sea to rescue a child would ever wish anyone harm.'

'That's as maybe,' Gemma went on, as if Ella's life was an insignificant nothing, 'but what's she doing here, Claire?'

'She made contact on Facebook,' Claire said, sounding confused. 'I told you.'

'Yes, but why now?'

Claire hesitated. 'Because of Dad's condition. I'd hardly have expected her not to once she realised that he might not be around for much longer.'

'Precisely. Have you considered that she might be after what she can get? Funds from the house, for instance,' Gemma suggested, causing Sophie's heart to pitter-patter frantically in her chest.

'But a huge chunk of the proceeds will have to go towards meeting the care home fees,' Claire pointed out. 'And anyway, she'd need proof of identity, wouldn't she?'

'Which can easily be obtained via a DNA test,' Gemma pointed out, feeding Claire ideas. As if she had some right to come here and turn her world upside down. Sophie couldn't believe Claire was listening to her. 'She won't even need that if Bernard's named her in his will, though. Have you checked it?'

'He wouldn't have done that,' Claire scoffed. 'Not without telling me.'

'It strikes me there are one or two things Bernard forgot to tell you about. Well, certainly one thing,' was Gemma's droll retort. 'Where does he keep it, do you know?'

'In his study, I think.' Claire now sounded flustered.

'I'd find it if I were you.' Gemma's tone was dour.

This was absolutely the last thing Sophie needed. The woman was trying to influence Claire, poison her mind against her. Paling, she backed away from the door.

'Look, Claire, I can't stop now,' Gemma announced. 'I have the bridesmaids' dress fittings to get to, but before I go, about Luke…'

Luke? Sophie's eyes sprang wide. Surely she wasn't going to poke her nose in there as well.

'Don't you think you might be judging him too harshly?' Gemma went on. 'I mean, I know he's been a bit of an idiot, but—'

'A bit of an idiot?' Claire laughed, incredulous. 'He cheated on me with some slut! It was you who sent me the photo.'

'I know I did.' Gemma sighed expansively. 'I meant about what happened afterwards. Have you given him a chance to explain? To tell his side of the story? I know he's cocked up, majorly, but…'

Time to intervene, Sophie decided. And then make an excuse to go out. She would have to now, urgently, thanks to this interfering cow.

'… he's always seemed to be such a nice person,' Gemma bleated on. 'To genuinely care for you and Ella.'

Care, my arse. Sophie stepped forward, rapping quickly on the door and going in. 'Sorry to interrupt.' She smiled apologetically at the friend Claire would be considerably better off without, then turned her gaze towards Claire herself. 'Ella's upstairs, playing a game on my iPad,' she said, making sure Claire realised *she'd* been concerned with her daughter's welfare, while her *friend* appeared to be oblivious to her existence. 'It's just that I have to pop out to the chemist for a prescription.'

'Oh no. You're not poorly, are you?' Claire looked at her, concerned. Put that in your pipe and smoke it, Gemma, Sophie thought, pleased. *She* was the one who was close to Claire now.

'No, nothing drastic,' she assured her. 'I had a chest infection a while back and it's lingered a bit. It's just that I forgot all about the antibiotics I was supposed to pick up, and as I've had a couple of bouts of pneumonia in the past…'

Now Claire looked stricken. 'God, Sophie! You'd better go and get them. There's a chemist on the high street.'

Walking towards the door, Gemma stopped in front of her. 'I'm just leaving,' she said, her eyes narrowed. 'I could give you a lift if you like?'

'That's really kind of you, but I actually think I quite fancy the walk.' Sophie declined the offer graciously. 'Plus, it's probably a good idea for me to find my way around now I'm staying.'

Offering Gemma another bright smile, she swung around, walking up the hall to grab her coat and bag from the pegs. She'd no intention of going anywhere near the chemist. Something else had just come up.

CHAPTER THIRTY-EIGHT

Gemma

Gemma's mind was still on Claire as she approached the village just outside Knowle where White Rose Wedding Gowns was located. She was worried about her friend, extremely. She looked utterly drained, and no wonder with all she had going on. She'd practically gone into hibernation while she'd been caring for her dad. She'd had no social life. Not many trips to the hairdresser or the shopping centre either from the looks of her. Poor thing. She needed to start looking after herself a bit more.

And what was the deal with this Sophie turning up out of the blue? Gemma had known Claire since they'd got their first job together, and she'd never even mentioned her. She was probably being judgemental, thinking Sophie might have made an appearance before if she was any kind of a sister, but there was something… Gemma couldn't put her finger on it, but she didn't like her. She had an idea the feeling was mutual. The woman had smiled readily enough, but there hadn't been any warmth in it. Might she be a bit jealous? Possibly. Whatever, Gemma intended to keep an eye on things. Claire really should get a DNA test done. Sophie wouldn't object if she was genuine. And she should make sure she had power of attorney over Bernard's affairs.

Making a mental note to ring her about that later, she headed along the main road into the village, and then hit the brakes, staring ahead disbelieving. They had to be joking. Roadworks? Right outside the only bloody car park. Typical.

Miffed, she turned around on the pub forecourt and went in search of a parking space, of which there were few. The parking was a major drawback, but otherwise the bridal shop was perfect, promising made-to-measure, bespoke bridalwear that was guaranteed to be completely unique. *Having an award-winning and creative dress designer is not cheap*, their online brochure said, *but we believe you're worth every penny.*

They were right about the not-cheap bit. She'd spent a *lot* of pennies. You'd think they'd use some of their designer prices to provide a car park for their customers. At this rate she'd miss the fitting altogether.

Forced to park miles away, down some obscure side street, she climbed out of her car and hurried back towards the main road, cursing the drizzle as she went. Her hair would be like candyfloss by the time she got there. She planned to have the full works the day before the wedding: spa, facial, hair treatment, the lot. She'd book Claire in for a treat, too. Her half-sister could help her out, which as far as Gemma could see she'd done precious little of in the past, and look after Ella while her mum had some necessary therapy.

Pulling her phone from her pocket, she selected one of her bridesmaids' numbers and stepped off the kerb, checking quickly for traffic. 'Sorry, Amy, the parking is hell,' she said. 'I'll be there in two… *Ouch!*'

She hissed out another curse as she went over painfully on her ankle. *Bloody shoes*. She'd seen them in the sale and couldn't resist them. It would be nice if she could actually walk in them. Glancing down, she attempted to reacquaint foot with mule, and then snapped her gaze sharply back up.

She didn't have time to scream before the car catapulted her into the air. She didn't even have time to wonder what had hit her before her body landed, her bones jarring excruciatingly painfully on impact with the tarmac. There was blood in her nose, in her mouth; she could taste it, warm, metallic. It was everywhere, bleeding into the ground beneath her. It was bound to be in her hair. It would take her ages to wash it out.

'Gemma? *Gemma!*' a disembodied voice called frantically from the phone at her fingertips.

Help me, she pleaded silently, her eyes clouding over as she watched the car disappear into the distance.

CHAPTER THIRTY-NINE

Julia

Julia was taking the opportunity to have a quick cigarette break. She smiled from under her umbrella as Bernard's daughter hurried towards her at the entrance of the care home, obviously keen to be out of the rain.

'Nice weather we're having.' Julia eyed the bulbous grey skies overhead.

'For ducks.' Running her hand through her short hair, the woman smiled shyly back, then turned her attention to her phone.

It was nice that she'd popped in again, Julia thought. It was heartbreaking when folk were abandoned here and then only visited once in a blue moon when relatives' consciences got the better of them. Some of the residents might have forgotten who their relatives were, but it didn't stop them feeling lonely, wandering aimlessly around looking for their missing memories. Bernard certainly hadn't been abandoned. He'd had his fair share of visitors in the short time he'd been here. The two sisters, whose names she got mixed up. The young man who'd said he was his son-in-law. He'd been two or three times, though he hadn't stayed long. Julia couldn't blame him. Bernard was openly rude to him. Why people bothered with him at all, she wasn't sure. He was a cantankerous old bugger.

'He's in his room,' she called after the woman. 'He refused breakfast this morning on the basis that it wasn't fit for pigswill.'

'God, he's a pain, isn't he?' the woman called back with a despairing shake of her head.

'Oh, he's definitely that,' Julia assured her good-naturedly. 'Not to worry. It keeps us entertained. You might want to grab him a cuppa and some bickies from the day room on your way up.'

'Will do.' The woman waved her phone over her shoulder and hurried on.

Twenty minutes later, Julia was on her way to the day room herself to serve the other residents tea when Bernard's daughter came back down the stairs. 'That was quick,' she said. 'Is he not in the mood for company?'

'In a mood, yes. For company, definitely no.' The woman sighed despairingly. 'He prefers his DVD to me, apparently.

The Great Escape, Julia remembered. When he was in his room, Bernard was superglued to his TV. But then, many of the residents were. She suspected the images on screen kept their minds occupied, reminding them of happier times and places they could relate to. 'I'm not sure whether it's Steve McQueen he's most fascinated by or the motorbike scene,' she said. 'He plays it over and over.'

His daughter looked sadly reflective at that. 'The motorbike, I think,' she said with a small smile. 'He still has his old bike in the garage. He's probably hankering after the days when he could impress the women with it.'

'Ooh.' Julia made knowing eyes at her. 'A ladies' man, hey?'

'He liked to think so,' the woman said, her smile now definitely on the melancholic side. 'I'm not sure Mum was overly impressed, though.'

'Oh dear.' Recalling the conversation she'd had with Bernard about the woman he'd been going to marry, Julia felt immediately contrite. 'I'd better not rib him about it then. Sorry if I've touched on a sore subject.'

'You haven't,' the woman assured her, with an unconcerned shrug. 'It's ancient history now. I'd better get off.' She smiled more easily and headed for the door.

'See you soon.' Julia called after her. 'Pass on my best to your sister.'

'Will do,' the woman called back.

Such a sad little thing. Julia watched her walk to her car, feeling for her. It was at times like this, watching someone's personality slip away, that relatives tended to reflect on the person they once were. Bernard Harvey had a history regarding his love life, it seemed. The sisters were similar in age, she guessed, but not that alike in looks. Could it be that they had different mothers? Somehow, Julia wouldn't be surprised to learn that Bernard Harvey had been a womaniser. He must have been quite good-looking in his heyday.

CHAPTER FORTY

Luke

Peeling open one grainy eyelid, Luke rolled over on the bed in his mother's spare room, and then winced as a hangover the size of a bus hit him. Served him right, he supposed, staring up at the ceiling, which had spun so nauseatingly above him when he'd crawled in here last night, it was all he could do to heave himself out again to the bathroom. He very nearly hadn't made it before he'd thrown up. The booze he'd purchased from the Tesco twenty-four-hour store hadn't been one of his brightest ideas. How the hell had he even got here?

His memory unobliging, he sifted through the soggy cotton wool in his head, and was relieved when he remembered that he'd found at least one brain cell and walked, or rather woven, here, leaving his car in the centre of town. He'd had a row with Derek, his mother's waste-of-space partner, when he'd arrived. He squeezed his eyes shut as his mind started to function, offering up a jagged recollection of their tussle in the hall. Luke had been seething with fury, ready to put the guy's teeth down his throat when he'd heard him call his mother a *silly fucking bitch* for letting him in. If he hadn't been so paralytic he could barely stand up, he might have done it, which – whilst highly satisfying after so many years watching the man disrespect her – would have been pretty stupid given his circumstances. As it was, all he'd succeeded in doing was getting an almighty crack to the jaw.

Running his tongue over the inside of his cheek, which was bloody sore, Luke sighed in complete despair at himself. Christ, he was a mess. Getting plastered was really going to help, wasn't it? But he'd needed to. He'd wanted to render himself unconscious; fall so deep into inebriated sleep he would forget that he and Claire were finished, despite the ridiculous hopes he'd been harbouring that they might get back together. She hated him. It was right there in her pretty green eyes just as surely as the love she'd once had for him used to be.

She'd found someone else. Swallowing back the sour taste of alcohol and bitter regret, Luke forced himself not to give in to the tears he felt like crying, which really would sum up how pathetic he was.

She wasn't letting him see Ella. He couldn't allow that. Right now, his baby girl was his only reason for living, the reason his heart kept beating. Whoever Claire was seeing, there was no way he wasn't going to have regular contact with his own daughter.

Heaving himself up, determined to try again to talk to her – to get down on his knees and beg her to listen if he had to – Luke hitched his legs over the side of the bed and massaged his temples, then buried his head in his hands, trying to still the nausea still churning his stomach, the throbbing like a pneumatic drill at the base of his skull. She'd moved on pretty damn fast, he reminded himself angrily, which meant he'd probably missed the signals telling him she'd wanted to. But then had he? He hadn't been able to do a thing right in Claire's eyes while they'd been living with Bernard: always in the way, which was why he'd figured it didn't much matter if he went out once Ella was in bed.

Was he there now? With his daughter? Some bloke he had no clue about staying overnight in his bed? How well did Claire know him? Well enough, obviously. He must have been blind.

Pulling himself to his feet, Luke steadied himself, reached for his shirt and tugged it on, then checked his jeans, which he'd ended up sleeping in, for his car keys. He would still be over the limit. The last thing he needed with the police on his case was to get pulled over. Worse, cause an accident and injure someone, or end up making Ella's worst fears come true and leaving her forever.

He couldn't let his baby girl down. Watch her growing up from a distance. He had been there himself. He'd tried to tell himself he didn't care, that it didn't matter, but it had. He'd felt like a complete failure when his father had walked away. That he wasn't enough to make him stay. His mother had tried to convince him the failure was his father's, not his. Luke hadn't believed her. He couldn't bear for Ella to feel like that: deserted, lonely, wondering what it was she'd done wrong.

He needed to see her. Needed to take a shower and get his damn act together. Hopefully he could do that and leave without encountering Derek. He really was not in the mood for another confrontation with him, which there would be if he had to listen to any more of his derogatory comments.

Ten minutes later, fresher, though still feeling sick and his head still banging, he hurried downstairs, hoping the lazy git was still in bed, where he usually was until mid morning, and that his mother was on her own so he could say goodbye to her. Apologise, too, for turning up on her doorstep drunk. He soon realised that Derek wasn't in bed. And whether he wanted to listen or not, Luke couldn't fail to overhear him in full bullying mode.

'Where's the rest?' he heard him growl from behind the partially open kitchen door.

Luke knew exactly what he was after: his mother's pension, which the bastard would then piss up the wall, after a visit to the betting shop en route to the pub.

'There *is* no more,' his mother said agitatedly, 'not unless you don't want to eat. Give that back.'

Luke pushed the door open, his anger simmering dangerously inside him as he took in the scene before him: his mother, who was no more than five foot four, trying to snatch her purse back; Derek holding it aloft, pulling everything out and tossing anything that wasn't of value aside before pocketing whatever paper money he found.

Luke's jaw tensed, his fists clenching at his sides as he watched his mother scrabbling around trying to retrieve her personal belongings. 'Leave it, Mum,' he said, his throat tight.

His mother looked up at him, and then at Derek, who glanced dismissively in his direction while grabbing half a slice of toast from a plate on the work surface and cramming it into his mouth.

'Get up, Mum.' Luke tried very hard to keep his temper in check as Derek sauntered towards him licking his fingers.

'Luke, leave it.' His mother paused in collecting up the few coins he'd left her. 'Don't start anything, please,' she begged.

Luke's gut twisted, his anger rising white-hot inside him as Derek locked eyes with him, a smirk curving his mouth. 'He'll pick it up,' he said, holding the man's gaze.

Derek looked mildly surprised for a second, then, 'Right,' he said, with a scornful laugh. 'And you're going to make me, are you?'

Luke answered with a short nod. 'That's right.'

'Yeah, yeah.' Derek sneered mockingly. 'You and whose fucking army? Move,' he said, stopping in front of him.

Too close. Luke could see the map of red veins in his eyes, smell the stale booze and the cigarettes he chain-smoked on his breath. His stomach curdled, but he didn't move.

'I said *shift*.' Derek pushed past him, shoving him hard as he did.

Luke stumbled back, felt for the hall wall behind him. Steadying himself, he wiped the back of his hand over his mouth and watched the man swagger up the hall, totting up the amount he'd stolen as he went. His rage exploded inside him.

'Luke! *Don't!*' his mother screamed as he took off, following Derek through the front door to see the older man breaking into a run, despite the beer gut he was carrying.

He caught up with him easily a few yards from the house. 'Say your prayers, you bastard,' he grated, sliding an arm around the man's shoulders, yanking it upwards and locking it tight with his free hand.

Derek grasped at his arm, clawed at it with his fingers. Luke felt the man's Adam's apple bob in his throat, heard the audible wheeze as he gasped for breath. He squeezed tighter.

'Luke!' His mother was behind him, tugging at his shirt, trying to pull him off. 'Luke! For God's sake, you'll *kill* him!'

He wanted to kill him. He really wanted to. His heart banged against his chest.

'Luke… *please*.' His mother was crying now. Luke heard her from a distance. The drone of a police siren, growing closer; he heard that too. Then nothing but the thrum of his own blood whooshing in his veins.

Through the thick red fog in his head, he noticed curiously that Derek was lying motionless on the grey tarmac, his complexion a strange shade of blue. Then two pairs of hands wrestled him away.

CHAPTER FORTY-ONE

Claire

Claire checked the peephole before opening the front door.

'Is it Auntie Sophie, Mummy?' Ella asked, emerging from the kitchen, Sophie's iPad clutched in her hands. Judging by the eager jiggling and the glint in her eye, she was excited to see her.

'It is.' Claire smiled, but she was concerned that Ella seemed to have bonded so strongly with Sophie. She was an only child. A lonely child, missing her father and her grandfather, therefore emotionally vulnerable. She was going to have to keep a careful eye on things, Claire realised.

'Yay!' Ella made no secret of her delight. 'I want to show her how good I am at Disney Crossy Road,' she said, squeezing through the front door almost before Claire had opened it.

'Hang on. Let her get in first.' Claire laughed, easing her gently out of the way.

'Auntie Sophie, Auntie Sophie, I won a Mickey Mouse,' Ella exclaimed, as soon as Sophie stepped over the threshold. 'And I've got lots of gold coins.'

'Wow! Well done you.' Sophie widened her eyes in mock amazement. 'I can see I'm going to have to brush up on my skills before challenging you to a game.'

Ella glowed with pride at that. 'I could teach you,' she said enthusiastically. 'And I'll give you a chance, obviously,' she added with an important little nod, as she twirled back to the kitchen.

Claire and Sophie exchanged amused glances, and then both laughed at once. 'She's growing up fast,' Claire sighed, her mind going to Luke and how much he would miss of her childhood. She desperately wanted Ella to have contact with him, but how could she countenance that after his recent behaviour?

'Did you get them?' she asked, following Sophie up the hall.

'Sorry?' Heading into the kitchen, Sophie dropped her bag on the worktop and turned to her, puzzled.

'The antibiotics?' Claire clarified, going over to put the kettle on.

'Ah.' Sophie nodded. 'Yes. Thanks. All sorted. I was thinking that next time I go into town, I should maybe get an extra key cut,' she said, walking across to the cupboard for mugs. 'You know, so you won't worry…' She stopped, glancing over her shoulder at Ella, who'd climbed back up onto her chair at the table. Her attention was glued to the iPad, Claire noted. She was going to have to keep her eye on that too. '… every time anyone knocks at the door,' Sophie finished diplomatically.

Claire was about to say she wasn't worrying, but the truth was, she was. She had no idea what was going on with Luke. She was angry, confused. Part of her was convinced that the man she knew would never do the things he'd been accused of. Another part of her simply couldn't believe they were fabricated. Luke had admitted that he and Anna had fought, after all, and a woman didn't gouge a man's face with her fingernails without good reason. She blinked back a tear as the steam from the water she was pouring into the mugs stung her eyes.

'I could get one cut on my way back, if you like?' Sophie offered, fetching the milk from the fridge.

'Way back?' Claire glanced at her curiously.

'I have to go back to Rhyl,' Sophie said, looking nervous. 'I'd rather not, but I have to get Cinder.'

'Cinder?' That got Ella's attention. 'Are you bringing her here, Auntie Sophie?'

'Only if Mummy doesn't mind.' Sophie glanced hopefully at Claire. 'Sorry,' she shrugged apologetically, 'but I'm a bit stuck.'

Noticing her worried expression, Claire smiled. 'Of course you can bring her here. Will you be all right going back on your own, though?'

'I'll be fine,' Sophie assured her. 'I'll be in and out in no time.'

'As long as you're sure.' Claire searched her face. She looked confident enough, but still… She wished she'd reported the assault to the police. 'You don't have to keep apologising, by the way, Sophie. And don't worry about getting a key cut. I have Dad's key,' she added, not quite able to keep the sadness from her voice.

'God, of course,' Sophie said, visibly wincing. 'I'm sorry. I should have thought.'

'You don't have to keep apologising, Auntie Sophie.' Ella slid off her chair to walk across and take hold of her hand. 'Mummy said so.' She blinked up at her, looking far more mature than her four years. She couldn't hide much from her, Claire realised. She was bound to start asking more questions about Luke soon. She was dreading that.

Sophie squeezed Ella's hand. 'I'll try not to,' she said, smiling affectionately down at her.

Claire couldn't help feeling concerned. Sophie was caring, helpful. Her fondness for Ella was obvious. Still, she worried about Ella growing too close to her. 'Come on,' she said, dismissing her anxieties for now. 'Time for an Oreo treat, I think.'

'*Yippee.*' Ella skipped back to the table, while Claire poured her a glass of milk and opened the cookies, and Sophie carried their drinks over.

Sophie reached for a biscuit, while Ella grabbed two, clutching them to her chest and making beguiling eyes at Claire.

'Just this once,' Claire said, wearing her best admonishing look. Her daughter was definitely taking advantage while Sophie was here. She really was going to have to keep eyes on her.

'I was thinking,' Sophie said, prising her Oreo apart to get to the middle bit, Ella imitating her every move, 'I could help you go through Bernard's things, if you'd like me to.'

Claire looked at her guardedly. She wasn't sure she wanted her involved in that. Half-sister or not, it felt like too much of an invasion into things that were personal; her memories of her father, some of which she dearly hoped she could salvage from a past that was now hopelessly tarnished.

'I noticed his motorbike in the garage,' Sophie went on. 'He was always talking about that. He came to Rhyl on it once when I was little, gave me a ride. I was scared to death, to be honest, but I didn't let on.'

He had gone off on one or two of his road trips on it, years ago, Claire recalled, a sudden stab of jealousy piercing her heart. It was painful. How could it not be, knowing now that he'd left her behind to be with his other daughter? 'I remember,' she said, placing her own cookie back on the plate. She no longer had much of an appetite.

Sophie reached across the table to squeeze her hand. 'I know you'll have your private memories, Claire,' she said intuitively. 'Things you'd probably prefer I didn't intrude on, but I do know how poignant and painful this sort of thing can be. I completely understand if you'd rather I didn't, but I'd like to help if I can.'

Claire swallowed, her gaze going to Ella, who was sitting by Sophie's side, licking the cream from her cookie and looking wide-eyed between them. She was right. It would be painful. She couldn't involve Sophie until she'd found her father's will, though. There would be a copy lodged with his solicitor, but she would much rather dig out the copy she'd thought was in his study, and which she'd so far failed to locate, before going down that route. 'Thanks, Sophie. It's lovely of you to offer—'

She stopped as her mobile rang. Pushing her chair away from the table, she went across to pick up her phone from the work surface to check who it was. Not Luke, she noted. Still, she was reluctant to answer it. But what if something had happened? Something awful. Luke's behaviour had been so erratic.

Her gaze shot to Ella. 'Luke's mum,' she mouthed to Sophie, and then nodded towards the lounge, indicating that she needed some privacy to take the call.

CHAPTER FORTY-TWO

Claire

Listening to Luke's mother pouring out what had happened in one garbled rush, Claire felt her blood run cold. 'He did *what*?' Shocked, she clutched the phone tight to her ear.

'He'd been drinking,' Joyce said, tearful and extremely upset. 'Last night. Because of the problems between you two, I suppose. I don't condone it, but…' She paused, drawing in a shuddery breath. 'He could barely stand up, Claire. He must have consumed a distillery. And then Derek made one of his usual nasty comments because I let him in so late. Luke was close to losing his temper then. I've never seen him like this before.'

Nor had Claire. But it was becoming more and more apparent that this was a side to Luke she hadn't been aware of.

'I was hoping to sit him down and have a talk with him this morning, once Derek had gone out, but he was up and dressed, about to leave, and then… God, *why* did Derek have to choose that moment to get up to his usual tricks?'

Those tricks being to act like a complete pig, bullying Joyce, no doubt. Claire had seen it with her own eyes. The man was obnoxious. She had no idea why Joyce hadn't thrown him out years ago, except, of course, he wouldn't go quietly. Whatever Derek had done, though, for Luke to have acted as he had… Claire's stomach twisted with confusion and fear.

'He'd got my purse,' Joyce went on shakily. 'He was helping himself to the contents when Luke came into the kitchen and…' Gulping back her tears, she stopped. Dread settled icily in Claire's chest. 'It all happened so fast. Derek pushed past Luke, almost pushed him over. Luke's face…' Again, Joyce broke off on a sob. 'Dear God, it was like thunder. I had no choice but to call the police when he went after him. I was so scared. I…'

She was crying in earnest now. Claire felt like crying with her. 'Where is he?' she asked, her throat parched.

'At the police station,' Joyce managed. 'He almost *killed* him, Claire. I have no idea what they'll charge him with. Whether they'll charge him at all if Derek refuses to press charges. He better had refuse,' she added angrily, 'or *I'll* bloody well kill him.'

Claire felt the frantic hammering of her heart abate a little. She'd thought… For a second, she'd imagined that Luke actually *had* killed him. She'd almost wished he had. Recalling an incident where Luke had squared up to him once before when Derek had made a derogatory comment to *her*, she realised how hypocritical she was being. She'd applauded him then, been pleased he'd defended her. Now, she was condemning him.

'How is Derek?' she asked, not that she much cared, other than about what the consequences might be for Luke.

'Sore. Nursing his bruised ego.' Joyce sniffled. 'I don't condone violence any more than I do drinking, but if you want my honest opinion, it's about time someone gave him a good beating. I told him as much, too. Mark my words, he'll come home from hospital to find the locks changed if he dares say Luke's attack was unprovoked.'

Was a push sufficient provocation, though? Luke had said he'd pushed Anna, that was all. Clearly he didn't think then that a push amounted to much.

'I'd better go,' Joyce said, taking a tremulous breath. 'I'm hoping Luke will call me.'

Claire nodded. She wasn't sure what to say. She could hardly ask Joyce to pass on her love to him. 'Will you let me know what happens?'

Joyce was silent for a second, then, 'Of course I will,' she assured her. 'But… will you talk to him? If he calls you? I've no idea what he's doing messing about with other women – that's unforgivable – but he's worried to death about Ella. He's frightened you won't let him see her. She's his whole world.'

She did know about the other woman, then. But did she know about the things Luke was being accused of, or had he been too ashamed to tell her? If he had, it wasn't Claire's place to do so. In any case, the woman was already upset enough.

'Yes,' she agreed guardedly. With Luke acting so aggressively, she'd been reluctant to talk to him at all, but she knew she would have to at some point.

'Thanks, Claire.' Joyce's voice flooded with relief. 'Bye, lovely. I'll ring you as soon as I know anything. Give Ella a hug for me.'

'I will,' Claire promised. Then, feeling as if all the blood had drained from her body, she ended the call and sat unsteadily on the sofa, trying to assimilate what she'd learned. She could understand why Luke would have reacted to Derek's despicable behaviour towards Joyce. The man would try the patience of a saint, let alone the son of a woman who was being abused right in front of his eyes. But how violent had he been that Joyce had been terrified he might actually kill him? Should *she* get the locks changed here? Luke still had his key. But he would never cause her or Ella any harm, she was sure of it.

Her heart aching with uncertainty, she was close to tears when Sophie tapped on the door and came into the lounge. 'Everything all right, Claire?' she asked her, her face full of concern.

'No,' Claire blurted, with a vigorous shake of her head. 'It's Luke.' She gulped back a sob. 'He attacked his mother's partner. According to Joyce, he very nearly killed him. He's been arrested. I've no idea what will happen now.'

'Oh no...' Sophie stared at her, looking as stunned as Claire felt. 'God, Claire, as if you haven't got enough to worry about.' Sighing sympathetically, she walked across to sit next to her, wrapping her arm around her and giving her shoulders a firm squeeze. 'Well, I can see now why you decided not to let him anywhere near Ella. A man who's done what he's done, someone who is clearly capable of killing someone, it would have been totally irresponsible to risk her safety like that. You've done the right thing, Claire, trust me.'

Hang on a minute. Claire knitted her brow. She hadn't made any such decision. Sure, she'd been wary of Luke seeing Ella until there'd been some kind of resolution to the situation with Anna and she could see he was behaving more rationally. But she'd never said she'd decided to stop him seeing Ella completely. She couldn't do that even if she wanted to, not without some kind of injunction.

'He would never hurt her. He loves her more than his life,' she said. She knew in her heart that that was true. He would never hurt Ella. Not ever.

Sophie looked at her, surprised. 'He's desperate, Claire. Why else would he leave dangerous things around the house? I'd bet it was him who slashed your tyre, making sure to curtail your freedom. And then there was his threat to inform social services of God knows what.' Her eyes were wide with worry as they searched Claire's. 'Have you considered that if you allow him access, he might abscond with her?'

'*What?*' Claire laughed, disbelieving.

'If he thinks he might go to prison,' Sophie went on, her expression deadly serious. 'He'll get bail, presumably, and if he thinks he might not see her again...'

Claire had heard enough. 'No. That's utterly ridiculous. He would never do something like that.' She got to her feet and headed determinedly for the door to check on Ella.

'Is it?' Sophie asked behind her. 'I lied to you about my cat.'

Confused, Claire stopped in her tracks.

'She's okay but… He took her, Claire,' Sophie said gravely, as she turned back to face her. 'Put her in a plastic bag and threw her over a canal bridge. From the description one of my neighbours gave me, it was definitely him. He's been harassing you, stalking you. You can't deny his behaviour was threatening when he came here and tried to let himself in.'

Claire didn't answer. She was too stunned to speak. The fact was, he *had* been harassing her.

'You say he loves Ella more than his life. It seems to me he's putting his own life above hers. Just be careful, Claire,' Sophie warned her ominously, 'for your little girl's sake.'

CHAPTER FORTY-THREE

Luke

'Bet this is beginning to feel like your second home, isn't it, Luke?' Standing over Luke in the interview room, Detective Sergeant Myers shoved his hands in his pockets and looked at him, unimpressed.

'Just as well.' The guy sitting opposite him, Detective Constable Simmons, leaned back in his chair, laced his hands behind his head and surveyed him with amusement. 'Since he'll be spending a considerable amount of time here – or somewhere equally salubrious.'

Luke closed his eyes, feeling sick to the pit of his stomach. He'd tried to convince them that Anna was lying, that the call she'd made claiming he'd been violent, the blood in the bathroom, her disappearance had all been a set-up. They were as likely to believe that now as they were him claiming the Pope was his father.

'Aggressive little git, aren't you, Elliot?' Simmons growled, sounding pretty aggressive himself. Luke swallowed back the hard knot of fear in his chest. He didn't answer. There wasn't a lot of point.

'Would you like to run over what happened again, Luke?' Myers suggested.

As if he had any choice, Luke thought, feeling petrified. He'd been here hours. Had no idea where this would end. There was nothing he could add to what he'd already said. He didn't remember half of it. He recalled wrapping his arm around Derek's neck. Possessed by pure, blind fury, he'd wanted to kill him. He remembered that much, the rage that had been burning inside him. After that, nothing but deep, dark red. He would go to prison. He would miss Ella growing up. He felt his heart crack inside him.

'Luke?' Myers urged him.

Luke wiped away the sweat beading his forehead with his sleeve. At least Myers wasn't being hostile or peppering his questions with sarcastic jibes. Luke wasn't sure how much more he could take of that. 'I told you,' he started, sucking in a tight breath and blowing it out slowly, 'he was—'

'Bad-mouthing your mother,' Simmons finished.

Luke sighed inwardly. 'Yes,' he confirmed, as he had done already, several times. 'He was helping himself to—'

'So you thought you'd throttle him,' Simmons cut in again. 'To death.'

Christ Almighty! Was he dead? Luke snatched his gaze away from Simmons, watching as Myers walked to confer with an officer who'd just knocked and poked her head around the door.

'Not much point refusing to answer, Elliot, seeing as you were caught in the act by two coppers.' Simmons dropped his hands from his head, laying them on the table in front of him instead, and then leaning forward to eyeball Luke meaningfully. 'Is there?'

Luke held his gaze. 'I'm not refusing to answer. And I wasn't thinking anything. I followed him out. Obviously I did that. I don't remember much after that until the police turned up.'

'So, you're sticking with the diminished responsibility crap, then,' Simmons sneered. 'Thought as much. I doubt it'll wash with the psych—'

'Leave it, DC Simmons,' Myers said, coming back from the door. 'You can go, Luke.'

He could… What? Not sure he was hearing him right, Luke did a double take. So did Simmons, staring at his boss as if he were insane.

'Derek Saunders has apparently decided not to press charges. Says it was just a family dispute that got out of hand. We'll need to do some paperwork, but you're free to leave. It goes without saying, don't do any disappearing acts on us, yes? We still haven't located your ex-girlfriend.'

Simmons muttered, 'I don't bloody well believe this. We should do them both for causing a public nuisance – and for wasting police time.' He scraped his chair back and got moodily to his feet.

Myers ignored him. 'Shall we?' he asked Luke, nodding towards the door.

They were letting him go? Incredulous, relief crashing through him, Luke shook his head. Then, running a hand shakily over his face, he pulled himself to his feet. He'd never imagined there would come a day when he would thank God that Saunders was alive. He was thanking God now.

'We'll need to verify you're still at the same address,' Myers said, catching hold of the door Simmons had yanked open and swung through.

'Right.' Luke found his voice. He'd got his mother to thank for this, he suspected, but he couldn't give them her address. Could he give Claire's? Would she back him up and say he was staying there even if he wasn't?

He would have to. He doubted they would settle for *no current abode*.

'About Anna,' he ventured hesitantly. Her name was beginning to stick in his throat, but he wasn't comfortable referring to her as his ex-girlfriend. That gave their relationship – whatever it was – some kind of credence. 'Did Claire come in? Did you check the text?'

'She did,' Myers confirmed, his eyes narrowing as they searched his. 'And yes, we checked it, once we'd retrieved it. The thing is, it doesn't give us much more information. We requested data from the handset and the SIM card it was sent from, including all calls and text messages. It seems there were only the texts sent to your wife.'

'Great.' Luke sighed, and dragged a hand disconsolately over his neck.

'We also located where the phone was first switched on,' Myers continued, studying him carefully.

'And?' Luke waited, another bout of nausea sweeping through him.

'Apparently it was activated at a Tesco store local to Anna's address. We checked the store CCTV footage, hoping the phone had been purchased there, but…'

'There wasn't any,' Luke finished, his heart dropping like a stone as he realised the implication. 'Which means there's no proof Anna purchased the phone or sent the texts.' Ergo, no proof that she was alive. He could almost feel the bars closing in on him.

'Correct.' Myers nodded thoughtfully. 'Anyone could have sent them. Including you.'

CHAPTER FORTY-FOUR

Claire

Claire's heart banged in her chest as she heard a creak on the landing overhead. She held her breath, and then almost wilted with relief as she heard Sophie talking to Ella. She was in her room, saying goodbye to her. She would probably be down soon. Where the *hell* was it? She pressed a hand to her forehead, turning full circle in her father's office and wondering where on earth to look next.

She'd been ignoring her own niggling doubts, Luke's serious doubts. She'd dismissed what Gemma had said as nonsense. What Sophie had said, though, about Luke slashing her tyres, it was *that* that was nonsense. He hadn't even known she was in Rhyl, so how could he have done it? As for the cat, there was absolutely no way he would ever do something as cruel as that.

She might be wrong – she'd been so devastated by events recently, her emotions were flying all over the place – but she couldn't ignore the suspicion growing inside her. She *had* to find her father's will. Why hadn't she been more organised, for God's sake? It had been in his bottom desk drawer, along with his insurance policy and the deeds to the house. And now it wasn't anywhere. There would definitely be a copy lodged with his solicitor – at least she hoped there was; she distinctly remembered him saying he'd done that – but she didn't want to ring him until she'd established it was actually mislaid.

Frustrated, she went back to the small filing cabinet where her father stored most of the household documents. Opening the various files, she spilled the contents onto the floor in case the envelope had somehow slipped inside one of them, and then dropped to her knees and sifted through the endless bits of paper. But still she came up empty-handed. She'd been positive it was here. Confused, she sat back on her haunches and tried to get her tumultuous thoughts in some sort of order.

He must have taken it with him. It was the only explanation. But why would he have done that? Surely he was no longer compos mentis enough to understand it. Did he intend to make changes to it, thanks to her stupidly reminding him about Sophie? Pulling herself to her feet, she tried to still the nervous panic knotting her stomach. If that was his intention, she would contest any changes on the basis that he wasn't capable of handling his affairs. His diagnosis would back that up. But if it was declared not legally valid, then from what she understood, the estate might be shared out amongst his children.

Why hadn't she listened to Gemma about the power of attorney? Yes, she'd been too exhausted to think straight, had had so much to do she'd hardly dared take time to breathe, but this was naïve. Negligent. God, what was the *matter* with her?

Shit! She looked up sharply, and then scrambled to her feet and flew through the study door as she heard Ella shout, 'Bye, Auntie Sophie. I'll miss you.'

'Bye, Ella. I'll miss you too, sweetheart,' Sophie called back. 'Be good.'

Her feet came into view on the stairs, and Claire dashed to meet her. 'You're off then?' she asked, her eyes flicking back down the hall. She'd left the study door open. *Please don't look that way.* Her mouth ran dry.

'I am. I hate the thought of you being on your own, but I'm really worried about Cinder.' Sophie smiled sadly. 'She'll pine without me.'

'It looks like Ella will too,' Claire said, glancing up the stairs.

'I shouldn't be gone for more than a day.' Sophie smiled and reached for her coat.

Claire took the opportunity to step past her, opening the front door to distract her from the view down the hall. 'And you're sure you'll be all right on your own?' she asked, arranging her face into a concerned frown.

'Positive.' Sophie gave her another reassuring smile. 'Don't do anything I wouldn't do while I'm away.'

'Chance would be a fine thing,' Claire joked.

She watched from the doorstep until Sophie had disappeared from view, then closed the door and started breathing again. Feeling hot and clammy, she charged upstairs and peered around Ella's door. 'All right, sweetheart?' she asked.

'Uh huh,' Ella assured her without looking up from the iPad Sophie had left with her. 'I won another Mickey Mouse.'

'Brilliant, but don't play too long on it,' Claire warned her, then froze at a knock on the front door.

It wasn't Sophie coming back for some reason, she told herself, trying to still the rapid palpitations in her chest. It couldn't be. She'd given her a key, her father's key. She must have gone stark raving mad.

Tentatively, she walked downstairs and peered through the peephole, taken aback to see Luke standing there. They'd let him go? Unsure what to do, she looked him over. He hadn't presumed to use his own key, and his body language didn't look aggressive. With one hand in his pocket, the other clutching the back of his neck, and his gaze fixed to the ground, if anything he looked utterly dejected.

Hesitating, she debated; then, needing to know he was all right despite the situation between them, she opened the door.

Luke's gaze snapped up, his expression one of surprise, as if he hadn't expected her to answer. 'Hi. I…' he started, and then stopped awkwardly. 'Can I see Ella?' he asked, his voice catching, his face clouded with uncertainty. 'I need to see her, Claire. Please?'

He was close to tears. Claire felt her heart twist. Still she hesitated. She had to get to the care home. She might be panicking about nothing, her mind feverishly trying to process everything that was coming at her, but now wasn't a good time. She desperately didn't want Ella upset either. If the conversation between them degenerated into the same kind of argument they'd had the last time he was here, then she undoubtedly would be.

She soon realised she had no choice, however, as behind her she heard Ella exclaim, 'Daddy!' The little girl almost bowled Claire over as she charged towards him.

'Hiya, pumpkin.' His expression was a combination of delight and tangible relief as he swept her into her arms and hugged her tightly to him.

Claire saw the tear squeeze from the corner of his eye, and her heart bled for him. She glanced at Ella. Her face was a kaleidoscope of emotion: concern, bewilderment. She could see her Daddy was upset. Studying him hard, she reached out, placing the palm of her hand softly against his cheek. 'You haven't shaved, Daddy,' she whispered, a worried little V in her brow.

She had to let him in, Claire realised, her heart breaking for her daughter. Ella's little world was already destabilised. She couldn't deny her contact with her father.

'Would you like a coffee?' she asked him, stepping back from the door.

Luke breathed out a sigh of relief. 'Thanks,' he said, giving her a small smile, which did little to diminish the exhaustion etched into his face. The dark shadows under his eyes were tinged purple, indicating he was sleeping as little as she was.

'Yay!' Plainly thrilled at that, Ella's face lit up. 'I can show you my new game, Daddy,' she said, her eyes now dancing with excitement. 'It's Disney Crossy Road. And I'm ace at it. Auntie Sophie said so.'

Claire didn't miss the flicker of agitation that crossed Luke's face. 'Auntie Sophie, hey?' He lifted Ella higher in his arms. 'She's staying here then, is she?'

'Yes,' Ella informed him with a decisive nod. 'She's nice. She doesn't shout at me.'

But her mummy did. Claire felt like crying. Innocent it might have been, but still that comment had stung.

'She's helping Mummy,' Ella chatted on, 'but she's not staying tonight. She's lent me her iPad. Would you like me to show it to you?'

Luke glanced at Claire curiously, and Claire guessed she'd been caught out about the man who'd supposedly been here last night. 'I'd love to,' he said, arranging his face into the special smile he reserved for his daughter. 'Why don't we go into the lounge and you can tell me all about Auntie Sophie while you're impressing me with your gaming skills. Okay?' he checked with Claire.

Claire nodded, and swallowed. It was clear that Ella did need contact with people other than her. Nice people.

Following them down the hall, she noticed Luke's gaze straying towards her father's study. The door was still open, the files scattered all over the floor. Should she confide in him? She'd been going to, before everything had fallen apart. She'd thought that when she told him of the plans she'd made with her father regarding his future, about what she'd promised to do, he would understand. Would he? she wondered.

CHAPTER FORTY-FIVE

Sophie

Letting herself into his building with the shopping she'd bought him, Sophie paused to pick up the post from the rubbish-strewn communal hall floor. There were two letters addressed to Jimmy O'Conner. Bills, judging by the envelopes. She doubted he'd have the money to pay them. He'd never had much, which was why her mother hadn't rated him, and now he had nothing.

Thoughts of her mother bringing her starkly to mind, Sophie swallowed back a sudden dryness in her throat as the flashback that plagued her dreams assaulted her. It was so full-on this time she could almost taste the petrol fumes thick on the air. Gasping in a deep breath, one hand on the wall for support, she felt the chassis of the van shifting beneath her, rattling her around like a ragdoll as it rolled; metal grinding and concertinaing before she was ejected through the flapping back doors. She felt a strange sense of weightlessness before she landed, every bone jarring agonisingly. Her teeth clenching sharply, shooting intense pain through her jaw, she gulped back the salty taste in her mouth and tried to move. She couldn't. She was acutely aware of the pain drilling through her leg like the red-hot point of a poker; vaguely sensed her mum dangling upside down in the front of the van. She tried to call out to her, but her tongue felt too thick in her mouth. Blinking hard against the film of crimson clouding her vision, desperation climbing her chest, she tried again – '*Mummy!*' – but no sound came out other than a rasping gurgle. And then she froze, lying stock still in the undergrowth, as two heavy biker-booted feet came into view, pausing directly in front of her.

She tried to still the panic twisting inside her as they moved onwards, heels clacking against the grit and ice on the road. He would help her. Relief flooded through her. He would save her mum. He would get her out. Praying hard, she squinted through the foliage half obscuring her vision. She could hear her own heart beating as a minute ticked agonisingly by; a bird chirruping high up in the trees above her. It was if her senses were heightened. She could hear herself breathing.

What was he doing? she wondered, fear tightening her tummy as the sickly-sweet smell of petrol filled her nostrils. *Help her*, she implored soundlessly, another interminably long minute ticking by. *Please hurry.*

And then she heard a new sound, sharper heels crunching on the gravel. Someone else coming? A scraping sound, too, like the strike of a match against the side of a box. Once, twice… three times. A silent scream rising inside her, she lost control of her bladder as she watched the lighted match fall to the puddle of fuel, igniting a fireball that swallowed her mother.

She took several slow breaths and tried to still the incessant shaking of her limbs that always accompanied the flashbacks.

No one had wanted to hear what she had to say when she'd eventually remembered what had happened. At first, when she'd woken up, she had no recollection. She'd felt nothing but a deep sense of terror, but she didn't know why. The shock, the doctors had said, had caused her to block the painful memories out. Soon afterwards, justice had been done, according to some. People at the pub had borne witness to the events leading up to the accident, recounting how much Jimmy had been drinking that night, how he'd been acting. No one had believed him when he'd protested his innocence. Just a farmhand who stank of pig shit and with a liking for the booze, he'd been convicted of causing death by dangerous driving. He'd been in love with her, consumed with jealous rage, the gossipers who revelled in the gory details thereafter had said. He had been in love with her. They were right about that bit.

Feeling more composed, Sophie continued along the hall. His flat – a poky, dingy hole not fit to house a dog – was on the ground floor, necessarily. He'd been four years into his sentence when he'd 'fallen' down the prison stairs, breaking his leg in two places. There'd been some kind of fight, apparently, Jimmy accused of starting it. He'd been carrying the knife that had pierced his lung as he fell, according to other inmates. Jimmy hadn't denied it. To have done that would have had him marked as a grass, he'd said. Better to do the extra time inside and live to tell the tale, he'd told her when she'd finally located him.

She'd been old enough then to choose what she wanted to do, rather than obey her gran's wishes. She smiled cynically when she thought of Gran. Far from the sweet old lady she'd portrayed for Claire's benefit, the woman had been a nasty, mean bitch. She'd had her mum young, so was only in her late forties when Sophie had gone to live with her, where she'd had to listen to the constant bumping and grinding through the bedroom wall whenever her dear gran had entertained one of her many men friends. She'd only taken Sophie in for the money that was paid into her bank account on a monthly basis, something she reminded her granddaughter of often.

It was Gran who'd unknowingly given her the idea of contacting Claire. 'Pity that bloke our Cath was seeing before she died didn't do the decent thing,' she'd said, with a wistful sigh. 'You might have been all right if they'd tied the knot.' Meaning *she* might have been. The woman was transparent.

It hadn't taken Sophie long to find Claire through social media sites. She hadn't been sure what her next step would be. Then, when she'd seen Claire's Facebook posts about Bernard's illness and how devastated she was… It had been fate really. The perfect opportunity to get in touch. And now here she was, installed in Bernard Harvey's house, which meant she couldn't stay long here. She had to get back, keep a close eye on the comings and goings of people who might put ideas in her dear half-sister's head. Ideas that Sophie definitely didn't want there.

Approaching his door, she heard his hacking cough as she pushed her key into the lock. 'Jimmy,' she called, letting herself in, 'where are you?'

Jimmy coughed heartily again. 'In here, love,' he managed from the bedroom.

Dropping her shopping bags in the kitchen, Sophie crossed the small lounge area, tapped on the bedroom door and then went on in. 'You all right, Jimmy?' she asked, her brow knitted into a worried frown as she looked to where he was sitting on the edge of his bed. He looked like death, his face pale and drawn. He was losing weight and she could hear the rattle in his chest from two yards away.

'Yeah.' He mustered up a smile. 'Just the old chest giving me a bit of gyp. Nothing to worry about, petal.' He coughed and wheezed, then reached for his cigarettes.

Sophie sighed and rolled her eyes as she walked across to him. She should reprimand him, but knowing he was hopelessly addicted, she'd long since given that up.

'You're staying with her, then?' he asked, lighting up and sucking smoke deep into his lungs.

'I am.' Sophie smiled. She'd texted him to tell him, warning him she wouldn't be able to make it over to see him until now. She hoped he'd been feeding himself properly.

He eyed her curiously. 'Getting on all right, are you?'

'Yep, good,' Sophie said, her smile widening. 'I think we've bonded.'

He arched an eyebrow and took another puff. 'You just be careful, Soph,' he warned her, after a contemplative second. 'I don't want you ending up getting hurt.'

'I won't,' Sophie assured him, grabbing his pillows and fluffing them up for him. 'Everything's going swimmingly.'

Apart from Ella almost drowning in her care, she didn't feel the need to add. She had been horribly worried for a second that she wouldn't get to her in time. Still, all was well that ended well. And at least it might make Claire appreciate what she'd got. She was inclined to feel sorry for herself, Sophie felt. She really shouldn't, considering the privileges she'd had growing up. Sophie would have given anything for her start in life.

'Cup of tea?' she asked Jimmy, going across to open his curtains and hitch the window open an inch. She didn't want him to catch cold, but a bit of fresh air would do him good. She made a mental note to close it before she left.

'I'll get it.' Jimmy stuffed his fag in his mouth, pressed his knuckles against the mattress and attempted to heave himself to his feet.

'Stay,' Sophie said, encouraging him back down again. It would take him ages with his limp and his shortness of breath. His health had deteriorated rapidly lately. 'Take your time. You know the sleeping tablets make you woozy. I'll do it.'

'I can manage, Soph,' Jimmy assured her. 'You don't have to keep worrying about me.'

Sophie wasn't so sure about that. 'Someone has to.' She sighed tolerantly. 'I can't stay long, though. I have to get back.'

Jimmy didn't ask why. He didn't expect or demand anything of her; didn't judge her. He just liked her company. And Sophie liked his. He was probably the only genuine person she'd had in her life.

'I've bought you some supplies,' she said. 'I'll warm you up some soup while I'm at it.'

'Thanks, Soph.' He smiled gratefully. 'You're an angel. If there's one good thing that's come out of all of this, it's you. Cath would have been proud of you.'

Would she? Her mum had never really paid her much attention. Sophie couldn't help feeling she would think she hadn't achieved much: no qualifications, no job. That was all going to change, though. Now that she'd found Claire, she would put the wrongs right and have something to show for her life.

CHAPTER FORTY-SIX

Claire

'Are you looking for something?' Luke asked behind her as Claire scrabbled about on the study floor, collecting up the paperwork she'd left there.

'No,' she said quickly. 'Just going through some bills, that's all. Where's Ella?' Getting to her feet, she glanced past where he was standing in the doorway.

'Fast asleep on the sofa. I'm obviously scintillating company.' Smiling wryly, Luke stepped in.

'That will be the film,' Claire assured him. 'She's watched it so many times, she mouths the characters' lines alongside them.' *Paddington 2* had become her latest firm favourite since Sophie had downloaded it, probably *because* it was Sophie who had downloaded it. Ella was besotted with her, but Claire had realised she might have made a huge mistake bringing her into her little girl's life. One she had to rectify.

His smile now tinged with sadness, Luke nodded. He was missing Ella, and Ella was missing him, but Claire had no idea what she was supposed to do. She could hardly pretend to their daughter that none of this was happening. 'Need any help?' he asked her.

'No. Thanks. I'm almost done,' Claire said, stuffing the last of the paperwork back into the cabinet. She couldn't confide in him, despite her desperate need to. He'd let her down so badly, become a different person from the man she'd thought he was. She'd struggled to believe the things this wretched woman Anna had accused him of. But now, learning that he'd been witnessed violently attacking someone… 'What happened, Luke?' she asked, turning to face him.

Luke squinted at her, confused.

'With Derek. Joyce told me.'

Nodding, Luke sighed wearily. 'She told you about what the prat was doing, then?'

Claire noted the hand he was running agitatedly over his neck. 'She did, though she didn't really need to. Trust me, I know what he's like, but… she said you almost *killed* him. Why, Luke? What on earth possessed you?'

Luke shrugged awkwardly. 'I don't know.' He glanced away and then back to her. 'I honestly don't remember. One minute I was following him out, the next the police were hauling me off him. In between…' He stopped, heaving in a shaky breath.

There was fear in his eyes, Claire noted. 'Are you saying you don't remember the actual attack on him?' she asked, incredulous.

Luke hesitated before answering, then, 'After a point, no,' he admitted sheepishly. 'I obviously lost it.'

Claire shook her head, her heart beating unsteadily in a combination of alarm and confusion. 'So are you saying you could have done what this woman, Anna, accused you of?'

Luke dropped his gaze and pressed his forefinger and thumb hard against his forehead. 'I'm saying I don't know. She says I did, but I can't believe I… What? Had some kind of mental blackout?' Raking a hand through his hair, he glanced upwards, as if searching for answers. 'I have no idea what's going on. What the hell happened in the first place.' His bewildered gaze came back to hers. 'I love you, Claire. I never meant to…'

'Hurt me?' Claire finished. Surely he must realise the ridiculousness of that statement.

Luke closed his eyes. 'I should probably go, while Ella's sleeping,' he said quietly. 'Save upsetting her.'

'Where?' Claire stepped towards him, stopping him as he walked to the door. 'Where will you go? I presume you're not at Steve's any more, since you went to your mother's?'

He turned back. 'No, I'm not at Steve's. I was making Lauren uncomfortable. She seems to think there's no smoke without fire, along with everyone else. I'll book into a bed and breakfast. Look for a room to rent at some point. Kiss Ella for me,' he said, smiling sadly. 'Tell her I'll see her soon.'

'Daddy, where are you going?' Ella had appeared at the living room door. Her eyes were wide and fearful over her Flopsy toy, and Claire cursed herself for not noticing her standing there sooner.

'Not far, sweetheart.' Luke moved towards her. 'I'll be back soon, and we can—'

'No!' Ella stepped back, dropping the soft toy to her side and clenching it hard in her fist. 'I don't *want* you to go.'

'Hey, I won't be gone long.' Luke attempted to pick her up, but Ella stiffened, so rigid in his arms he was struggling to hold onto her.

'Yes you will!' she cried, as he managed to straighten up with her. 'Sophie said you have to go away because you made Mummy cry, but I don't want you to. I don't *want* you to go away, Daddy.'

'*Jesus*,' Luke muttered, shooting a worried glance at Claire. 'I'm not going away, pumpkin,' he said throatily, easing his now sobbing daughter's head to his shoulder. 'I promise you, I will never, ever do that.'

Claire swiped an angry tear from her own face. Sophie had no right to interfere in any of this, let alone feed worrying information to her child.

'Stay,' she said, as Luke turned his gaze once again towards her. His face was pale, his eyes deeply troubled. 'I have to visit my father this evening,' she went on falteringly. 'Could you… would you stay with Ella?'

'Do you honestly think I would go anyway, seeing her like this?' Luke's tone was quiet, but he was working to control his emotions. Claire could see that, and she couldn't blame him. Not this time. Why would Sophie intimate that he would no longer be part of Ella's life? She must have known how devastating that would be to a child. She'd claimed she wanted to be part of Claire's family, but little by little, Claire was losing everyone who mattered to her. Suddenly even Ella seemed to be pulling away from her.

What had Sophie been thinking? Did she want her to have nothing and no one? Gemma had been right. Claire should have looked more closely into Sophie's motives.

Where *was* her father's will?

CHAPTER FORTY-SEVEN

Sophie

It was a shame about the cat. Sophie sighed sadly as she drove back to Birmingham. Still, it had had a good life, well fed and looked after. She consoled herself with that thought, and switched her mind to Jimmy. She couldn't help worrying about him. He didn't look at all well. His cough had been painful to hear, and his complexion was sallow, tinged yellow, she'd noticed. To add to his problems, the letters that had arrived were to inform him that his benefits had been suspended thanks to some internal error. Sophie quashed her anger that the system should treat him in such a way. Hadn't he already been punished enough?

Arriving in the city centre, she parked the car Peter had kindly purchased for her as close to P&K Financial Services as she could. The little Ford Fiesta hatchback was second-hand, but it did the job. And it had earned Peter one or two brownie points, as he had known it would; hence the gratifying sex session – gratifying for him, anyway. She hadn't let on about the car to Claire, of course, for the same reason she hadn't mentioned Peter. She was glad that she hadn't now. It was a terrible shame about the dent in the front of it. There was a repair shop in Rhyl. Maybe they could knock it out?

Checking her watch as she pondered, and noting that it was almost five o'clock, she called Peter on his office number as she approached the building, cutting the call without speaking when he answered, and then waited across the road until she saw his receptionist leave before going in.

She beamed the security guard a smile as she sailed by. 'Hi, how are you doing?' She'd guessed she would have no trouble getting past him. His eyes had been all over her last time she'd been here.

'Yeah, good. You?' he said, addressing her arse as she headed for the lift and the second floor.

She was aware from her previous visits – all of which had been after hours – that Peter's glass-fronted office overlooked the open-plan sales area; his wife's desk was located in the office next door to his. He would be surprised to see Sophie, but not delighted, she suspected. With his wife looking on, however, she was sure he would play the part of financial adviser to her client seeking impromptu advice, and invite her in cordially.

She needed that element of surprise. For him to know that she could turn up in his life any time she pleased. That she could ruin it, and would, without compunction, if he didn't do as she asked.

Granted access to the outer office by one of his sales team, she caught Peter's attention and gave him a wave. His face was an absolute picture when he realised who it was. Blanching to a pale shade of white, he got shakily to his feet, his eyes swivelling to the partition wall between his office and his wife's. The woman glanced curiously up from her phone, and Sophie gave her a bright smile to allay any suspicion. She had no gripe with her. She didn't want Peter. His wife was welcome to him. It was his services she wanted. He owed her that much.

Clearly guessing that he didn't have much choice, Peter braced himself, straightened his tie and came out of his office. 'Hi, Peter Davies,' he said, forcing his face into a professional smile. 'Can I help you, Miss…?'

'Tyson,' Sophie supplied, shaking the hand he extended. 'Sophie Tyson. You gave me your card when you came into the café where

I work,' she added for the benefit of those in earshot. 'I was hoping you could offer me some advice.'

'Regarding?' He scanned her eyes, a combination of suspicion and fear in his own, Sophie noted with satisfaction.

'My father's estate.' She smiled pleasantly. 'I'm sorry I came on spec. I was going to ring and make an appointment, but it is quite urgent, and as I was passing…'

'No problem. That's what we're here for, to offer friendly but professional financial advice,' he said, stepping away to gesture her towards his office, his eyes sliding again in the direction of his wife as he did so.

Poor man. Sophie felt a smidgen of sympathy for him. She noticed the sweat popping out on his forehead, which was obviously also wetting his armpits. He looked as if he might actually be sick.

Leading the way to his office, he opened the door for her, allowing her to go in before him – such a gent – and then indicated his visitor's chair and smiled again, a little more stiffly.

'So, Miss Tyson, what can we help you with?' he said loudly, going around to his own chair, where he picked up a file and tapped it nervously on the desk. 'What the fuck do you want?' he added, his voice now a strangled whisper.

The gracious manners hadn't lasted long. Sophie sighed, and reached into her bag. 'A signature,' she said, sliding the document she retrieved from it across his desk. 'Two signatures, actually. I'm sure you can convince one of your eager sales team to oblige.'

Peter eyed her warily and then picked up the document and perused it. When he had finished, he snapped his astonished gaze back to hers. 'I can't sign *this*. It's a witness signature; it has to be signed in the presence of the person the document belongs to. And it's backdated. You'll never get away with it.'

'I will with a sworn statement from you, should it be required, which of course you'll also be happy to oblige with.' Sophie surveyed him coolly.

'I can't. It's illegal,' he croaked, tugging his collar loose with his forefinger as he studied the document again. Sophie watched him swallow back his Adam's apple. 'It's dishonest, for God's sake. Have a heart, Sophie, I'll lose my licence.'

'Ah…' Sophie smiled scornfully. 'And *you* would never be dishonest, would you, Peter?' She glanced pointedly at the partition wall; then, seeing he'd got the implicit message, passed him his pen.

CHAPTER FORTY-EIGHT

Claire

'Hello, lovely,' Julia greeted her, as Claire went into the day room in search of her father. 'We're a bit late tonight, aren't we?' Walking across to her, she checked her watch. 'Everything all right?'

'Yes, thanks.' Aware that she probably looked more than a little flustered, Claire forced her face into a smile. 'I had a bit of trouble getting a babysitter. I didn't want to bring Ella along now that Dad's… you know, becoming more unpredictable.'

Julia nodded understandingly. 'I know that scenario well. It took me forever to find a decent babysitter,' she said, going to the table where endless cups of tea were served. 'Does your sister not help out then?'

Her sister? Claire's stomach lurched. How could she possibly know about…?

'She seems like a nice girl.' Julia smiled, oblivious to Claire staring at her stunned.

Sophie had been here? She'd actually come to see him, despite Claire asking her not to?

'Always dashing in and out, though,' Julia went on. 'You'd think she was the one with children. She doesn't have any, does she?'

'No,' Claire managed, panic rising inside her as she realised Sophie must have been here more than once. Her gaze went to her father, who was sitting in one of the armchairs, his gaze fixed on the television and looking the picture of innocence. 'She's busy moving house.'

'Ah. To somewhere nearer?' Julia enquired pleasantly as she carried a cup of tea across to one of the residents.

'That's the idea,' Claire said, following her across the room. 'How is he?' She nodded towards her father.

'Cantankerous as always, hey, Bernard?' Julia called good-naturedly across to him. He arched an eyebrow in reply, unimpressed. 'He was a bit muddled after your sister left. I think he gets the two of you mixed up.'

Claire would bet he was. 'Did she come today then?' she enquired, attempting to keep her tone casual.

'Early this morning,' Julia clarified. 'You could probably have given it a miss tonight.'

Claire sighed demonstratively. 'I could have, couldn't I?' she said, thinking it was a bloody good job she had come. 'Ah well, I'm here now. I'd better go and say hello.'

Her smile now plastered in place, she veered off to walk across to him. 'Hi, Dad,' she said brightly, positioning herself between him and the TV. 'It's Claire.'

Since he couldn't avoid her, Bernard looked up at her. 'Hello, dear,' he said, smiling uncertainly.

'I hear Sophie's been to see you?' she went on chattily. 'That was nice of her, wasn't it?'

Bernard scanned her eyes, his own seemingly uncomprehending and his forehead creased into its usual puzzled frown. 'Has she?' he asked.

He wasn't pretending he knew nothing of her existence then. Fury burned in Claire's chest. He'd *always* known she existed. Despite his failing memory, there was part of him functioning, she was growing more certain of that. He was still capable of the lies that had destroyed the woman he was supposed to have loved. The deceit that had stolen Claire's childhood. She might be wrong, there was always that possibility, but she very much doubted it.

'Did you have a nice chat?' she asked him, dumping her bags on the floor, perching on the arm of his chair and taking hold of his hand.

Bernard looked her over, the wheels of his mind seeming to turn as he tried to place her. 'Yes thank you, dear,' he said eventually. Was his confusion real? Or was it manufactured to avoid him being found out? *I know!* Claire wanted to scream at him. *I know what you did. Everything!* But she didn't know everything, did she? She would never know the answer to the question that really haunted her: *Did you hit her? Did you cause my mother to fall to her death?*

'That was nice for you, catching up with her.' Smiling encouragingly instead, she squeezed his hand. 'So, what did you talk about? Old times, I bet.' Cathy? she wondered. The woman whose unimaginably horrific death might never have happened if not for him.

The furrow in his forehead deepening, he appeared to contemplate her question. Claire watched him. Might he finally confide in her, she wondered, his legitimate daughter?

But, 'I don't really remember,' he said flatly, causing the knot of anger in Claire's chest to tighten. She stared hard at him, willing him to look at her, to see her, see the pain he was causing. The guilt she carried, because of the promise she'd made him.

Bernard, though, looked away.

'How are we doing?' Julia asked, coming across to them. 'I was about to help him get ready for bed,' she told Claire. 'I'm off duty soon. You could go up once he's ready, if you like.'

'Oh, don't worry about that. You get off. I'll do it.' Claire smiled reassuringly and got to her feet. 'I'll just drop my things upstairs and then I'll be right back. Won't be a sec, Dad.'

Picking up her handbag and the plastic carrier containing chocolate biscuits and choux buns – his favourites – she headed for the door. Tears welled in her eyes, distorting her vision as she glanced briefly back at him. Was he really the monster she was imagining he was?

Once in his room, she pushed the door to and leaned against it, her chest heaving as she gulped back her sobs. She was wrong. She *had* to be wrong. He wasn't capable, surely, of cutting her out of his life, out of his will, in favour of his fucking love child. *God!* Realising she only had minutes, she tore herself away from the door, dropped her bags on the bed and glanced around the room. Her eyes travelled to the top of the dressing table – and her heart skittered to a stop in her chest. Her mother's photograph was there, where she'd left it. But it was laid flat.

Bastard. Her chest tightening painfully, she walked across to it and righted it, then yanked the drawers of the dressing table open, quickly searching through them. She still didn't know what she hoped to find. It wouldn't be so obviously hidden. Deviousness required an amount of cleverness, and he'd certainly been that over the years.

Shoving the drawers shut, she flew to the wardrobe, to find his shirts and trousers hanging in colour-keyed rows. His jackets, two of them. Swiftly Claire searched the pockets, finding nothing but his expensive Montblanc fountain pen, a comb and an out-of-date credit card.

Frustrated, she closed the wardrobe door, her eyes flicking once again around the room. What was she doing? He might not even have taken it. It might genuinely be simply mislaid. The house had been in upheaval, after all, with her and Luke moving in, her father moving out. The stress of all that had happened was causing *her* to lose her mind.

She stopped, attempted to take stock. He'd tried to be there for her since her mother's death. Business trips aside, which she cared not to dwell on, he'd done the absolute best that he could to be both mother and father to her. Whatever had happened between her parents, whatever he'd done, it was in the past. She needed to stop this. She needed to move on. If she didn't, it would shape the rest of her life.

Feeling a little calmer, she went back to the bed to collect her bags. She'd been tempted not to leave him the things she'd brought him, but even knowing now how imperfect a father and husband he'd been, she couldn't deny him the few little luxuries he still had left in life. Was anyone perfect, at the end of the day? Retrieving the cakes and biscuits from the carrier bag to place on the bedside cabinet, her gaze fell on the drawer in the top of it.

She almost resisted opening it. Almost. When she did, it took a second for comprehension to dawn.

She'd never even considered it, the fact that her father might still be able to sign his own name. Her stomach clenching coldly, she lifted out the notebook and stared incredulously at it. Apparently he could. Over and over he'd scrawled it. Page after page, filled with his signature, shakily written with his expensive Montblanc pen. Now why would he do that – Claire felt something harden inside her – unless he was planning to sign something? An official document, to replace one that was missing.

Bypassing the day-room door, Claire sipped quietly out of the care home. Would she grieve for him? she wondered as she walked to her car. Would she carry around the same aching loss inside her she had for her mother? Learning what she had about his past, she'd been devastated. Now, she felt as if a piece of herself had died. She was numb inside. Detached almost.

CHAPTER FORTY-NINE

Bernard

Bernard sank back into his pillows, glad of the peace and quiet that night-time brought. He found constant chatter bothersome. He could never keep hold of the thread of the conversation. It was easier lately just to nod and smile, rather than try to converse. They seemed placated by that, the people who drifted in and out of his life, whose faces were vaguely familiar but whose names increasingly escaped him. He preferred to be alone, except he never was, quite, with ghosts from his past whispering around him. Waiting, Bernard felt, for him to right the wrongs he'd done them in life.

Closing his eyes, hoping sleep would soon claim him, his thoughts drifted to the young woman who'd visited him tonight. She wasn't happy with him, he sensed, but he was buggered if he knew why. He was bemused as to why she kept calling him Dad, too, but he'd smiled and nodded when she'd addressed him, hoping to appease her, and eventually she'd gone away. Had she been crying when she'd left? He tried to recall, but his brain was uncooperative, sluggish, desperate for respite from the effort of thinking.

He attempted to empty his mind, allow it to meander to some happier place where his night terrors wouldn't haunt him. He was tumbling softly, pleasantly, like a kite on a summer's breeze, when it snagged on the one memory he could never expunge, the smell of petrol and burning flesh, like pork crackling on Sundays, jerking him wide awake. Sweat pooled at the base of his neck, wetting the sheets beneath him, but he didn't dare move to wipe it away. Ruth hated it when he disturbed her. She could never get back to sleep. The alcohol she drank was an anaesthetic – Bernard had tried to explain it to her – and once it wore off, sleep would be impossible. He should know. He'd once drunk his fair share, too. It never helped him forget, bringing the horrific details into sharp focus instead: the terror in eyes that would soon be bulbous and opaque, the piercing scream cut suddenly short, details that would haunt him to the grave.

Shifting his position slightly, once he was sure he hadn't disturbed his troubled wife, he lowered his eyelids and tried again. A short time later, or it could have been hours, his mind lurching frantically from thought to disjointed thought, he couldn't tell if he was awake or still dreaming. A moment ago he'd been running, the long landing in front of him stretching on to eternity, the door ahead of him growing more distant, the floor like treacle beneath him, sucking his feet in. The room he was trying to get to was empty when he reached it, stark walls, nothing to tell him why he was there. And then the door slammed behind him and the dark descended, and there was no door, no window, no way out of his nightmare.

Guessing he was awake, as the sounds of the night reached him – the resident in the adjoining room coughing, the lonely hoot of a tawny owl – he raised his head from his pillow, and a new sense of panic started to take root inside him. He wondered at first whether the figure on the other side of his room was a figment of his imagination. When it approached, he didn't recognise the person looming over him. The features were familiar, yet not. Fleetingly he had a memory, but it floated away before he could grasp it, disappearing into the night like a soft white djinn. Tormenting him. Always the memories tormented him, hovering on the periphery of his recollection.

But he wasn't hallucinating, he soon realised. This person was real, tangible. He could hear the controlled breathing, as if they were holding their rage in. By the amber glow of the fire escape light spilling in through the bay window, he could see the seething sheen of malice in eyes that seemed to be looking right into his soul. He smelled the cloying odour of floral cologne, and he knew it; knew who it belonged to. He groped for the name of the face that danced just out of his reach, sifted through the quicksand in his mind. He couldn't catch hold of it before the face was lost to him.

This individual meant him harm. Cold certainty settled like an icicle in his chest. 'What do you want?' he rasped, his throat thick with fear.

The loud silence that followed was filled with tacit threat. And then, 'I know what you did,' the person whispered. The voice, tight with suppressed emotion, tugged at the frayed edges of his consciousness.

Another soundless minute ticked by. And then the figure moved, its penetrating gaze holding his briefly before it turned away from him. His heart thrashing wildly, he strained to hear the sounds above it: soft footsteps; the window opening; rain plopping heavily from the roof. Her name – the woman who was long ago lost to him – he heard that, too, carried mournfully on the wind that whistled through the trees in the grounds. A distant dog howled, soulful, blood-chilling, the primeval cry of an abandoned animal. And then…

'She's here, Bernard,' his visitor said softly. 'She's waiting for you.'

Bernard had known she would be. He'd sensed her waiting over the years, nothing but the flimsy shadow of death between them. He'd imagined her lying next to him, sharing his bed again. He'd searched often for her lately, hearing her treading quietly along the landing, calling out to him, urging him to stop fighting. His heart heavy with guilt and grief, he'd wanted to give in, to be with her, as they once were. He'd struggled, though, to find his way, the doorless walls confounding him, the landing a maze of obstacles, defeating him.

She was here now. Shivering with cold though he was, Bernard experienced a blessed sense of relief as he gazed down at the gravel path leading through the lush gardens below. She'd always loved her garden, found solace in it as she'd pottered. She would show him the way. He'd been devastated when she'd turned away from him. He hadn't blamed her. He'd never intended to hurt her so badly. He'd meant to console her, to calm her, not push her. If only she hadn't been drinking. If only she hadn't been about to say out loud what they'd promised each other not to, and disillusion their little girl about him forever.

'Do you think she'll forgive me?' he asked his visitor, his voice almost drowned out by the heavy patter of rain against the metal frame of the fire escape.

'Why don't you ask her?' his visitor suggested.

Bernard felt an acute sense of panic as he flailed forward. Then his skull cracked on the iron steps as he bounced and tumbled his way down, and he didn't feel anything more.

CHAPTER FIFTY

Claire

Hearing the creak of a floorboard on the landing, Claire wondered whether it really was just the wood settling. Might it be a ghost, after all? she wondered. That of a woman whose life was cut cruelly short, searching endlessly for some sense of closure. Imagining how that might feel, lost and lonely as she tried forlornly to make contact with those who still lived, a shudder ran through her. She was glad that Luke was downstairs. She felt safer with him here.

He was as furious as she was about Sophie's inflammatory comment, she could see it in his eyes, but had diplomatically said it was a subject better not pursued tonight. She still didn't know the truth about what had happened between him and Anna, whether a switch had flicked and his emotions had spiralled out of control, the shock of what he'd done causing him to bury it. It was possible. She wished she herself could forget so easily. She doubted she ever would.

Sitting at her dressing table, she studied the photograph she'd extracted from her memory box – a beautiful photo of a couple seemingly very much in love – and then went back to her task. She found manually editing her father out of the photographs therapeutic. She couldn't banish the memories from her mind, as he had, but she could obliterate any physical reminders of him.

She placed the remaining half of the photo back in the box and selected another, one of her and her father together on their long-ago trip to Rhyl. There was no point keeping just half of it – herself smiling adoringly up at a man who wasn't there – so, wielding the scissors carefully, she snipped it into halves, and then halved it again, cutting until she'd obliterated every recognisable part of him. Sighing at the loss of something that should have been special, but obviously never was to him, she sprinkled the bits of photograph into her waste-paper basket like so much sad confetti, and reached back into the box for her mother's perfume, the smell of which she found so comforting. She frowned as she noticed the top was loose. That was odd. She always pushed it back on tightly. Someone had been using it. Not Ella. She knew how precious it was to Claire. Sophie, no doubt, poking around, as she obviously had been.

Picturing her pretty little pixie face, Claire reached for another photograph of her father and hacked sharply through it.

It would be interesting to see what she had to say for herself when she got back. Claire had been on the verge of ringing her but had thought better of it. She wanted to talk to her face to face, read what was in her deceitful doe eyes when she confronted her.

Hearing another distant creak, she felt a shiver prickle her skin. She'd been icy cold since she got back, chilled to the bone after getting soaking wet tonight. It was late. She hadn't realised how late. Noting the time on her bedside clock as the digits clicked over to four a.m., she pushed the bits and pieces back into her box, placed it in the drawer and went across to the bed.

She paused before climbing in, ran her hand over Luke's pillow, wished he was here, that there wasn't a floor separating them, an ocean between them. She craved the warmth of him, his hard body next to hers. Wished dearly that things could be the way they had been before their lives had been turned upside down. But he hadn't wanted to be with her. He preferred sadomasochistic sex with a complete lunatic… according to Sophie. Claire had actually started to believe her, thought that in some mysterious way, finding her half-sister might have been a blessing, an antidote to her deep sense of loneliness. She'd thought the woman had truly cared about her. She stifled a scornful laugh. It had all been bullshit and lies, and she'd been ready to believe it because she'd been desperate.

Rubbing at the goose bumps on her arms, she pulled back the duvet and crawled under it, curling herself into a ball and squeezing her eyes closed, attempting to block out the images that played on a loop through her mind, but to no avail. They were scorched on the insides of her eyelids: images of her father's bewildered face as she'd glared accusingly at him. How much bullshit had he fed her over the years? It seemed to her that his whole life was an intricate web of lies. How could he have done that, lied so consistently to his own child? Had he been lying this evening? Even though his mind was failing, had his first instinct still been to protect himself, no matter how much hurt he caused her? Claire curled herself smaller, listened to the sounds of the house breathing.

She heard it again, a ghostly creak on the landing. This time it was louder, nearer; definitely not wood settling. Emerging from her cocoon, she listened, and then threw back the duvet. It was probably just Luke going to the bathroom, but still she felt the need to check on Ella.

Coming quietly out of her room, she paused to peer over the stair rail for signs of him. Seeing none, she carried on to Ella's room, hesitating outside her door when she found it open a fraction. Strange. She'd stopped leaving the door ajar when her father had taken to wandering at night. Perhaps she'd gone to the loo, which was also a bit strange. Ella was scared of the dark. She would normally come and find Claire first.

She pushed the door further open, cursing silently as the hinges squeaked, and squinted across at Ella's bed. Unable to make her out by the pale glow of her night light, she tiptoed further in, poised to reassure her should she wake – and then froze.

'Ella?' she whispered, her heart catapulting into her mouth as she realised there was an empty space in the bed where her little girl's body should be. 'Ella?' Attempting to quell her panic, she glanced quickly around the room, and then flew across to the wardrobe in the vain hope that her daughter might be playing some sort of hide-and-seek game.

Nothing.

Icy fingers ran the length of her spine.

She must have gone downstairs. Claire took a deep breath, breathed it out. Of course she had. Aware that Luke was down there, she'd snuck out of bed and crept down. She was probably snuggled up fast asleep on the sofa with him. Nodding reassuringly to herself, her chest pounding, she was about to go back to the door when a tiny glimmer of light from Ella's bed caught her eye. Steeling herself, unable to imagine what it was, she reached for the duvet and peeled it back. Her heart jolted violently and her stomach turned over, nausea climbing her throat as she stared down disbelievingly at the sharp shards of glass. A broken wine glass, red wine staining the white sheet beneath it.

Oh, dear God. 'Ella!' Whirling around, Claire flew to the landing, swinging round the stair rail to thunder down the stairs. Her whole body lurched as she lost her footing partway down. Instinctively, she flailed for the rail, catching hold of it and pulling herself upright to scramble down the rest of the way.

'Luke!' Thrusting the door wide, she raced into the lounge. 'Luke?' It took another terrifying second for her to assimilate what she was seeing, as she took in the blanket haphazardly folded and placed on the pillow. *He might abscond with her…* Sophie's dire warning rang loud in her head, and Claire's heart stopped dead.

CHAPTER FIFTY-ONE

Claire

'Yes, we've split up. He was staying overnight, that was all.' Claire tried again to explain to the police officer who'd taken her call why she would be worried about her husband leaving in the middle of the night with her daughter.

'And you're concerned he might harm her?' the officer asked.

'No,' she answered instinctively. Then, 'Yes,' she said, thoughts of his blackouts – if that was what they were – rushing to mind. 'I don't *know*. He attacked his mother's partner, possibly his girlfriend. You arrested him, for God's sake!'

'Okay, calm down, Mrs Elliot,' the officer tried to placate her. 'I'm dispatching officers to your address now. It would be useful if you could have a recent photograph of your little girl to hand,' he suggested, causing the harsh reality of what was happening to hit her. Her child was missing. Her husband had taken her.

Closing her eyes, she tried to focus, and then emitted a sob. 'The only recent photographs I have are on my mobile,' she said, her voice raw. 'I can't find it. I don't know where it is.'

'Do you have a paper photograph?' he asked gently.

'I...' Claire tried to think, but her thoughts were leaping over each other, a jumbled mess in her head. 'Yes.' She remembered the photos they'd taken at Alton Towers. She'd printed some off.

They were in her wardrobe. She was sure they were. 'But they're over a year old.' Ella had grown so much since then.

'I'm sure they'll be fine,' he assured her. 'The officers will be with you shortly. Meanwhile, can you provide us with some details about your husband? His current address and—'

'He hasn't got one! It's four thirty in the morning, he's deranged, and he's taken my daughter!' Claire cried, and then banged the phone down, frustrated and sick with panic. She couldn't stand here talking. She had to *do* something.

Where would he have taken her? She needed to ring Joyce. She couldn't imagine he'd taken her there, but she needed to find out if his mother knew what might be going on in his head, because Claire certainly didn't.

Reaching again for the phone, she stopped, her heart jolting as it rang, shrill and loud against the silence. She snatched it up. 'Luke?' She wouldn't berate him, she wouldn't scream at him, she would just ask him, beg him, to bring her baby back.

'Claire? No, hi, it's Amy.'

Amy? Claire racked her brains, agitated, desperate, hopeful. Please God this had something to do with where Ella was.

'I've been trying to get in touch with you,' the woman went on, 'but Gemma's phone was damaged in the accident and I couldn't find your number.'

Accident? Claire's throat constricted. 'What accident?'

'She's okay,' Amy said carefully. 'Out of surgery. It was a hit-and-run. Some cowardly bastard knocked her over and then drove off without stopping. She has a fractured pelvis, cracked ribs. Her jaw's broken too. I have no idea what kind of animal would…'

Claire's head swam. *Well, that was a really shitty thing to do, wasn't it? Still your best friend, is she?* She recalled what Luke had said when he'd learned it was Gemma who'd sent the photograph from the club. His tone had been full of contempt. He'd been drinking, consistently. Enough to fill a distillery, Joyce had said. He'd been volatile, aggressive, possessive; all the things Anna and Sophie had said he was. Unbalanced. He didn't want to be in Claire's life. He didn't want her to have anyone else in her life. Not Sophie. Not Gemma. Not another man. Not even her father. It was as if he wanted her totally isolated. To have no one.

Oh God, please, no. A primal moan rose inside her. *Don't let him hurt my baby.*

CHAPTER FIFTY-TWO

Luke

It took a minute for Luke to realise why Myers was asking whether Ella was with him. 'Why do you think she would be?' he asked, fear slicing through him.

'Do you mind if we come in?' Myers indicated the hall beyond him.

Luke stepped back, allowing him and the two officers with him access. 'Did Claire call you?'

Pausing in the hall, Myers turned to face him. Luke's heart pounded painfully as he tried to read his expression.

'She's missing, isn't she?'

Myers nodded – a short, apologetic nod – and Luke's heart seemed to explode. 'Jesus Christ, no.'

'Oh my *God*.' His mother pressed a hand to her mouth, her eyes petrified as she looked at Luke, and then she was at his side, attempting to hold him up as the blood drained from his body and he dropped heavily to the stairs.

'What's going on?' she asked the police officers. 'For God's sake, don't just stand there. He's her father. *Tell* him!'

Myers glanced uncomfortably between them. 'We received a call from Claire Elliot at approximately four thirty a.m.,' he said, 'informing us that her daughter had been taken from her bed.'

'No. No, no, *no.*' Feeling the breath sucked from his lungs, Luke buried his head in his hands and stifled a throaty moan. He couldn't breathe.

'She seemed to think her father had taken her.'

'Don't be bloody ridiculous,' Joyce snapped. 'Does he look like he's taken her?' She nodded towards Luke, who was levering himself shakily from the stairs.

'We need to search the premises nevertheless,' DS Myers informed her apologetically.

'She's not here. You should be out *there*, looking for her!' Joyce bawled, flailing a hand in the direction of the street.

'We have officers going door-to-door,' Myers tried to reassure her. 'We're organising a search of the local areas and circulating—' He stopped, glancing past her to the sudden commotion at the open front door.

'Where is she?' Claire seethed, her eyes a whirl of palpable pain and fury as she pushed past the police officer positioned there.

'She's not here, sweetheart.' Joyce tried to intervene. 'Luke hasn't—'

'Where *is* she?' Claire screamed, shrugging her off to fly at Luke. 'Tell me where she is, you bastard!' Tears streaming down her cheeks, she drew her hand back and slapped his face, hard. 'Tell me!'

Staggering backwards from the impact, Luke's own hand went instinctively to his cheek. 'She's not here!' he shouted. 'Why the *hell* do you think I would have—'

'You *shit.* You absolute piece of shit!' Claire sobbed, her eyes, red-rimmed and raw, now full of nothing but loathing. 'Why are you doing this? Why would you hurt Gemma? To hurt me? Is that it?' The flat of her hand curling into a fist, she stepped after him, landing a hard blow to his chest. And another. 'Gemma's done *nothing* to you. Why would you do this? *Why?* Tell me where my baby is!'

Propelled into action, the officer from the door was behind her, catching hold of her wrist, as Luke stumbled back under the impact of another blow. 'Come on, Mrs Elliot. This won't help,' he said gently, feeding an arm around her torso to heave her bodily away from him.

Luke moved after her, his gut wrenching as a female officer joined her colleague, both of them attempting to subdue her. 'Leave her,' he said throatily. 'She's upset. She—'

'I'll *kill* you.' Claire glared dementedly at him as she struggled to break free. 'I swear to God, if anything happens to my baby—'

'I don't know where she is!' Luke insisted. 'Claire, for God's sake, I came here because my mother needed help. Derek was trying to… *Jesus!* I left you a note, on the coffee table. Please… you *have* to believe me.' A sob escaping his own throat, he swiped a hand across his face and moved towards her again, only stopping when Myers grabbed his arm.

The detective indicated the kitchen. 'A quick word,' he said, relaxing his grip a little.

Luke noticed the cautionary look in his eyes, and his gut twisted afresh. Glancing back to Claire, who was now sobbing like a child – for her lost child – comforted by Joyce and the female officer, he nodded and reluctantly followed Myers.

In the kitchen, the detective pushed the door closed. Then, scratching his forehead with his thumb, he drew in a breath and eyed Luke hesitantly. 'I'm telling you this because you're going to need to keep it together,' he said. 'Be there for your wife, at least until we've established the facts.'

'Facts?' Luke searched his face impatiently. The facts, as far as he could see, were that his daughter was missing and they were standing around here doing nothing about it.

'Gemma Taylor was involved in a road traffic accident,' Myers said quietly, searching Luke's face in turn, as if to gauge his reaction. 'She was the victim of a hit-and-run.'

Luke couldn't speak for a second, then, '*Fuck*,' he muttered, dropping his gaze.

'We haven't yet been able to identify the driver. You can see how it looks like this might not just be coincidence,' Myers went on guardedly.

Bewildered, Luke nodded slowly.

'We also received a call from the Lawns care home,' Myers added, as Luke scrambled to make some kind of sense of it. 'They tried to contact your wife, but they couldn't get hold of her.'

The care home. His gaze snapped back to Myers. 'Her father?'

Myers nodded gravely, and Luke guessed what was coming next. 'He passed away early this morning; somewhere between midnight and three thirty a.m., I gather, when someone went to check on him. He was found at the foot of the fire escape outside his window.'

'You have to be joking.' Luke glanced back to the door, beyond which he could hear Claire breaking her heart. 'Does she know?' he asked, though he knew the answer.

Myers shook his head. 'They left a message for her to call, but they didn't say anything other than that it was urgent. The thing is…' he paused, his expression darkening, 'we haven't yet been able to establish whether it was an accident. One of the other residents claims to have seen someone in the grounds. We're not sure how reliable the information is but we have to follow it up. The staff informed us that Claire has a sister,' he went on. 'Do you have a name and address for her?'

Nausea crashing through him, Luke swallowed hard. 'Sophie,' he said throatily. 'Her half-sister.'

CHAPTER FIFTY-THREE

Claire

They sat in silence on his mother's sofa, no words between them that could ease their separate torture. Claire stiffened when Luke reached tentatively to place an arm around her shoulders. She felt his tense intake of breath, but he didn't move, waiting quietly instead – and her will to resist crumbled. A guttural moan escaping her, she turned to him. She needed to feel the solidity of him. She couldn't bear it. She could feel her baby's pain. Hear her. *Oh God.* She pressed her face into Luke's shoulder, tried to block out the graphic images playing through her mind. Her little girl's face, pale and petrified, her summer-blue eyes recoiling in fear. Her small voice, bewildered, filled with terror as she cried out for her mother. She couldn't bear it. She couldn't. *Don't hurt her. Please don't hurt her.*

'I'm so sorry about your father.' Luke squeezed her still closer.

Claire drew a breath; tried to stop the sobs rising in her chest. 'You hated him.'

'I didn't hate him, Claire,' Luke said, with a weary sigh.

He didn't, she knew. He'd hated Bernard's lack of respect for him, had despaired of the way he'd treated him, but he didn't hate him. She could hear the sorrow in his voice. He would grieve for him, she suspected, where she felt she couldn't. She cried harder.

Luke tightened his grip as the sobs racked her body. Claire allowed him to hold her. She needed him to. Needed him.

Why had he done it, taken the first opportunity he could to do to her as her father had done to her mother? She couldn't have stayed with him. Lived a lie; died a slow death until her life became unbearable, as her mother had done, part of her withering away each day as she'd waited, living in hope that the man she loved would choose her. He'd killed her as surely as night turned to day. He'd also killed part of his daughter. Claire's ability to allow herself to be loved, to believe that she was worth loving. She'd prayed that Luke would never put her through that kind of pain. That she could trust him. That he would be the one person on earth who would understand the promise she'd made her father. Perhaps deep down she'd considered it inevitable that he would stray. Her survival instinct driving her, she'd pushed him away. And now this. She blamed him. But she blamed herself more for the pain she'd caused their precious child.

Another desperate sob shook through her. 'Where is she?'

'They'll find her,' Luke said, his throat hoarse from the tears he'd tried and failed to suppress. Was it worth it? Claire wanted to ask him. She didn't. She hadn't got the strength to. She didn't want to argue any more. She just wanted her daughter.

Her hands strayed to her tummy as a new wave of empty helplessness swept through her. The space where she'd been able to keep her baby safe until she could survive independently of her. She should have always kept her safe. It was her duty as a mother. She'd failed.

'They'll find her,' Luke repeated, taking hold of one of her hands, squeezing it gently. Was there the same conviction in his heart that there was in his voice? Claire wondered. Did he really believe that?

'How?' Pulling away, she looked up at him – and was shocked by the raw pain she found in his eyes. He was hurting just as much as she was. Had she really imagined he wouldn't be?

'Sorry to interrupt.' Detective Myers had come in. 'Claire,' he said, his expression giving nothing away as he stopped in front of her, 'you wouldn't happen to have a recent photograph of your half-sister, would you? For identification purposes. We've sent officers round to her address in Rhyl. She's been back there, according to neighbours, but doesn't appear to be there now. We need to locate her and take a statement.'

Searching his face warily, Claire pulled herself to her feet and fetched her bag from where Joyce had left it on the armchair. She'd found her mobile, eventually, in her car. She'd imagined all sorts of things when she couldn't find it: that Luke had stolen it in order to stop her getting help, which was ridiculous. He would hardly have done that and not cut the landline. They'd used a photograph of Ella from Luke's phone in the end, one he'd taken in the park the day Claire had been settling her father into the care home. She swallowed back an overwhelming sense of guilt and tried not to linger on him: where he was now, how he would look. At peace? His mind finally free of his torment? She wasn't sure she wished him that much. Her mind would never be free.

She wiped a hand across her wet cheeks and went back to Detective Myers. She didn't have many photographs of Sophie, just one or two she'd taken at Children's Village, the best likeness one she'd taken as Sophie came off the helter-skelter. 'I only have a couple,' she said, handing the phone to him. 'I'm not sure how helpful they will be.'

'Extremely,' he assured her.

Luke got to his feet and walked across to look at the photos. Claire watched him, feeling for him. His face was deathly pale, his body language tight. She noted the tense set of his jaw as he studied them, the hand going through his hair, then he turned and walked away. '*Fuck!*' he growled, slamming the heel of his hand against the partially open door. 'Where the *hell* is she?' His shoulders heaved as he pulled in a deep breath.

Her heart pounding with fear, Claire watched him carefully, wondered if he would ever breathe out.

'I'll get one of my officers to forward these to the appropriate people, and then let you have the phone back,' Myers said, drawing her attention back to him.

In case someone tried to contact her? she wondered, her stomach twisting afresh.

Myers walked to the door, pausing behind Luke. 'We'll find her,' he said quietly, placing the flat of his hand briefly against Luke's back before heading out.

'Luke?' Claire took a step towards him.

Kneading his forehead hard, Luke turned to face her. 'Do you know of any places she might be?' he asked her, his voice gruff, his face now pale to the point of grey. 'Sophie,' he clarified. 'Does she have any friends or relatives in Rhyl?'

Claire shook her head. 'I was only there for two days. We just took in the sights and then went to the beach. She said she didn't have anyone…' She stopped, hope rising briefly inside her, followed by a new kind of terror as she remembered the derelict pub. Sophie had said she'd spent much of her childhood there. Talked nostalgically about it, as if those were her happiest memories of growing up.

'The village pub,' she said, locking fearful eyes on his. 'It's in Meliton. It's being demolished. Sophie's mother worked there. She—'

'I'll let Myers know.' Luke spun around, heading abruptly for the door.

Minutes later, hearing raised voices in the hall, Claire headed after him.

'Luke! Hold up!' She saw Myers catch up with him at the front door. 'Where are you going?'

'Where the hell do you think?' Luke yanked his arm from the detective's grasp, his eyes blazing as he turned to face him. 'To look for my daughter. I can't just sit here doing fuck all.'

'Luke!' Claire called, alarmed at the state he was in.

'It's Anna!' Luke yelled, and raced out, slamming the front door behind him.

CHAPTER FIFTY-FOUR

Luke

Approaching on foot across the fields, Luke paused opposite the pub. It was obviously under demolition. He noted the shuttered windows, the door to the main entrance hanging off its hinges. The stone walls at the front of the building were crumbling, the thatched roof caving in. The place looked as if it hadn't seen a soul for years. But for his instinct screaming at him that his daughter was near, he might have doubted anyone was here.

He swept his gaze over the building again. Claire had rung him. She'd told Myers he was searching the streets for Ella in the hope that she'd wandered out. She'd bought him some time. Luke was now debating the wisdom of coming here, though. Wouldn't the police be better equipped to deal with the situation if Anna was inside with his daughter?

Imagining that scene, armed marksmen all over the place, he shuddered inwardly. Anna had no problem harming herself. Luke doubted she would have reservations about harming anyone else if she thought she was cornered. His hand going involuntarily to his cheek, anger burned steadily inside him.

Slipping further into the foliage at the perimeter of the field, he made his way along until he felt it was safe to cross the road unnoticed. If she was inside and she was keeping a lookout, he guessed – hoped – it would be from the front of the building.

Minutes later, he was in the grounds at the back of the pub, scanning the shutters on the doors and windows as he approached. Only one window wasn't boarded up, and that was on the first floor. His heart sank. *Shit!* There had to be another way. He couldn't just walk in through the front door. Squeezing behind old beer crates stacked behind the pub, he cursed silently again as he crunched broken glass underfoot, and then stopped and listened. Not a sound. Growing desperate, he glanced around – and his gaze snagged on the doors to the beer cellar. They were probably locked, but there was a chance they might not be.

He moved carefully across to them. *Bingo.* The doors were wooden, rotting, the long hinges flapping. It didn't take him long to prise one loose and slide down the barrel skids to the floor. He stayed crouched for a second and tried to orientate himself. The place stank of stale beer and mould. There had clearly been no one down here in ages. Apart from the rats. His stomach recoiled, a cold chill running through him as something bulbous, trailing a scaly tail behind it, scurried over the hand he'd placed flat on the floor. *Shit!*

Snatching his hand away, he pulled himself to his feet and squinted through the dark to the thin shaft of light filtering under what he assumed was the door up to the pub. Praying that it was open, that there were no surprises on the other side of it, he headed towards it. Once up the steps, he pressed down on the handle and breathed a considerable sigh of relief when the door gave. His heart thudding erratically against his chest, he waited a second, and then eased it further open and stepped cautiously out.

The bar area was dark behind the shuttered windows, the same stale beer smell hanging in the air. The furniture, dark oak in keeping with the antiquated feel of the place, still stood where he imagined it had been when the final last orders were called. There were no signs of life other than another scuffling rat and the spiders that had taken up residence in the absence of humans. Venturing into the corridor, he was about to check out the lounge bar and the living quarters when he heard the floor creaking overhead. He froze, his heart skidding into his throat. He heard it again. There was something up there. He had no idea whether it was animal or human. Whatever it was, it was heavier than a bird or a rat – and it was moving.

His gaze snapped to the stairs at the end of the corridor. Every sinew in his body tensing, he moved silently towards them, his heart rate slowing to a dull thud in his chest as he grabbed hold of the handrail. He'd never thought there would come a day when he would be terrified of a slimly built woman, but he was; terrified for his child. Bracing himself, he mounted the stairs, checking ahead of him as he went.

Once on the landing, he pressed the flat of one hand against the first door he reached, pushing down the handle with the other, and eased it open to find a small bedroom, empty apart from an old bed frame and a stained mattress.

He went to the next room along. Seeing that was also empty, he moved silently to a third room, located at the back of the pub over the living quarters, he guessed. His mouth parched, his hand visibly shaking, he reached for the door handle, prayed hard and eased it down. A movement from inside made him shove the door open. When he did, his heart careered to a stop in his chest.

Anna was standing on the opposite side of the room. A section of floorboards running around the edge of the room supported her. Above her, the roof was open to the elements. Between her and Luke there was a direct drop to the rubble-strewn floor of the room below. His blood froze as she adjusted her footing, causing more debris to fall and crash into the twisted beams and broken brickwork beneath them – just as surely as his child's small body would if she dropped her. Noting the hatred in her eyes as she glared at him, he didn't dare look away; other than to glance at his daughter, who appeared to be sleeping in her arms. Not through this she wasn't. Not unless she was drugged. Luke felt something splinter inside him.

'Anna,' he said hoarsely.

'Sophie!' she spat. 'Fuck off, Luke.'

Luke didn't react. Didn't move, even to wipe away the bead of perspiration rolling down his cheek. 'Let her go, Sophie,' he said, his voice calm, terror tightening his stomach.

'Try to get anywhere near me and I will.' Her gaze slid meaningfully downwards.

Panic climbed Luke's throat. 'She's four years old. Just an innocent child,' he tried. 'She's done nothing—'

'*Precisely!*' Sophie shrieked over him. 'Do you think she deserves any of this?'

Luke's gut turned over. He had no idea what she was talking about. Holding his breath, he watched helplessly as she heaved Ella higher in her arms. She hadn't stirred. Hadn't so much as twitched. Was she even breathing? His own breath hitched in his chest.

'To have a lying, abusive bastard as a grandfather?' Sophie went on nonsensically, her face contorted with rage, her tone full of acid venom. 'And as a father, a man who was prepared to sacrifice his daughter by cheating on his wife?'

Luke quietly assessed her. He'd got that right, if nothing else. The woman was a complete fantasist. 'But I didn't cheat on my wife, did I?' he pointed out.

Confusion played across her face for a second. Then, 'It was only a matter of time,' she said, smiling contemptuously. 'You know it, Luke. Claire knows it, too, but she's just too needy to tell you to piss off. As for her,' she nodded down at Ella, 'she's better off dead. I mean, what kind of a future would she have with you as a father and a self-centred bitch for a mother, too busy bleating on about her problems to care properly for—'

'It's over!' Luke shouted. He was a breath away from telling her about Bernard, but stopped. There was a possibility she might have had nothing to do with it and didn't know he was dead. If so, that information could tip her over the edge. 'It's over, Sophie,' he repeated quietly. 'Whatever Bernard did, it's in the past. Claire had nothing to do with it. No more than you did. You must realise that. Please, don't do this.'

Her dark eyes hardened, but she didn't flinch.

Luke's gaze darted to the side of the room and back to her. The boards looked intact enough round the edge. What would she do if he tried to get to her? 'Sophie, whatever you think of me, please don't take it out on—'

'You're pathetic,' she sneered over him. 'Poor hard-done-by little man, whose wifey was too busy trying to look after his child and her demented father to find time to pander to him. Do you honestly think I would have wanted a selfish bastard like you anywhere near me if I hadn't wanted to get to Claire?'

His mind on how to reach his child, Luke couldn't think how to answer. She'd used him, that was clear. To what end? She must know they would have reported Ella missing, that the police would be looking for her. Did she think she could just walk away from this? His stomach clenched painfully as he realised that she was probably so out of touch with reality she wasn't even considering the consequences. 'What do you want, Sophie?' he asked her.

'To even the score,' she said matter-of-factly.

Sweat wetted Luke's shirt, ran in rivulets down his back, as he noticed her hoisting Ella up again. She was growing heavy. Too heavy.

Fear lodged itself like a shard of glass in his windpipe. '*Why?*' he asked frantically. 'What did Claire ever do to you? What did—'

'Exist!' she yelled. 'My mother died in absolute *terror* because of your wife's parents! I had no one! Nothing! While poor sorry-for-herself little Claire had everything! Everything *I* should have—' She stopped, her eyes growing wide with alarm at the sound of a door banging downstairs.

'Who's with you?' she hissed. Her gaze shooting past him, she gathered Ella tighter to her, and then, glancing down, shuffled sideways towards the unboarded window.

Jesus Christ. What was she going to do? Luke's heart froze, and then slammed against his chest as her foot slipped, causing more debris to rain down on the rubble below.

Fuck! Instinctively, he moved. His focus on his baby, panic driving him, he stepped onto the jagged boarding to the side of him. He'd managed two precarious steps when the rotten wood snapped beneath him.

CHAPTER FIFTY-FIVE

Claire

'Luke!' Claire felt the thud resonate through her as his body landed, sending a thick plume of dust into the air. Horrified, she watched him lying petrifyingly still for a second, before attempting to raise himself, craning his neck to look down at the twisted piece of metal skewering his leg. It took another second, as she scrambled over the rubble to get to him, for the blood to spurt upwards, a bright red parabola arching through the air and then stopping. Until his next heartbeat.

Oh, dear God! 'Luke!' He was losing consciousness. Gulping back her panic, swiping the steaming blood from her face as she kneeled over him, Claire realised his injury might kill him. Instinctively, she pressed her thumbs to his thigh above the wound. The blood kept spraying. It was slippery, pumping everywhere. *Shit. Shit!* She had to stem the flow. But how? A tourniquet. She didn't know whether it was the right thing to do, but it was the only thing she could think of. Reapplying the pressure, she glanced desperately around, seeing nothing she could use. She hadn't got time to search. He could bleed out, bleed to death. Quickly she tore off her own shirt, which was already sodden with blood, fed it under his thigh and tied the sleeves. Then, with all of her might, she pulled the knot tight.

'I'll be back, I promise,' she whispered, close to his ear. 'Hold on, Luke. *Please* hold on.' Stifling her tears, she leaped to her feet, pulling her phone from her pocket as she turned to climb back over the broken debris. She needed to call an ambulance. She needed to find the sick creature who'd caused all of this mayhem. To find her little girl and take her home.

After giving the information regarding Luke's injuries as succinctly and precisely as she could, Claire paused at the doorway back to the hall, where she bent to pick up a similar sharp piece of metal to the one that had pierced Luke's thigh. She weighed it in her hand. She had no qualms about using it. If her half-sister had caused her baby harm in any way, so help her God, she *would* kill her.

Breathing deeply, she went to the stairs. Clutching the handrail determinedly, she kept her gaze fixed upwards as she climbed, her antennae on alert for any sounds. Her heart stalled when she reached the landing. And then kicked up again, adrenalin pumping through her veins as she focused on her aim: to retrieve her innocent child from the clutches of a madwoman, whatever it took.

She wasn't surprised to see Sophie standing there, her huge dark eyes, now far from sympathetic and caring, glinting with malice. Claire's gaze darted past her, her anger festering like poison inside her as she saw no sign of her daughter.

'Where is she?' she asked, her throat dry, her gaze coming back to the woman who'd taken her. How could she have done this? What kind of sick individual would cold-bloodedly win over the affections of a four-year-old child only to use her so cruelly to punish those she imagined owed her?

'Sleeping,' Sophie said, with an indifferent shrug. 'She's not up here, so I wouldn't waste your time looking.'

Claire felt her hatred harden for this woman she'd once thought she could care about. 'Have you drugged her?' Nausea rose sickeningly inside her as she spoke.

'Just sleeping tablets,' Sophie said matter-of-factly. 'She'll be fine. How's Luke?' she tacked on, as if she cared.

'You're sick.' Claire took a careful step along the landing towards her. 'You need help.'

'Maybe.' Sophie shrugged again. 'Luke, how is he?' Smiling sweetly, she repeated her question.

Icy fingers ran the length of Claire's spine. The woman was utterly insane. How could she not have seen it? 'He's bleeding,' she answered, trying to speak calmly. 'Badly.'

'Oh dear.' Sophie sighed dramatically. 'Perhaps he'll do us both a favour and bleed to death.'

Claire's chest constricted. She was pure evil. 'You twisted fucking freak,' she seethed, her anger perilously close to spilling over.

'Claire… such language.' Sophie blinked in feigned shock. 'Honestly, some people are never satisfied, are they?'

What in God's name was she talking about? Claire's blood thundered through her head as she tried to make sense of any of it.

'I didn't think you'd be that bothered if he died,' Sophie went on, smiling like a demented Cheshire cat. 'You really are better off without him, you know. At least this way you won't have to waste any more emotion worrying about whether he'll—'

'Where *is* she?' Claire lunged for her.

Sophie backed away fast. 'How does it feel to have nothing, Claire?' she taunted. 'No money, no parents, no perfect man—'

'I'll kill you, I swear, as God is my witness…'

'He *was* pretty perfect, you know, determined to stay faithful to you no matter how much I tempted him,' Sophie went on, with a melodramatic sigh. 'But you were too busy looking for his imperfections to realise what you had. You were bound to lose him one way or another.'

'Where's my *daughter*?' Claire screamed the words.

Sophie ignored her. 'I'm sure you're beginning to realise now, though, aren't you? What you've lost? What it's like to have nothing in your life, to wonder why you weren't good enough,' she continued, each word like an icicle through Claire's chest.

She tightened her fist around the jagged piece of metal, itching to drive it through Sophie's black heart. Sophie's gaze travelled towards it. Claire didn't doubt she would be ready for her if she tried. What if she was too strong for her? What would happen to her baby then?

'Bernard was quite keen to amend his will, by the way. Did he tell you? Or did it slip his mind?' Sophie looked her over with amusement. 'He owes me, you see. I knew he would never admit it, though, without a little incentive. That's why I sought you out.'

Claire's head reeled. She had to stop her. She had to shut her vile mouth. 'Why did he owe you, Sophie?' she asked calmly, thinking fast, swallowing her anger. 'Because he fucked your whore of a mother? Produced an abhorrence?'

Sophie's face darkened. 'You *bitch*,' she snarled, advancing towards her.

'You didn't seek me out.' Claire backed away. 'Did you think I didn't know you were the sordid little skeleton in his cupboard, you pathetic creature? That I wouldn't know why you'd crawled out of the woodwork? I sought *you* out!' She glared hard at her, despite her heart breaking inside. Her own desperation to have Sophie as part of her family, to have a sister, someone who would always be there for her, had blinkered her to the evil she'd invited into her life. She'd been fooled by Sophie's false sympathy and kindness because she'd wanted to be. Luke had been right. She'd imagined they shared a bond, but she hadn't known her. In setting out to uncover her father's secrets, she'd risked the lives of the people who truly mattered to her. Allowed Sophie access to Luke, to Ella. She would never forgive herself for that.

'I knew who you were as soon as I saw your Facebook profile. I'd been searching for you for years,' she embroidered the truth. Sophie's location had sent her mind flying back to that distant day in Rhyl, right here in this very pub. Even as a child she'd wondered about the intimacy between her father and the woman with the leopard-print shoes and red-painted lips. She'd listened to that child. Acknowledged her fears. Encouraged Sophie – and waited. 'All I had to do was mention Dad a few times on my profile and I knew you'd seek me out. I found you, Sophie. I caught you!' she went on, summoning her courage to spit the words out with the same vitriol Sophie had spewed out her nonsense. 'I knew *exactly* what you wanted.'

'Did you, Claire?' Sophie's lips curled into a sneer. 'Did you really?'

'I was one step ahead of you all the way.' Claire pushed it, baiting her, wanting her to come just a little bit closer. 'All that oozing sympathy you did over Luke – did you think I was that *weak*?'

'You let him walk all over you,' Sophie scoffed contemptuously. 'He wouldn't think he could fuck other women if you hadn't allowed him to.'

'He didn't, though, did he?' Holding her gaze, Claire took another step back. 'He felt sorry for you, Sophie. Of course, he didn't realise the game you were playing; that far from being terrified and suicidal, you were a nasty, disgusting little trollop who obviously takes after her sluttish mother!'

'*Shut up.*' Her eyes narrowing to icy slits, Sophie moved closer.

'You failed, Sophie,' Claire taunted, her mind racing. 'You're a failure, a mistake, just face it.'

Sophie stopped, her chest heaving, her eyes ablaze with humiliation and rage. And then she exploded forward.

Claire twisted sideways as Sophie flew at her, then watched, fascinated by the startled expression on her face, the dull *thud... thud... thud*, as her half-sister's soft body tumbled and bounced down the stairs. Her heart pelting manically, she stood frozen for a second. And then, realising that Ella might be anywhere, in mortal danger, she thundered down after her.

CHAPTER FIFTY-SIX

Sophie

It hadn't felt like much more than a low punch to her back when she landed. Sophie guessed she was badly injured, though, when she couldn't raise herself. It was as if she'd been stapled to the floor. She knew she was in deep trouble when, straining her neck, she saw the telltale crimson stain flowering beneath her. She must have landed on some sharp piece of debris, broken glass possibly – ironically.

Claire would undoubtedly be delighted, knowing she'd won. That she would have her inheritance and carry on living her perfect little life with her perfect man and her perfect daughter. Her claim to have known who Sophie was all along was interesting. She was no doubt congratulating herself on her cleverness at having worked it all out. *Not quite clever enough, Claire. You really should make sure you're one hundred per cent certain of the people you invite into your life.* Gulping back the warm, salty taste in her mouth, Sophie watched as she descended the stairs, the look in her eyes one of absolute fear. *That's right, sweetie,* she silently urged her. *Keep that gaze fixed firmly on me.*

'Where's Ella?' Claire begged, dropping to her knees at her side.

Sophie furrowed her brow as if thinking, and then, 'I can't quite remember,' she said, a mocking smile curving her mouth.

'You sick bitch.' Claire moved her hands to her shoulders and pressed down hard, causing excruciating pain to rip through her.

'You would never have been part of this family,' she hissed, leaning closer, her face a breath away from Sophie's, her eyes burning with hatred. 'You're not wanted. You never were, not by my father, not even by your own mother.'

Sophie didn't answer, wincing instead as the woman who pretended to be oh-so-caring applied a little more pressure.

'Your whore mother's affair with my father killed my mother!' Claire pressed still harder. 'You robbed me of my childhood, my memories. I won't let you take my daughter from me. Did you honestly think I would let you steal what was mine?'

Intolerable though the pain now was, Sophie focused, fixing her gaze on Claire's. Claire looked shocked when she laughed, spattering her white vest top with rich red speckles of blood. 'No, sweetie,' Sophie managed, with effort. 'I think you'll find it was your darling mother who was the murderer. It was her who struck the match that caused the fireball that killed my mother.'

Claire pulled back, blinking uncomprehendingly for a second, and then, 'Liar!' she spat.

'Bernard was trying to protect her,' Sophie continued. 'He'd followed her.'

She stopped, tried to draw breath past the wet gurgle that rose in her chest. Closing her eyes, she was transported back there, hurting and bewildered as she lay in the undergrowth. She heard it again, as clear as day: the second set of footsteps, sharper heels crunching on the gravel. The scraping sound, like the striking of a match against the side of a box. Once, twice… three times. Desperation constricting her throat, she tried to call out. And then clamped her mouth shut as a male voice yelled, 'Jesus Christ! What the bloody hell have you done?'

'It's your fault, you bastard! You drove me to it!' the woman screamed. 'I told you to stop. I told you to end it!'

'Go!' the male voice roared. 'Get back in the car!'

'But what if someone sees me? I can't just—'

'For God's sake, just get in the *car*. Go back the way you came. Now!'

Sophie forced her eyes open. She was struggling, but Claire had to know. 'It was your father's motorbike that was witnessed driving away from the accident…' a sharp cough rattled through her, 'not *my* father's.'

Claire stared hard at her, her expression now one of stunned disbelief.

'Jimmy's my dad. Mum's ex.' Sophie smiled, a small smile of satisfaction. 'He went to prison because of your mother. Your father died because of her – didn't he, Claire? I wouldn't want to be part of that family.'

Shifting her gaze, she looked past Claire. 'Would you?'

CHAPTER FIFTY-SEVEN

Claire

Claire's heart dropped like a stone as realisation dawned. Swallowing back a sick taste in her throat, she looked over her shoulder to find Luke standing behind her, his weight on his good leg, his face white, their baby girl nestled close to his shoulder.

The emerging sun filtering in through the open entrance door threw slanting shadows across his strong features as he stared hard at her. 'Did you mean the house?' he asked her. 'When you were talking about what was yours, did you mean Bernard's house?'

Claire couldn't answer. She didn't know how to. How much had he heard? How much had he seen? Her back had been towards him, but she had no way of knowing.

'The proceeds of which were to pay for his care home fees,' Luke went on, pressing Ella closer as she stirred in his arms. 'Unless, of course, there are no care home fees.'

He knows. Claire read what was in his eyes: disbelief, slowly giving way to stunned comprehension.

'Did you know Bernard was dead, Claire?' he asked her bluntly. 'When Myers told you. Did you already know?'

'No! Of course I didn't!' Seeing the accusation now in his eyes, panic clutched at Claire's chest. 'How could I have?'

Luke appeared to consider, then, 'Tell me something,' he said quietly. 'Did it ever occur to you to think about the effect on Ella when you sought this woman out? The effect on anyone, not least Bernard?'

Claire scrambled to her feet. 'Of course I thought about the effect on Ella,' she said tearfully. 'Ella adored her. And I know she's just a child, but… Oh God…' She squeezed her eyes closed. 'Please try to understand, Luke. I needed someone who would be there for me. I didn't even know whether she would make contact, but when she did… I thought I'd found that someone.'

'And your father?' Luke asked, his expression unimpressed.

Claire searched for the right answer. There wasn't one. How could what she'd done ever be right in Luke's eyes? She tried desperately to explain. 'I had to find out,' she said. 'My dad wasn't going to tell me. I don't even know whether he remembered. How else was I going to do it? I didn't know Sophie would turn out to be a monster. I thought it was better to be aware of anyone out there who might make some claim against his estate, before…' She faltered, realising that she was about to confess to having contemplated her father's imminent death. 'I never wanted to harm anyone,' she went on, her heart squeezing painfully as she acknowledged that she had, irrevocably. 'Not you. Never Ella. I would have died before doing that. Things got out of hand, and the more you told me that Sophie might not be who she appeared to be, the more obsessed I became with the idea that she was. I should have listened to you. I know I should have.'

'Right,' Luke said flatly. 'But your first priority when she fell…' he indicated Sophie 'was to go to her, rather than find your daughter?'

'I didn't know where Ella *was*.'

'She was here!' Luke shouted. 'She brought her down, left her behind the bar! There's broken glass everywhere!'

'I didn't *know* that,' Claire cried. 'I thought she might have hidden her in some dark, lonely place where we would never find her. Don't you see?'

Luke continued to study her for a long, silent moment. Then, 'No, Claire, I'm not sure I do,' he said. He shook his head sadly and turned away.

'Luke, *please*…' Tears squeezing from her eyes, Claire followed him towards the entrance, where rotating blue lights indicated that the emergency services had arrived. 'I'm sorry! For everything. For not believing you. I never stopped loving you. I just couldn't bear the thought of you not loving me. Please forgive me. *Please*… don't walk away.'

Luke hesitated, then squeezed his little girl closer and limped on.

EPILOGUE

Claire approached Luke's bed cautiously. He was sleeping fitfully, his eyelids fluttering as his mind chased his dreams. Nightmares; she had no doubt he would have those. Placing the things she'd brought him on the bedside locker, she reached to ease the visitor's chair closer.

Luke awoke with a jerk, his eyes flooding with panic, as the chair leg clanged against the bed frame. He looked relieved for a split second when he realised it was her. And then his expression changed, his eyes filled with obvious disillusionment before he averted his gaze. Claire instinctively reached to help him as he attempted to ease himself up the bed, but he pulled away from her. 'I can manage. Thanks,' he said tightly.

'I brought you some things,' she tried. 'Some juice and biscuits, and overnight things you might need.'

Luke tugged in a breath and sighed it out. He nodded, but still wouldn't meet her eyes.

'Can we talk?' Claire asked tentatively. He'd only just come round from the anaesthetic when she'd visited him yesterday. There'd been no eye contact then either, nothing but stilted conversation between them.

Luke took a second, and when he finally looked at her, she wanted to curl up and die. His look was now one of pure anger. As if he might even hate her for what she'd put him through. She felt her heart fold up inside her. She couldn't bear that, for him to have nothing but contempt for her.

'About what?' he asked, raking a hand unencumbered by tubes furiously through his hair. 'The fact that you didn't trust me, that you were willing to believe the worst of me. Christ, it almost seemed to me that you *wanted* me to cheat on you.'

'I didn't!' Claire's heart squeezed. 'I wanted you *not* to. I wanted to be able to trust you.'

'Right.' Luke laughed scornfully. 'But you didn't, did you? You weren't prepared to listen to a word I had to say.'

Seeing the hurt now in his eyes, Claire dropped her gaze. 'No,' she said, inhaling deeply, trying desperately to keep the tears he wouldn't want to see at bay. 'I should have done.' She looked back at him, willed him to try to understand her insecurities, her need to be loved wholly, to be confident that she was worth loving. 'When I saw you smiling at that girl in the pub, though—'

'What girl? When?' Luke furrowed his brow in confusion.

'A while back. Dad had a sitter and Gemma took Ella for the evening. I came to the pub with you and…' Claire stopped. It sounded ridiculous. Ludicrous.

The look on Luke's face told her he agreed. 'I think it might be best if you go, Claire,' he said quietly, after a loaded pause. 'I'm not sure there's any point—'

'I didn't want to be not good enough that you wouldn't stay!' Claire blurted, tears springing from her eyes, despite her best attempts to stop them.

Luke studied her curiously for a long, silent moment, and then he nodded, almost imperceptibly. He understood. She knew he did. He knew how it felt, the crushing hurt inside when you found yourself abandoned by the person you loved most in the world, the person who was supposed to love you back.

'You didn't have to allow Sophie to drape herself all over you, Luke, whoever and whatever she was pretending to be. You must have been having a pretty intimate conversation for her to do that. At least, that's how I see it,' she pointed out hesitantly, hoping he wouldn't think she was looking to apportion blame, to incite argument. She didn't want that. Not any more.

Again he nodded, conceding her point. 'There's still something I need to know,' he said, wariness now in his eyes as he searched hers. 'Your father, did you…' Glancing away, he faltered, and Claire felt a prickle of apprehension run through her. 'Did you end his life?' he went on, his gaze fearful as it came back to hers. 'Out of kindness, maybe? It's just, with someone being seen in the grounds and from what Sophie said about Bernard dying because of your mother—'

'No!' Claire denied it emphatically. 'I could never contemplate such a thing. It was one of her games, Luke, her manipulations. Please believe me.'

Luke searched her eyes as she stared beseechingly at him. Was there a flicker of doubt in his? She couldn't be sure. 'So you never discussed it with Bernard?' he asked. 'When he was first diagnosed?'

'Never,' Claire insisted. 'It wasn't me who was seen in the grounds that night, I swear. I was at home, in my room. You were downstairs. I'd already been to visit him earlier that—' She stopped, her heart leaping in her chest, as she saw DS Myers approaching through the viewing pane to the corridor.

Luke followed her gaze, and then glanced at her anxiously as the detective came into the side ward.

'Luke, Claire…' Myers nodded a greeting. 'I have some news,' he said. His tone was grave, Claire noted, her stomach churning with nerves.

'Regarding?' Heaving himself higher against his pillows, as if bracing himself, Luke's gaze shot again to hers.

'It's about Sophie, the woman you knew as Anna.' Myers glanced guardedly between them.

A shudder of relief ran the length of Claire's spine. Sophie couldn't have told him anything. She'd still been breathing when they'd taken her away in the ambulance. Claire had cried for her as she'd watched the resuscitation team fighting to stem the internal bleeding, genuine tears for the sister she might have had, had things been different. DS Myers had been at the hospital, waiting to speak to her, but she'd never regained consciousness. She couldn't tell tales from the grave.

'We've finally located the owner of the Birmingham apartment she was staying in,' the detective went on.

'And?' Luke said, clearly wondering where this was leading.

'He wasn't in Ghana. Turns out he came home for a visit,' Myers continued, his expression grim. 'He never went back.' He paused, scanning each of their faces in turn, as if wondering how much to tell them. 'We found his body this morning.'

'Oh my God.' Claire pressed a hand to her chest, horrified. 'Where?'

'Hidden in a storage cupboard,' Myers supplied, with a terse intake of breath.

Paling visibly, Luke stared at him, stupefied for a second, and then, '*Jesus.*' He swallowed hard. 'In the apartment?'

Myers shook his head. 'In one of the other apartments he owned. Wrapped in polythene, otherwise it might have been more obvious that he was there before now. We have enough forensic evidence to be confident Sophie Tyson was involved in his death.'

He paused, looking now at Claire. Apprehensively, she noticed. 'There's something else,' he said, with an inscrutable smile. 'There was a note on your father's person when he fell. Not a suicide note. It was typed on a pc.' He pulled out a notebook from his jacket pocket. 'It said, "Give my love to my mother. She died because of you." Knowing what we now do about her mother – that she was involved with your father when she was killed by her ex-boyfriend – we believe it was left by Sophie Tyson. It looks like flagrant disregard for other people's lives was in the DNA.' Sighing, he stepped aside as a nurse approached indicating she needed to take Luke's observations.

He was likening Sophie to her father, Jimmy, who'd been convicted of killing her mother. Claire's heart skittered inside her.

'I'll leave you two alone,' Myers said, his smile now one of commiseration as he glanced again at Claire. 'You know where to find me if there's anything you need to discuss.'

'Thank you,' Claire said shakily as he turned to go.

Her thoughts whirling, aware that she had to tread very carefully, she waited for the nurse to finish and move on, and then took a breath. 'She tried to forge my father's signature, Luke,' she told him. 'I found evidence she'd been doing that in his room, signature after signature scrawled in a notebook. She was obviously insane. I wish I had listened to you.'

She wiped a tear from her cheek as Luke met her gaze, his eyes still shot through with shock and confusion. This would be an end to it, she thought, relief coursing through her. He needed to heal now. She would help him. They needed to heal together. They could, Claire was sure of it. Fate, is seemed, really did move in mysterious ways. She'd been desperate to talk to Luke about the burden of the promise she'd made her father to save him from the final cruel ravages of the disease. Now, she thanked God that she hadn't had the opportunity to confide in him. Luke had turned out to be more trustworthy and honest than she'd ever given him credit for. He might never have been able to reconcile what she'd done and keep her secret.

She'd never imagined she would be capable of fulfilling her promise.

A LETTER FROM SHERYL

Thank you so much for choosing to read *The Perfect Sister*. I really hope you enjoy it. If you do, please do sign up for my newsletter to get alerts on my future books. You can unsubscribe at any time and your details will never be shared.

www.bookouture.com/sheryl-browne

As the title of this book implies, this is a story about past secrets and lies and the effect they might have on other people's lives. It's about how our past might shape our future. How certain paths chosen by those people closest to us might impact on our perception of ourselves. So often as children, when we are not loved and nurtured as we should be, we see the failure as our own, thinking ourselves unworthy, perhaps predicting what bad things might happen in later life because, though resilient and optimistic on the outside, on the inside that sense of unworthiness stays with us. In a way, I suppose, this is a way of preparing ourselves for the problems that will inevitably face us throughout life. Are we not painting our own landscape, though, our past memories influencing our future?

The Perfect Sister follows Claire's journey as she tries to unravel historical secrets that are affecting her life. In doing so, she has to dig into the past of a man whose memories of the events that shaped her might be unreliable. Her father has early-onset Alzheimer's. How can she trust that his recollections are accurate? Is he capable of lying still? Can Claire banish the ghosts that force her to push away the people she loves? Can she learn to forgive and let go of her fear in order to move forwards?

Writing her father's story, documenting his progress through this, one of the cruellest of diseases, was difficult, as I imagine it will be for some people to read about. My heartfelt sympathy goes out to anyone caring for a loved one who is suffering in such a way. I didn't have to rely too much on research for this character. I, too, have been a carer. It's one of the hardest things in life one has to do. Please know that, while writing, my thoughts were with you.

As I pen this last little section of the book, I would again like to thank those people around me who are always there to offer support, those people who believed in me even when I didn't quite believe in myself.

To all of you, thank you for helping me make my dream come true.

If you have enjoyed the book, I would love it if you could share your thoughts and write a brief review. Reviews mean the world to an author and will help a book find its wings. I would also love to hear from you via Facebook, Twitter or my website.

Keep safe, everyone, and happy reading.

Sheryl x

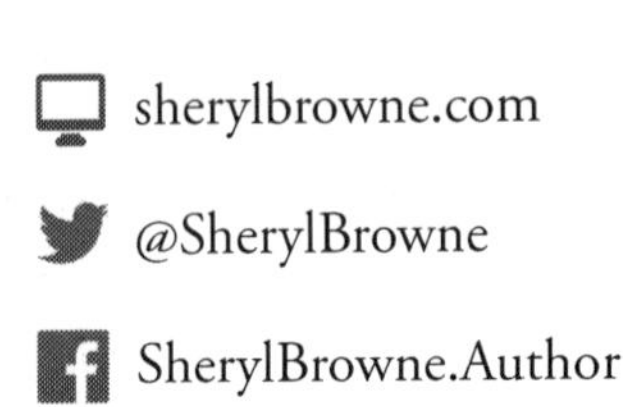

ACKNOWLEDGEMENTS

Massive thanks to the fabulous team at Bookouture, without whose expertise, dedication and patience *The Perfect Sister* might have remained a secret! Special thanks to Helen Jenner for her faith in me and her amazing editing skills. Not only does Helen make my books shine, where my first draft might have been a bit lacklustre, but she is super-supportive, especially when life does what it does. Massive thanks to head of publicity Kim Nash, and publicity and social media manager Noelle Holten, who work their socks off to help get our books out there. I have no idea how they do all that they do. Thanks, too, to Alex Crow, Bookouture's head of digital marketing, for the brilliant graphics, and also to the fantastic cover artists. I adore my book covers! To all the other wonderful, talented authors at Bookouture, I love you. Thanks for your shoulders when I needed them!

A special mention to Stuart Gibbon, former UK detective and author of *The Crime Writer's Casebook* and *Being a Detective*, for his excellent police procedural advice. Thanks so much for answering my questions at short notice, Stuart.

I owe a huge debt of gratitude to all the fantastically hardworking bloggers and reviewers who have taken time to read and review my books and shout them out to the world. Your passion leaves me in awe.

Finally, thanks to every single reader out there for buying and reading my books. Knowing you have enjoyed my stories and care enough about my characters to want to share them with other readers is the best incentive ever for me to keep writing.

Made in the USA
Middletown, DE
07 March 2020

86017309R00182